THE
SHEPHERD
OF
WEEDS

Also by Susannah Appelbaum

The Hollow Bettle
The Poisons of Caux, Book I

The Tasters Guild
The Poisons of Caux, Book II

THE POISONS OF CAUX

BOOK THREE

THE SHEPHERD OF WEEDS

SUSANNAH APPELBAUM

illustrated by Andrea Offermann

Alfred A. Knopf   New York

THIS IS A BORZOI BOOK PUBLISHED BY ALFRED A. KNOPF

Visit us on the Web! www.randomhouse.com/kids

Educators and librarians, for a variety of teaching tools,
visit us at www.randomhouse.com/teachers

Library of Congress Cataloging-in-Publication Data
Appelbaum, Susannah.
The shepherd of weeds / Susannah Appelbaum ; illustrated by Andrea Offermann. — 1st ed.
p. cm. — (The poisons of Caux ; bk. 3)
Summary: With an army of scarecrows, a legion of birds, and her friends and uncle by her side, it is up to Ivy Manx to wage war against the evil Vidal Verjouce and the Tasters Guild, defeat her own father, and restore order to the plant world.
ISBN 978-0-375-85175-9 (trade) — ISBN 978-0-375-95175-6 (lib. bdg.) —
ISBN 978-0-375-89897-6 (ebook)
[1. Poisons—Fiction. 2. Scarecrows—Fiction. 3. Uncles—Fiction. 4. Fantasy.]
I. Offermann, Andrea, ill. II. Title.
PZ7.A6445Sh 2011
[Fic]—dc22
2010051351

The text of this book is set in 12-point Caslon.

Printed in the United States of America
October 2011
10 9 8 7 6 5 4 3 2 1

First Edition

For A.M.R.,

who stayed until the Wind changed

Lo, I the man, whose Muse whilom did mask,

As time her taught, in lowly Shepherd's weeds . . .

—The Faerie Queene
Spenser

Contents🌿

Part 1: The Well Keeper

Part II: Inkworks

Part III: The Creatures of the Air

Part IV: The Army of Flowers

Part V: Poisoned Pen

Part VI: The Stones

Elegy

Previously in

THE POISONS OF CAUX

Times had changed in the ancient land of Caux. The Deadly Nightshades were no longer, and while many in the realm awaited news of the previous ruler, the beloved King Verdigris, a stubborn few hoped for the return of a more dangerous way of life . . . a way of poison.

The world of botany was a deadly one, but there existed an arguably worse evil—and sadly for Ivy, this was her father. Vidal Verjouce was not only the Director of the secretive Tasters' Guild but a true specter of destruction. And he now had a masterful ally, the deadly and treacherous plant called scourge bracken, a weed so potent, so perilous, that nearly all who encountered it were annihilated. One needed to be a powerful and mighty king to handle its dark and unpredictable character.

A powerful king—or eleven-year-old Ivy Manx.

Ivy was a poisoner of some skill, and she soon found that her vast knowledge of herbs made her a remarkable healer. But her talents were mysterious and unpredictable, and a cure came with a hefty price: a visit to her father's terrifying Mind

Garden. This was Verjouce's realm, a dark destination found only in his ruined imagination, where nightmares thrived like weeds.

Ivy and her friend Rowan Truax entered Rocamadour by way of the dank sewers, and were welcomed by the revered Professor Breaux and his granddaughter, Rue. But a wrong turn down a twisted alley delivered Ivy to Irresistible Meals, the dreaded course taught by the subrector Snaith. Before the entire class in the vast lecture hall, Ivy was poisoned with scourge bracken. Risking everything, Rue saved her.

Sickened and feverish—but to Snaith's utter disappointment, somehow still alive—Ivy arrived in Pimcaux, Caux's sisterland. There, she recuperated atop the cheery lighthouse of the alewives—the banished companions of Caux's trestlemen. Rowan was left to explore a nearby village. For his efforts, he was rewarded with a peculiar shop, eerie and abandoned, its inhabitants long gone. A weathered sign announced the place as once being the *Four Sisters Tapestries of the Ancients and Royal Haberdashery.*

Meanwhile, with the help of the alewife Wilhelmina and a pair of enormous seabirds, Ivy found the ailing King Verdigris. Unfortunately, she also found her wicked former taster, Sorrel Flux, who had adapted quite well to life in Pimcaux. Appallingly, Ivy's mother, Clothilde, appeared to be under his command. King Verdigris, from his gruesome throne of hawthorns, issued Ivy a command. Giving his great-granddaughter two strange stones—fruit pits—he told her to plant them in Caux.

Dismal, desperate—and pursued by Flux—Ivy and Rowan returned to Underwood, to their first glimmer of happiness. Ivy's beloved crow, Shoo, had emerged from the enchanted tapestries, where, alongside a mysterious woman in white, he had been imprisoned.

But the reunion was to be a brief one. The Prophecy—the future of Caux—still rested heavily upon Ivy's small shoulders. She had yet to cure the King, and time was running short—for the trestleman Axle, her wisest friend and the famed author of *The Field Guide to the Poisons of Caux,* had been captured. His was an existence of woe; the trestleman was being kept for the amusement of the Director in his chambers atop the dreaded spire in Rocamadour. And each day, Vidal Verjouce was growing stronger, his powers greater, and scourge bracken more tempestuous.

Ink

A good and durable ink may be made by the following directions: 3 drams of clear rainwater, a vessel of powdered galls, and a sizable bath of eau-de-vie. Add gum arabic and rasped logwood. Warm with summer's sun or winter's fire for 2 days. Strain.

—

WARNING

Under no circumstances should you distill an ink or dye from an unknown weed or untested recipe, for this might very well result in unforeseen and highly unpleasant consequences.

—The Field Guide to the Poisons of Caux
Axlerod D. Roux

Part 1

The Well Keeper

What of someone from the darkworlds,
who is returned to the light?
They rejoice as the sun sets,
and find solace in the shadows of the night.

—Prophecy, Sparrowhawk fragment

Chapter One

Mrs. Mulk

hrough a gate of jagged iron needles sat a decrepit brick building. At some point in its long life, the fence along the gate had endured a botched repair and was bandaged in places with barbwire, which sat rusting in sharp and dangerous clots. Behind it was a plot of rubble that could never be mistaken for a play yard, but in some sad coincidence was indeed just that. It was littered with stones, bits of broken glass, and scraps of rusting metal. The only visible toy was a small, weathered doll that sat headless and dejected. When there was a thin window in the brick building, long, uneven bars stretched across it. A faded sign announced this destination as a final one.

The Wayward Home for Indigent Orphans and Invalid Hotel

It was, in fact, a picture of perfect misery. But appearances did not matter for the Wayward Home for Indigent Orphans

3

and Invalid Hotel, as there were never any visitors (unless you were unfortunate enough to be an orphan or an invalid).

No visitors, that is, except tonight.

From somewhere up the battered pathway and in the general vicinity of the crippled entry, a blast of impatient knocking shook the old front door. And then, *rat-tat-tat-tat*, a second. From the stoop, in the silence that followed, there was an irritated complaint, a muffled swear, and the thud of a large package hitting the ground.

Stillness followed.

Above, the worn slate roof was the same color as the cold night sky, except where a yellow incision of moon was carved beside a crumpled weather vane. Dark thornbushes scraped against the old walls, making strange, unsettling whispers. Vines edged over the creaky windows in a tenuous green curtain.

Finally, the peeling wooden door opened just a crack and a slash of weak firelight escaped from the orphanage.

"Who goes there?" accused a falsetto voice, the matronly one of Mrs. Mulk. "We are not due for another delivery." She attempted to close the door but found a stranger's shoe to be preventing this. Examining the shoe, she saw it was of unusual quality—possessing an oily sheen—and terminated in a silk stocking that bagged upon a bony ankle. It wriggled, trapped. Mrs. Mulk narrowed her eyes, and contemplated squishing it.

"Wanda," the visitor murmured.

It was a whisper of a word, and the darkness somehow made it more potent. The name—the softness of the letter *W*, the gasp of the final *da*—was a name of broken promises.

"*Wanda,*" he said again.

The name stayed her hand.

"Who's there?" the custodian hissed. She brought an eye thick with mascara to the opening and peered out. The tar upon her lashes clumped together rebelliously, and when she blinked, it threatened to seal her eye altogether in a gluey mass. "If you prefer your foot attached to your body, I suggest you remove it at once. Otherwise, it will become the property of the orphans and invalids in my care. They are, it just so happens, in need of a new toy."

"Wanda. It's *me,*" the nasally voice repeated, this time louder. It took on a pout. "Surely you have not forgotten?"

Mrs. Mulk thought for a moment. Few knew her by her given name. Could it be? While there was something familiar about the voice, there was something quite different, too—and it had been so long.

Times had changed in the kingdom of Caux. The Deadly Nightshades had been deposed, and while many in the land awaited news of their previous ruler, Good King Verdigris, a stubborn few hoped quietly—sinisterly—for the return of a more dangerous way of life.

Mrs. Mulk was one such person. She saw that now there were far fewer poisonings, and fewer poisonings meant fewer orphans. It was bad for business. Wanda Mulk did not like the current state of affairs in the least.

She thought for a moment, a name upon her lips.

"Sorrel?" Mrs. Mulk was suddenly tentative. "Dear Sorrel— Sorrel, is that really you?"

"Yes, Wanda. It's me."

The door was flung open and the generous form of the orphanage's lone custodian filled the frame. Wanda Mulk greeted her old friend and cohort with a look of genuine pleasure. Theirs was a friendship born from great misfortune— not their own, but that of others.

"Oh, Sorrel!" Mrs. Mulk's hands met at her bosom and her fingers laced and unlaced themselves in nervous expectation. Between them on the ground was a large and unwieldy package, wrapped tightly in an old rug and finished with rope.

"And, as usual, Wanda," Sorrel Flux continued, "I come bearing gifts."

Chapter Two

The Package

In the parlor the orphan maker and orphan minder conversed in low tones while the package lay unopened at the bottom of the cellar stairs, beside a few crusted barrels of saltpeter in the tallow room. The reunion was punctuated with Mrs. Mulk's muffled trills, Sorrel Flux's nasal tones threading between. Soon the tinkling of glasses grew more boisterous, while—perhaps in a trick of the candlelight—the woven carpet that haphazardly wrapped Sorrel Flux's gift seemed to pulse and swirl. It possessed a weave that was at once complex and captivating, and dark and discouraging, and, above all, ancient. But the years had not been kind, and the carpet was threadbare in places, and matted and overgrown in others— and the entire thing possessed an overwhelming odor of rotting vegetation.

While Sorrel Flux allowed himself the attentions of Mrs. Mulk, and liberal cupfuls of her sherry, he plotted the package's demise. This came quite easily to the miserable taster, as his dislike of anyone other than himself was what commanded the weak pulse in his sallow wrists. He talked long into the night, quite happy to hear his own voice—dripping with vainglory and tinged with conceit.

The package, he explained, contained a child.

"An orphan?" Mrs. Mulk asked hopefully. They were so much easier than invalids.

"No. Not yet," Flux allowed.

And then he opened his pasty mouth, a slit in his yellowed face, and told Mrs. Mulk the reason for his visit.

Indeed, Flux was right in that the package did not contain an orphan. But, in an interesting coincidence, the package, when it awoke, would wish to be one. It was, in fact, a bitter coincidence that the package should find itself within the walls of an orphanage, for the package most definitely possessed two parents—each more treacherous than the other. The package's mother had seemingly slipped it a very potent sleeping potion, resulting in this current situation. And its father, well, the package's father was bent on world destruction.

So, in the hands of its former, fiendish taster, the package slept—and dreamed.

The basement was composed of walls of bare rock, and dotting the various crannies were dingy candles, dripping molten wax upon everything beneath them. Many more had burned themselves out, nothing but greasy stumps, but the smell of the rendered fat remained.

To look on the bright side, the room was well lit. Sadly, the view was one perhaps better relegated to the dark.

Above a far door to the laundry room was an embroidered sign.

DON'T BOTHER DOING ANYTHING NICE
FOR YOUR CHILDREN.
THEY'LL ONLY REMEMBER
THE BAD THINGS ANYWAY.

Chapter Three

The Boil Pile

I t was the laundry room where all these bad things happened.

As awful as the basement was, the laundry room was far worse. It could be found, beneath the embroidered sign, through a small, riveted steel door. Inside, industrial-sized machines *clugged* and *sloshed* the sheets and tattered uniforms in a syrup of gray suds. Next, a large cylinder with a hand crank would squeeze out most of the dreary water, preparing the laundry—normally—for the drying process. But since Mrs. Mulk's clothes dryer had long ago expired, the washing was then unceremoniously returned to the various cots and shoulders whence it came, damp and discouraging. And then Mrs. Mulk would turn her attentions to what she found to be a far more agreeable project: the Boil Pile.

In one corner of the laundry room, a boiler sprouted many crooked pipes and occasionally belched a cloud of steam. Beside it was a vat—indeed, a cauldron of sorts—which was heated from a vast, glowing orange coil of wire beneath. From a broken metal hatch below it all, tangles of frayed cords and bulging tubes spilled forth along with the occasional spark. There was no off switch. There were no windows. A thin vent pipe threaded through the damp foundation and led to the orphanage's exterior, and was the only clue of the room's existence to the outside world.

For it was here Mrs. Mulk practiced her pursuit of perpetual youth.

Because Mrs. Mulk had it in her mind that there was nothing as precious as youth, she had long ago concocted a way to get herself some. With youth came the promise of longevity and vitality, both in short supply in Caux. But this obsession of Mrs. Mulk's did not translate into perhaps a more healthful lifestyle—the occasional enjoyment of the outdoors and an appreciation of fresh air and good deeds. No, Mrs. Mulk intended to *steal* herself some youth. And from whom better than the youngsters in her care?

The custodian of the Wayward Home for Indigent Orphans and Invalid Hotel found herself thinking that youthfulness could be *extracted*—quite simply, albeit horribly—from cherished objects belonging to her children. Upon arrival, the orphans (already parentless and destitute) were forced to relinquish their only beloved objects—their last possessions, filled with the sweat, kisses, tears, joys, and fears of their miserable lives.

A short list of things upon the Boil Pile:

1. One teddy bear, left eye missing, lovingly replaced with a battered button
2. A child's blanket, silken edge rubbed raw from cuddling
3. A broken locket
4. An odd doll's shoe
5. A thick book, titled *The Field Guide to the Poisons of Caux*, by Axlerod D. Roux

Mrs. Mulk would carefully boil down each of these treasures and, from the burnt dregs at the bottom of the vat, produce a mass of creams, powders, and lotions that would—she hoped—imbue her with eternal life.

Chapter Four

"It Is Done."

orrel Flux's eventual departure from the orphanage brought with it an uncheery moment of silence.

He pattered down the creaky steps. He skulked through what was once a small rose garden, which now grew nothing but vicious thorns. He made his way along the dark hedgerows that lined the walk, covered in a stingy winter's snow, past a few tattered scarecrows made from the cast-off clothes of abject orphans. The scarecrows were silent. A slight wind moved through their straw arms, causing a few to sway worryingly, but Sorrel Flux paid them no mind. His was a nature not to be troubled by nightmarish things—he preferred, instead, to cause them.

The grounds that surrounded the orphanage were, if possible, even more dire than the place itself. Much of the countryside was riddled with wetlands, and in the warmer months, the impassable earth was thick with deadwood and slime-covered puddles. Round hills rose from marsh, and fell back again into field. Tonight, everything was frozen and unwelcoming, even beneath a blanket of snow.

The moon was high now, a sulfurous wedge of yellow in the dark pool of Cauvian night. It easily illuminated the dented pipe from Mrs. Mulk's laundry room, and Flux made a beeline to it. He unwound the silken ascot from his yellowish neck and balled the fine fabric into a small clump, which he then stuffed satisfactorily into the ductwork before him. It was thoroughly jammed. Satisfied at his handiwork, he turned his back on the orphanage.

Sorrel Flux then found his way cautiously in the low light to an old crab apple tree, where he stopped and shifted his weight from one foot to the other. He shook off some of the snow from his polished shoes and waited. He coughed once, and then thought better of it. He stifled a yawn.

Finally, from the deep recesses of the winter night, another figure emerged. It was a grand one, tall and glorious, especially beside the insignificant silhouette of the taster. The moon shone down, revealing a dress of such spectacular fabric as to mimic the celestial heavens above. A deep, night blue—devoid of all stars.

This was Clothilde. She appeared, as if stepping down from the ether, hands upon her hips. Her long hair—once fiercely black—was now a wintry silver, icy. The moonlight coursed through it like a waterfall. With an elegant sweep, she pulled it back into a tidy bun, securing it with a flash of a silver hairpin.

Sorrel Flux, his eyes narrowed, regarded his companion. But he was distracted not by his companion's utter resemblance to the child he had just delivered into Mrs. Mulk's questionable care. No, instead, he was preoccupied with a fantasy. It surged within his scrawny ribs, a dream of his future, one to which he was now one step closer.

"It is done," Flux smirked.

The unlikely pair then turned, bound for Templar.

Damp Idyll No. 1

In the gloaming—before the light falls away completely in the evening—a trio was gathered in an overgrown garden. They were sisters, these three, from a time in Caux's history when great feats of magic were performed by cherished kings and hands wove spectacular tapestries made from silken ribbon and strong enchantments.

But these ladies, like Caux, had seen better days.

The first sister had long ago succumbed to a fungus, and her face was lumpy and porous with hundreds of small mushrooms. The next was wrapped in a cloak of moss so old and formfitting it was hard to distinguish where it began and her flesh left off—if indeed there was such a place. And the last of the sisters was like a very ripe cheese—mold had converged within her veins, and her skin was aged and crumbly. Hers was not a skin but a rind.

These were the Mildew Sisters, and they were gathered together for a spot of tea. A weak fire had been lit beside the garden's stricken scarecrow, and a dented kettle warmed between them.

"We are too late," the aged-cheese sister muttered. "The tea leaves do not lie."

The other two nodded, thoughtfully appraising the soggy pile of brewed nettles on the ground between them. They leaned in, divining.

"You are right, as always, Lola. The girl has returned to Caux, a failure. The Prophecy is unfulfilled. The King has not been cured."

All three nodded, agreeing.

They took a moment to look about the garden. At one time, a young girl's hand had tended the rows—growing with great skill deadly poisons right beside their antidotes. Not far from the crumbling walls, an old millhouse stood abandoned. A sign for a tavern swung from a single nail.

The Hollow Bettle

"And see, Lola"—a weedy hand pointed again at the tea leaves—"it says here she is in grave danger." This was Gigi, and Gigi wrapped her moss shroud about her shoulders tighter, disturbing a nesting spider in one of the folds. "They call her a false prophet."

"Deceitful. A fraud," agreed Lola.

"She must harness the power of the forest to succeed," continued Gigi.

Again they nodded agreeably.

Lola and Gigi looked at the third sister, the fungus-strewn one, a bit hesitantly. This was Fifi. Fifi, realizing something was currently expected of her, leaned in to the soggy pile, squinting.

"Er—" She looked up at the expectant faces of her sisters and then quickly back at the pile of tea leaves. She tentatively gave the mound a nudge with a worn boot.

"It says . . ." She tried again, resolute. "The tea leaves are telling me . . ." A look of frustration settled upon her porous features and then renounced itself.

"It's no use!" Fifi squeaked. "I think I need another cup."

Gigi and Lola scowled at their youngest sister, and then with a resigned sigh, Lola turned to the drooping scarecrow and plucked a generous handful of its stuffing from a fraying hole in its side. From this, more tea was made—the cup finally shoved indelicately in Fifi's direction.

"Now, divine," they ordered.

Surrendering, Fifi sloshed the contents around the dented cup and threw them to the ground. Staring intently, she avoided her sisters.

An uninspired moment passed. Then suddenly, to both Lola and Gigi's great astonishment, Fifi was seized with a rolling shudder— followed by another, more powerful one, after which she appeared frozen in place. The shock of this fit caused her mouth to drop open, a dark hole among the erupting mushrooms upon her face, her knees locked in an indelicate squat where she had bent to examine the earth.

For a stunned moment, the only sound was the hiss of the fire. Then, at once, Lola and Gigi overcame their surprise and rushed to their ailing sister's side.

"Fifi!" they called. "Fifi—what has happened?"

"*Awaken! Blink, dear, if you can hear us!*"

There was no response.

After a minute of continued quiet from Fifi, a different tone from Lola—a suspicious one. "Fifi! Stop this charade at once! When I suggested you apply yourself more diligently to your tea-leaf readings, I hardly had this *in mind. . . ."*

The small walled garden in which they had settled was silent, which made the slap delivered by Lola to her sister's lumpy cheek that much louder. Lola lowered her blue-veined arm.

Progress!

Fifi did blink now—her puff face roiled, producing a contorted scowl.

But before the other two could react, she sputtered. And spoke.

From Fifi's misshapen mouth came a single name in a deep baritone.

She spoke not of Ivy Manx—nor the ancient Prophecy on which they were now called to action—but instead another. A name the three had not dared utter in many, many years. One that, for the Mildew Sisters, was a reminder of their unspeakable past. An unpleasant reminder.

"Babette!" Fifi whispered, her voice raspy and dry, and not at all her own. "Babette is here, and she is coming for us—"

But before she could finish, her other pitiable cheek was met with a forceful slap—this time from Gigi.

The darkness around them pressed in.

Chapter Five
Orphan'd

ost of the putrid candles in the cellar had gut-
tered, and a pungent smoke was all that remained in the unusual half darkness. Thick snores punctuated the parlor room
above, as Mrs. Mulk succumbed to the effects of her sherry,
while below, a pair of hands worked quietly, feverishly, on the
hemp rope of the oblong package. The binds were erratic and
thoughtless—redundant in their loops and often reversing
themselves maddeningly. But the small hands were patient,
and after nearly an hour the rope lay in a cluttered pile and the
strange carpet was all that remained between the contents of
the package and the rank basement air.

A crooked seam joined the edges of the textile, and large
stretches of knotted thread crisscrossed the closure—the work
of a maniac with a fishhook. With a loud *rip*, these parted,

and, along with a large waft of concentrated mildew, the sleeping contents of the package were revealed. Inside: a girl with strands of golden hair, skin abnormally pale even in this low light. She wore a tragic dress made of the blackest soot.

"Ivy!" the owner of the hands called softly, and then again—this time shaking her sleeping form. "Wake up!" the voice pleaded.

After a moment, Ivy's eyes did flutter open, but with a blank stare, unrecognizing. A frown. Then nothing, as her heavy eyelids fell closed.

"Ivy Manx," the girl's voice whispered. "Listen to me. You have been betrayed. Poisoned! You were given a sleeping potion and brought here—to this awful place. You must wake up! And quickly—Mrs. Mulk will be here soon!" The hands carefully smoothed Ivy's untidy hair.

It was useless. Ivy's sleep was deep and profound.

And in it, she dreamed.

Currently, Ivy was hearing distant chatter. Bird chatter—annoying and insistent. She scowled. Her mind rolled over, and to escape the intrusion, she burrowed farther into the dark and springy loam that cradled her in her deep sleep. She pulled a dreamy cloak of woven grass and dried leaves over her head and sighed. The earth was her domain! She had found a restful place finally, no heavy expectations upon her shoulders here, no Prophecies, no voices.

Except the one.

When it arrived, peaceful slumber became a nightmare.

Where are you, my child? came the harsh whisper. A rolling hot wind accompanied it—sickening, poisonous. Ivy held her breath, hiding in her resting spot.

You cannot stray, you know. You and I are one—you shall see. I will find you. There is no escape—no escape from me. From King-maker!

The voice. It was her father's. She knew it at once. He had found her—here even, beneath the earth! She knew something else, too. He was right. There was nowhere she could go that he would not find her.

But in the distance, that bird.

A chatty bird—it refused to hush. In fact, it was louder now, and it was drowning out her father's despicable rant. And the creature's song! Persistent and vital, it sang of strange things, of broken enchantments and drifting ash.

The bird was singing her name, over and over.

"Ivy Manx," it crowed. "Ivy Manx! Wake up!"

Suddenly Ivy was overwhelmed with the vision of her old friend Axlerod—an awful image of the trestleman locked away in a cage, forgotten. Dying.

Ivy struggled to open her eyes, battling furiously against the deep desire to sleep. She forced her mind to retreat from its earthy hole, the deep blanket of crumbling leaves and soil it had fashioned for her nest of artificial slumber. She moved endless piles of earth and her breath felt stale.

With a gasp, she sat up—awake.

But where was the bird? It was not here. Someone else was calling her name softly, shaking her shoulders, chasing the poisoned sleep away. It was a girl—a pale and sickly girl wearing a filthy robe.

Ivy blinked. Where she was, she had no idea. But she knew one thing: the girl before her was completely and utterly familiar.

"Rue!" Ivy gasped. Rue had saved her life at the Tasters' Guild, leading her to the safety of her grandfather's compound after Ivy had been publicly poisoned in the infamous class of Irresistible Meals. Ivy never saw her again, having escaped her father's clutches into Pimcaux. Judging by appearances, Rue had not fared well. She was thin and drawn, her smooth skin a host to blooms of some sort of angry red rash.

"Rue—what's *happened* to you?"

Rue shook her head, looking over her shoulder in a panic. "Not now. Listen to me carefully. You are in an orphanage—"

"An orphanage?" Ivy allowed herself a moment of pleasant contemplation of a world without her parents.

"Not just any orphanage," Rue growled. "The Wayward Home for Indigent Orphans and Invalid Hotel. The oldest and worst orphanage ever built!"

"That's quite a distinction!" Ivy smiled.

From upstairs an unsteady clatter of heels upon the thin floorboards, and Rue's whisper abruptly stopped. A creaking as the door to the basement was thrown open, and a stretch of anemic light hit the stairs.

"Rue?" Ivy looked for her friend, but she was suddenly alone.

Mrs. Mulk was not long on the uneven steps—this was a trip she made often, and in any variety of the teetering footwear that she favored. Something was most certainly amiss with her delivery. As her eyes adjusted to the dimness, she heard a voice from the floor.

"Oh, hello," Ivy said sweetly. "May I trouble you for a glass of water?"

Chapter Six

The Dress

Mrs. Mulk spun around to the package, which was now unwrapped and transformed into her newest charge.

"What did you say?" Her voice was that of an opera singer's after a strenuous performance, high and wavery. Her lips, from where the voice emerged, were penciled dramatically and smothered in a savage pink.

"I'm parched!" Ivy explained. Indeed, whatever potion she had been given had made her mouth dry and stale, and left behind the taste of bog. "Is there any water around here?" she repeated.

"You little savage!" Mrs. Mulk drew herself up to full size. "Where are your manners?"

"Sorry. May I *please* have some water?" Ivy smiled her most endearing smile—one that charmed nearly everyone—but it faded quickly when she saw the look upon the woman's plump face.

Mrs. Mulk inspected this new, pitiful creature before her with interest. Flux had told her the child was a special one. But if looks were anything (and to Mrs. Mulk they were *everything*), there was some mistake. The orphan's hair was wild and uncombed, her fingernails ragged and dirty. But the carpet she came in was salvageable. Wrinkling her nose at the stench of mildew, Mrs. Mulk decided it would make a fine blanket for one of the children in her care.

The caretaker drew herself up.

"Well, orphan," Mrs. Mulk said. (She addressed all her charges thusly—even the invalids.) "Which is it?"

"Which is what?" Ivy wondered.

"Don't take that tone with me, orphan! Do you have the power to heal? Or, is it like I said, that all children are born liars?" Mrs. Mulk challenged.

Ivy blinked.

The custodian noticed that the creature's face had a strange pallor and her eyes were flecked with glittering gold.

"All of Caux is clamoring about your supposed healing powers. 'Child of the Prophecy,'" Mrs. Mulk scoffed. "You've got everyone fooled—but me. Those who expect the return of the old King will soon be disappointed, if I have anything to do about it."

"I am *not* an orphan." Ivy narrowed her eyes at Mrs. Mulk.

"Indeed?" She'd heard that one before.

Mrs. Mulk turned to go, but as she did, a strange look passed over the woman's face—a niggling thought of a lost opportunity.

"Although . . . I am nothing if not fair."

"I can see that," Ivy lied.

Mrs. Mulk leaned in then, her ravaged skin and rouged cheeks aflame with desire. "I will give you one chance."

"For what?"

Mrs. Mulk's words were coming quickly now. "I'll give you one chance to prove yourself. Make me young again. Use your powers and restore my youth. Do it—and I'll free you. You, and that bag of bones that's hiding behind the stairs." Mrs. Mulk wheeled about, pointing at Rue's hiding place. Rue stood, frozen and panicked, and Ivy's heart sank.

"I'm afraid I can't do that," Ivy whispered. Even if she wanted to, she could not chance a cure—for every time she did, she found herself in her father's Mind Garden. The risk was too great.

"Just as I thought."

Satisfied that she had proven yet again that children were nothing if not worthless, the custodian stepped nearer to Ivy. Mrs. Mulk brushed her hands together briskly as if the entire matter was dismissed, and peered closer at the tedious, conniving creature.

The child was wearing a tattered dress the color of a

gravestone's shadow. Mrs. Mulk could tell that at one time it had been a desirable, expensive frock, the product of fancy tailoring and unique lace, and this realization caused a deep surge of envy to bound about her insides. Yet the dress had seen better days and appeared to be falling apart at the seams—the girl could obviously not be relied upon to maintain it. One of the girl's shoulders was exposed where the dress had failed. An old family heirloom, she decided. Perfect for the Boil Pile.

"You will tender that dress to me, young lady," Mrs. Mulk informed Ivy. "The orphans in my home wear this." She produced a gray flannel rag with a pair of armholes.

"But I'm not an—"

"Hand it over. It's going to the Boil Pile."

The history of Ivy's dress now bears a moment of reflection.

The unusual fabric from which it was sewn is unknown, but its origins are not. Ivy received this dress in an encounter with her father, Vidal Verjouce, in his abominable Mind Garden. His carefully manicured retreat had been laid waste by his appalling desire for a potent and despicable weed, once thought extinct. To consult *The Field Guide to the Poisons of Caux* for a further explanation, a careful reader would soon realize this weed was known by two names. Kingmaker—for those who had fallen under its spell. And scourge bracken—for those who had yet to. Furthermore, Axle wrote, it was just a matter of time before you *would* fall—succumbing to parched dreams of brutal domination—for scourge bracken would stop at nothing, calling to it ever more power for its evil designs, until all of Caux was laid waste.

Ivy's Mind Garden dress was tight enough to restrict her breathing and made from an unusual lace with a chaotic, menacing pattern—jagged teeth and eerie shapes, not some pretty doily. It was made, too, by the ruined imaginings of her wicked father. She was happy to see it was decomposing here, back in Caux. The dress came off her in clumps like dried moss.

"Water, you say?" Mrs. Mulk wanted very badly to punish the offending orphans before her, but a greater desire coursed through her now. She wanted to throw Ivy's dress into her despicable vat. She turned to Rue, who stood shaking in the shadows beneath the stairs. "What are you waiting for, you wretched brat? Show her where the well is."

Chapter Seven
The Well

he parlor streamed with welcome light, after the dim
and smoky cellar. The barred windows were decorated with a
faded calico—a pattern of which women of a certain age seem
fond—and the flooring was a worn and stained carpet of similar taste. There was an overabundance of cozies, normally little
lace coverlets sewn to shroud a teapot, but here, in the parlor,
they protected Mrs. Mulk's large collection of miniatures.

The room, despite the light, possessed an inexplicable re-
pellency. The few orphans still in residence were reluctant to
enter it, and the invalids—well, upon this subject they would
all agree their mite-infested beds were preferable to Mrs.
Mulk's parlor. If forced to conclude just what the nature of the
unpleasantness was within these four walls, the task would not
be easy. Perhaps you might point to the smell—the whiff of

decay, a pinch of desperation—but this would be explained away easily, since the room was directly above the molten vat bubbling in the laundry room. The place was a threshold of loneliness.

And it held one occupant. A small one.

It, too, had a cozy.

The door to the basement creaked as Rue and Ivy entered the parlor, and the creaking seemed to have some sort of effect upon a creature beneath a splash of lace suspended from the stained ceiling.

It emitted a frightened *cheep*.

This, after a moment, was followed by the most mournful of songs Ivy had ever heard. The two girls paused beside the cage.

"Is that . . . a bird?" Ivy asked incredulously. The song stopped abruptly.

Rue nodded dismally.

Ivy lifted the cage's cover enough to see two things. It was a small warbler—nearly featherless. And, like the residents of the orphanage, it lived in squalor.

"This is unacceptable!" Ivy shook her head in dismay. The wood warbler was her uncle Cecil's favorite, and she had grown up with many of them beside the Hollow Bettle, the tavern that was her home. Together, Ivy and Cecil had made small houses for them out of worn brandy casks, which they nailed to posts beside her garden and the nearby river. The tiny warblers belonged in the field, flitting about at dusk near the orchard with their tiny wings cutting through the air and feasting on insects, not moldy scrapings.

"We shouldn't—" Rue looked behind her, worried. "We're not supposed to go near it."

Ivy shifted her decomposing carpet to her far shoulder—she would not leave anything further for the Boil Pile—and flung off the lace cover of the birdcage. She pried open the little door.

"For shame!" Ivy scowled. "How dare she keep a wild bird caged like this!" She bent close to the opening. "Hello," she coaxed. As Ivy reached her hand in, the bird began flapping madly, disturbing its litter and upending a small tin of dreary seeds.

"Ivy—"

"It's okay," Ivy cooed. "I'm not going to hurt you.

Here—I'll leave the door open. Stretch those wings! But don't take too long—you-know-who's likely to return!"

Ivy turned to Rue, grabbing her hand. "What is it with this place?" she whispered. "He looks nearly as bad as you."

The well was not far from the orphanage and bordered the encroaching marshes. But it was in an appalling state. The stand of bricks teetered, and in one very worrying place appeared to be missing entirely. An old bucket was discarded beside it, a length of decaying rope attached. The well bespoke weariness and caution—not a cheery spot to put down a picnic and pass a pleasant afternoon. Winter's grim light left the slight hill bleak and frozen. Ivy dumped the appalling carpet upon the frozen turf and Rue set herself wearily down upon it, and then Ivy approached the stand of bricks.

"This is the place?" she asked with some trepidation. Rue nodded.

Inching forward, Ivy peered in. A familiar smell hit her nose—of swamp and disuse—and she was reminded at once of Rocamadour's deepest tunnels and crypts. Her stomach lurched. She peered down the long hole—several dead mice floated on the water's dull surface. Pulling back quickly, Ivy looked at Rue.

"Surely she can't expect us to drink this?"

"Mrs. Mulk says this is just fine for the orphans." Rue nodded.

"Well, I'm not an orphan." Ivy frowned. She pondered for a moment. "Where does she get *her* water?"

Rue paused. She shivered, and pulled the carpet around her.

Then she told Ivy about the other well.

Chapter Eight

The Other Well

Mrs. Mulk drew her water from a well found at the end of a walk over rolling hills and down a long, rough path, said Rue. Once a week, she would saddle up an orphan or two in harnesses that held a yoke and secured two wooden pails, one on each side, and they would journey to the spot. The well was clear and pure, and it was rumored that something very special—but long forgotten—was buried deep beneath it.

It was hard and drenching work to collect Mrs. Mulk's water, made worse—much worse—by the fact that the orphans were under strict orders not to drink it lest they contaminate Mrs. Mulk's personal supply with their orphanness.

"Ah," said Ivy. "That's more like it! Show me where this well is, Rue."

The well at her childhood home was prized for its taste—and made the brandy of the Hollow Bettle famous. But Ivy's memories of clear, fresh water drawn by her millhouse were shattered as Rue slumped against a small, ruined tree, crooked and charred from a lightning strike.

"Rue?"

Ivy could hear that Rue was crying quietly.

"How awful of me! You're tired, of course. We'll just rest until you feel more like yourself—"

But Rue's sobs grew louder and more miserable.

"Rue?" Hesitating, Ivy finally sat down beside her, smoothing the mildewed rug. "What is it? Don't worry about *her*—I've seen worse, much worse! Why, if I can handle my own father—"

At the mention of the Guild's Director, Rue's crying only increased. Ivy was quite concerned—this seemed to be unusual behavior for Rue, although Ivy could not say for sure. Rue had been Rowan's friend and classmate, and upon meeting her in Rocamadour, Ivy had somewhat petulantly disliked her. Ivy remembered Rue had once desired to be a subrector herself, and had even apprenticed under the detestable subrector Snaith. She had been well on her way when she risked everything for Ivy, rescuing her from scourge bracken poisoning. If Rowan were here, Ivy thought bitterly, he'd know what to do for Rue, but the last she'd seen of him was on the journey home from Pimcaux. They'd shared a few private words before she awoke in Mrs. Mulk's clutches.

"Rue," Ivy said suddenly. "How did you get *here*—to Mrs. Mulk's?"

"Snaith—" Rue turned to her. "Snaith sent me here. As punishment. For . . ."

"For helping me?"

Rue nodded quietly. Ivy felt awful. The harrowing trip from Snaith's lecture hall, as the scourge bracken in the irresistible chocolate cake took effect, would forever be burned into Ivy's memory. Ivy had been losing the battle when Rue stepped in to help her. The streets of Rocamadour were a swirling menace of darkness, and indeed, from then on, Ivy would never again feel right in the shadows. She was now—at best—a wounded healer; the scourge bracken poison within her was biding its time, she knew, waiting for her to falter. And if she did, it would be ready.

"I could have gotten worse . . . ," Rue added quickly, and Ivy knew she was right.

"And my father . . . ?" Ivy hardly dared to wonder what evildoings he practiced in his broken chambers atop the tall spire. Time had passed while Ivy was in Pimcaux—it was winter now in Caux.

"The last we heard from your father"—Rue's expression turned fearful—"he was babbling, and made little sense. Most of his talk was of ink, some ink he is making beneath the city. He is close to perfecting it. He terrified us—the younger ones were crying. There was no comforting them."

Ivy's stomach lurched. Her father's madness was complete.

"Did he say anything else about the ink?" Ivy demanded.

"Only this: 'What is written can be unwritten.'"

"What is written can be unwritten," Ivy whispered. What did this mean?

"We didn't hear from him again. Instead, we were addressed by his Watchmen—usually Snaith. And the stench! No learning happens in that foul air; there is some sort of fire belching out yellowish fumes from beneath the city. What few students remain are fearful and desperate. We were herded into a lecture hall to pass the day. Grandfather"—Rue gulped back a sob—"tried to make the best of it. He carried on his lessons as best he could, but he, too, is considered an outsider. They locked us in."

Ivy's heart sank. Her last memory of Rocamadour was not a pretty one—a crypt beneath the ancient city in the heart of the catacombs. There, they had found hallowed ground, the only place where scourge bracken grows. All was lost if Hemsen Dumbcane, the traitorous forger from Caux, was successfully making ink from the diabolical plant—for scourge bracken was at its worst when concentrated into the deep, rich ink, and Dumbcane was the only one who knew the recipe. He had inadvertently discovered it scrawled in the margin of an ancient, stolen text—and he then, unknowingly, produced the perfect vehicle for the deadly plant. The recipe made the weed impeccably concentrated, irresistible, and portable. And poised for destruction.

After a gloomy moment passed, Rue wiped her tear-stained face and tried to smile.

"How was Pimcaux?" she asked hopefully.

If possible, Ivy felt even worse.

In a low voice she told Rue of her trip, of the tiny alewives and her ride on Klair and Lofft—two magnificent seabirds with ribbon harnesses and the power of speech. But King Verdigris had sent her home, back to Caux, with a task—and an unusual pair of stones.

"He called them *an old King's burden*," Ivy recalled. "And told me to plant them here, in Caux, when I returned."

"What are they, these stones?" Rue frowned.

"They look like the pits from some sort of fruit—like a peach or a plum. Their coloring is strange—deep gray, with pinkish, fleshy ridges. And they're quite heavy. They're—they're like nothing I've seen before. But . . ." A distant memory tugged at her. "But at the same time, they are so utterly familiar."

Something from deep within the fetid well gurgled.

"If *you* don't know what sort of tree they are from, I doubt anyone in Caux does." Ivy's spectacular expertise in botany was known even to Rue.

"I can think of someone," Ivy replied glumly.

Rue sagged. Together, the girls thought of Axle, Ivy's friend and traveling companion—and expert author of Caux's famed *Field Guide to the Poisons of Caux*. His future was dim—even if Ivy managed to escape Mrs. Mulk, he was behind the impenetrable walls of the Tasters' Guild, a captive of Vidal Verjouce himself.

"Ivy—" Rue began, alarmed. "The stones. Mrs. Mulk—?"

The wind had picked up and a deep chill was settling in. Ivy stood and carefully wrapped Rue tighter in the old rug. The thing was appallingly dirty and smelled damp like mildew, but Rue needed its warmth.

"They are safe."

Ivy looked around, appraising the hills. Somewhere out there was Rowan—she hoped. And her uncle, in Templar. But the wintry hills of this far corner of Caux looked dismally unfamiliar. Ivy spotted something upon a nearby branch and reached for it, snapping off a small, delicate spike. "Here." She handed it to Rue. "A maple icicle. They're delicious! Sweet and cold, the best of winter."

As Ivy stood, Rue remembered something.

"Ivy," Rue warned. "Beware of the well keeper."

"The well keeper?"

Rue swallowed nervously and nodded. "Yes. Her name is Lumpen Gorse."

Chapter Nine

Lumpen Gorse

Nestled in a nearby valley among swollen hills lay a pile of mossy stones. In the center was a deep, dark hole, the well of which Rue spoke—one of great depth and clear, satisfying water. No one knew what lay beneath the well that lent it such marvelous clarity and taste—not even Lumpen Gorse (or if she did, she had long forgotten). The well was only accessed by a small meandering path that left all who approached open for inspection.

Beside the ancient well was the well keeper.

Lumpen Gorse squatted in all seasons near the pile of stones, one arm grasping her yarrow stick—a thin Y-shaped branch she regarded as both a necessity to her profession and a weapon. When she was awake, her large brow protruded in a permanent scowl. She had a colony of red capillaries upon her face, and the sackcloth that made up her rudimentary skirts splayed out about her in a succession of faded and pulled patchwork. Her bones were sore from resting upon the stones of the well, and she had remedied this with padding; her threadbare coats and long pantaloons were stuffed with straw from nearby fields. Her lips appeared to be sewn to the corncob pipe protruding from one corner of her mouth, which glowed with red embers even when she slept (which she managed to do with one eye open—for such was her suspicious nature that she had long ago learned to keep guard on the water even while she rested).

And Lumpen was indeed currently asleep, her one eye staring mindlessly at the large clot of thorns and burrs that made up a hedge nearby. Little gurgling snores poured out of her pipe. But suddenly the listless black pupil within Lumpen Gorse's bloodshot eye shrank to a pinprick—and the eye assumed an intensity and focus, an awakeness, while the craggy eyelid held virtually still. From all outward appearances, Lumpen Gorse slept on.

Within the hedge a pair of hummingbirds flitted.

Or, to be more precise, a single hummingbird darted from branch to branch, encouraging her mate, who was hopelessly entangled within a deadly shroud of burrs. The suffering of the male hummingbird was observed by the well keeper for a quiet minute. Then the twiggy eye blinked finally, and with a grunt, Lumpen rose and plodded over to the hedge.

With surprising agility and patience, the well keeper assisted the ensnared bird, carefully peeling away the tiny hooks embedded throughout the creature's miniature feathers while the other hummingbird nervously droned beside the well keeper's mass of strawlike hair. Her considerable fingers were unusually deft.

And only then, after the final pesky barb was removed and the exhausted creature sat resting in her callused hand, did Lumpen Gorse remove her pipe from between her sluggish lips. While the relieved mate looked on, she popped the liberated bird into her mouth and ate it for breakfast.

The delicate bones had barely cleared her gullet when, from behind her, a voice called.

"Miss Gorse?" it spoke.

The shock Lumpen felt was twofold. First, she had never, in her long history of well-tending, been surprised in such a way as this—the path to her well was a long and open one, and by the time a thirsty traveler had arrived at her skirts, she had already summed him up quite appropriately. And second—and this she discovered as she wheeled about—the hummingbird was partaking of his final revenge, and was stuck in her craw.

Before her was quite an unusual group. It consisted of half a dozen red-cloaked men—a deep, rich scarlet, Lumpen noticed, the color of blood—and one very particular gentleman in their midst. *Gentleman* might be a stretch, Lumpen now thought, but he was evidently important enough to warrant such an impressive escort. He was, for one, entirely covered in what appeared to be some form of paint. A dark, inky splatter reached across his white shirt and freckled his thin, lumpy neck. His frail fingers and cuticles were a permanent deep, rich black.

It took Lumpen Gorse a complete minute to recognize him.

"Hemsen Dumbkin?" She coughed suspiciously. A few emerald-colored feathers accompanied the words and floated lazily between the two.

A satisfied look crept across the calligrapher's inky face. "A pleasure to see you again, Lumpen."

The well keeper's eyes merely narrowed.

"I have come, with your permission, to draw more of your fine water."

Damp Idyll No. 11

A great gasp penetrated the small walled garden and drifted out in the bitter air as a rolling cloud of misted disbelief.

"She did not just say what I think she said!" Gigi sputtered, appalled.

"It's your fault, you know—you're always so tough on her—" Lola accused.

"Me? You hit her first!" Gigi retorted.

"I was merely trying to break whatever swoon had overtaken the poor thing," Lola insisted.

"Still—she did say the name, you know. Babette—"

"Shh!"

The two sisters peered at the third. Fifi was quiet now, after her outburst.

"Let us agree to put this off to the trials of the journey; you know that she is decidedly unused to keeping such a pace," Lola decided.

Indeed, the Mildew Sisters had been on the move, leaving the seclusion of their dilapidated compound on the island of the Eath, traveling together in silence through ancient forests to find themselves at a small, dark, and shuttered tavern.

The three sisters were not there for the famous brandy (they were, after all, teetotalers). They had journeyed not to the tavern but to the small garden behind it. For within the crumbling walls was a potent source of information, if not herbs. This was not any garden. This was the garden of Ivy Manx—or Poison Ivy, as she was known by her clients. And notably, this garden was one of great wonder, and great danger to the uninitiated. Just the place to make tea and divine the fortunes of the garden's wayward proprietor.

Among the old stones, Ivy Manx had long ago propped a broken mirror, and standing before it currently were the three huddled figures of the Mildew Sisters. Frost crisped the damp hems of their decrepit dresses. Steam threaded up from a discarded pile of tea leaves. Yet it was as if the mirror had met with daylight and held it hostage, for quite clearly the reflection was of a meeting beneath the afternoon sun. More curious still, the Mildew Sisters—the ones in the mirror—were very much the picture of youth and beauty, unburdened by their various afflictions.

Gone were the shroud of greenery, the rindlike skin, the roiling mushroom eruptions.

Within the shard of glass, three impossible dresses clothed three impossible beauties, the color of each so bewilderingly beautiful, to

name it would be a frustrating exercise in poetry. Crowns of posies kissed their dewy temples, while a garden lush with life was in full bloom beside them.

Yet in the dismal garden, beneath the brooding clouds, Fifi was coming to, and, realizing she was the subject of some concern and vexation, she spoke.

"The strangest thing—I had the most peculiar dream!"

"Never mind." Lola straightened and looked around the dimness purposefully. Flashing Gigi a warning look, she was determined to forget the whole shocking affair. She pointed. "The author's trestle is just there. Ivy's friend—the little man who wrote the Field Guide."

"Yes," Gigi agreed. "Let us go. There still is a chance."

"A last hope," Lola concluded.

A small path strewn with white pebbles led from the garden to the tavern in the twilight. From behind the crumbling walls a few ungraceful footsteps crunched; the snap of deadwood called out an enormous owl from his hunting perch. The Mildew Sisters emerged.

Through dark, misted fields, Fifi, Gigi, and Lola proceeded past the Hollow Bettle's limits, over broken casks and rusting hoops, to find the old Northward Corridor rail line. The eldest, Lola, paused to breathe in a chestful of the damp air.

"The Southern Wood," she said, satisfied, "has a delicious chill to it tonight, wouldn't you say, mes chères?"

The others paused and eagerly agreed.

"A night such as this, it seems a shame to be doing the bidding of another." She was thinking of the forest and its deep and uncharted fens and glades, what nibbles she might find within them.

Again, all were in agreement.

"But that we must," she sighed. "For we have a promise to keep."

With that, the three strange silhouettes made their way across the treacherous rail ties to a place mid-trestle and, through a dewy spiderweb, disappeared down a small painted door.

They were followed, quite unbeknownst to them, by a shadow—a strange shadow, one not black, but white.

Chapter Ten
Spies

Ivy neared the top of a stark hill, and noted the scenery seemed positively inspiring the farther she got from the dismal brick prison. It was quite evident that the rolling hills and open fields had been carefully tended by knowledgeable hands. The land opened into a patchwork, and Ivy could see, posted as sentries, the occasional scarecrow on guard.

She struggled to find a familiar landmark. The frozen farmland was sparse and stretched out forever, crisscrossed by crumbling stone walls and the occasional shade tree. Rowan, she knew, came from the north, where the dark, rich earth was perfect for farming. But this was not the Northward Corridor, her friend's homeland, for there, the ancient Craggy Burls rose in jagged peaks.

How far is Templar? she wondered.

A few small birds flitted nearby—alighting upon the crumbling stone walls and hedgerows. They chattered at the happy discovery of some hayseed, and in the weak light of winter made a meal of it. A lazy shadow played across these fields now, a vast jagged V, and Ivy felt a sudden chill. The bird party departed abruptly after several shrill warning cries. The shadow glided, its shape stretching monstrously as it passed over an outcropping of rocks, a crooked menace. Looking into the stark sky, she saw the vast wingspan of a vulture, circling lazily.

Ivy froze.

The bird was a Rocamadour vulture. They were the Director's messengers, his spies. She fell quickly into the relative safety of a thicket, the rough growth scratching her skin through the threadbare cloth of Mrs. Mulk's orphan uniform.

From Ivy's vantage point, she could see the valley beneath her, the small puffs of hills topped with the prickly remains of a grain harvest poking through the anemic snow. Below, where the valley leveled out, there was a pile of round gray stones. Normally, it would be here that the well keeper would begin her assessment of the oncoming visitor, wearing her trademark scowl and her corncob pipe.

But Lumpen Gorse was otherwise occupied.

And Ivy only needed to see the scarlet cloaks and deep hoods of the Watchmen to know that no matter how thirsty she was, she would have to wait to drink.

Chapter Eleven

"Dumbkin"

nly after several quiet minutes did Ivy dare to peek out, slowly. Her breath was coming quickly—after her deep sleep, her heart beat uncomfortably in her chest. She had not been spotted.

At the well, there were half a dozen of Snaith's henchmen, or Watchmen—the newest and most brutal sort of subrector at the Tasters' Guild, all dressed in blood-red robes. The sight of them sent a surge of cold fear through her. These figures surrounded an irregular fellow, somewhat slight and bent, whose skin was oddly mottled and splotchy. From the distance, Ivy couldn't place him. They appeared to be in discussions with by far the oddest-looking person of the group—a woman seemingly made of straw and dressed in patchwork.

Ivy had no choice but to watch and wait, for there was

nothing—not the slightest wisp of a word—that might be heard from high on the hill.

Down below, Dumbcane was finding his negotiations were not going as planned. After Lumpen Gorse's initial greeting, her face had turned more dour (if that were possible) and her substantial arms were now crossed upon her broad chest. She shook her head fiercely, demonstrating a remarkable fearlessness around the Guild's infamous servants.

Hemsen Dumbcane inhaled sharply, and again attempted to explain his errand to the well keeper. He needed her water for his ink—and he was prepared to bargain. Only her water would do. After several disastrous attempts at re-creating his scourge bracken ink for Vidal Verjouce, he came to realize his error—and just in time. His original inks from his private stock in his shop upon the Knox were successful because they were produced with the waters of Miss Gorse's well, and of this he now reminded the well keeper. Without the water, there would be no ink.

Without the ink, there would be no Dumbcane.

"Not again, Dumbkin." Lumpen took a stab at his name. "That's the last time you swindle me. You're cut off. Besides, I got no use for yer faded papers—the last one you gave me was nothing but gobby-glook."

Dumbcane opened his palms outward to signify he was empty-handed. His hands—even the bony wrists and slight peek of a hairy forearm—were splattered with ink. "All I have to trade—all I've ever had, my dear, dear Miss Gorse—were papers and books and the occasional chart—which, I assure you, are all of inestimable value."

"Not to me."

She glared at the group. She experienced a moment of regret for eating the hummingbird, for her throat was now as prickly as a whisker, and she wanted to tell them all to leave. As she attempted to clear it and continue, Hemsen Dumbcane glided forward, an inky arm extended before him. It was an odd gesture to Lumpen—admittedly not a woman of the world. The scribe approached, his outstretched thumb aimed at her head. His inky, black-stained digit bobbed at her, eye level, while Lumpen Gorse felt her arms roughly pinned behind her and a red sleeve snaked about her neck, pulling her back.

"Sadly, Miss Gorse, it has come to this."

"Dumbkin?" Lumpen croaked.

Hemsen Dumbcane held his soiled thumb to her forehead, and in the spot just between her eyes where her weathered brow was fretting, the calligrapher anointed her with a sticky, inky thumbprint. There was a singeing sound, as if a hot coal had been extinguished in a bucket of water. The swirls of the tip of the scribe's thumb were remarkably clear upon her skin, the idiosyncrasies of its unique design visible as a raised black blot on her forehead. A wisp of smoke dispersed.

Lumpen gasped—nearly inhaling her corncob pipe—and collapsed.

"Thief!" she squawked. "Scoundrel!"

An eerie ripple coursed through the tall, dry grasses in the stark snowfields around them, catching the Watchmen off balance. The waves finally settled at Lumpen's feet, where they took a moment to dissipate. A few of the Guild's assassins surveyed the hills tensely, but seeing nothing further, they resumed their guard.

"Dumbkin, I will hunt you down—" Lumpen attempted to raise her head, but it would not cooperate. And then her words came no longer. The Watchmen relaxed. Stepping back, they were indifferent to her curse.

They were now tasked to collect her water.

Chapter Twelve

Calyx

vy waited a long time after the Watchmen had stolen Lumpen's water—filling large, squat skins and dozens of barrels and stacking them on a cart. She had observed as they turned away from the still figure of the well keeper and busied themselves with the chore of moving the water back to the Tasters' Guild and Rocamadour, to where Dumbcane had set up shop. The large beast responsible for the transport was tethered to the cart, and until this time had been enjoying a lunch of what remained of the hay underfoot.

At one time, this beast was not one of burden; rather, he was an impressive steed in the long regiment of horses kept in the once-stunning stables of Rocamadour. His bloodline was celebrated, and he was amazingly long-lived. His father, and his father before him, were said to ride with the crest of the cinquefoil upon their foreheads—that is, they were descended from the Good King's own steeds. King Verdigris's horses were a rare breed—possessing brutal war instincts and amazing strength and intellect.

This particular horse, while once standing regal and tall, was now old and tired. At one time in his life, he had worn a bridle and saddle of the most supple leather, the color of the evening sky; draped in the finest of jewels, he rode out of the night carrying the very stars upon his back. Now he was the last of the great horses to inhabit the Tasters' Guild. But his name remained, a relic of his respectable past—although his beloved master had long abandoned him. He was called Calyx. And indeed, if you looked close enough, you would still spot dignity in Calyx's eyes.

Calyx's lunch was over when his head was rudely jerked upward from the ground cover. He shook his shabby mane in protest and fussed. Before the whips came down on him, though, he knew to move forward, pulling the heavy load of water from Lumpen Gorse's well. Pulling a cart—pulling anything other than a chariot of the finest silver—was beneath him. But he had long been broken.

Ivy debated returning to Rue, but the extensive trip and her own parched tongue kept her there above the dangerous scene. She knew she herself was wanted—more, even, than Lumpen's water. And she had returned to Caux, tasked with a command from the Good King himself to plant the strange stones. She could not be captured.

The Director's henchmen were efficient, and quite soon they were advancing up the only path—the very one by which Ivy now crouched.

Calyx came first. His war instincts still very much alive, he sensed her there, and even chanced to turn his head before remembering the debilitating blinders he wore.

So there lurks a child, he thought as he plodded uphill, a froth beginning in the corners of his bridled mouth. His senses were still keen, and, like Ivy, he was royalty. He knew her at once as noble, and in a swell of pride he lifted his bony profile. *Let her be safe from this bunch.*

The scarlet-clad men walked in step behind the cart, silent, ominous.

It was the last in the fearsome parade that nearly made Ivy gasp.

His skin was splotchy from the caustic scourge bracken ink he concocted from a secret recipe, a recipe he had chanced upon in the margins of one of his stolen manuscripts. But Ivy recognized him. He was Dumbcane, the forger from the Knox, and she now knew his presence here could mean only one thing. This water would be used to make his ink.

Chapter Thirteen

The Garden Angel

The prone figure of Lumpen Gorse lay quite still beside her beloved pile of stones as Ivy approached. The wind played about the straw padding that emerged in clumps from her wrists and old-fashioned pantaloons. Still, Ivy was guarded and, with narrowed eyes, approached cautiously. The sun was behind the hill, lighting her golden hair aflame, and in the valley all shadows were long and arched.

Lumpen's poor, bloodshot eyes were open, and her tongue was swollen and discolored and lolled about awfully. The black thumbprint in the center of her forehead was now depressed into the flesh, wrinkled and cracked. It was for this reason that Ivy missed a sudden dilation of the well keeper's pupils—for Lumpen's body remained completely motionless. But her eyes shifted ever so, and took on an awareness. Her fingers tensed into balls, her arms like clubs beneath her. She watched Ivy, who, with the sun at her back, looked, Lumpen would later remark, like a burning, flickering flame.

The very one she had been waiting for.

Quietly, Ivy approached the well. With a final look over her shoulder at the still well keeper, she peeked down the deep hole. The smell was nothing like Mrs. Mulk's, or the awful sewers of Rocamadour. It was of the earth, of fresh, damp wholesomeness and infinite pleasures.

Falling to her knees, she began pulling the long rope upward to her, and when the pail finally arrived, she drank directly from it, letting the clear, pure water that escaped fall down her front and pool in her lap.

This was some thirst. Whatever potion she had been given had now worn off, and with Lumpen Gorse's delightful water, she felt her strength and purpose return to her. The world seemed at once bright and alive; the fields in the valley coursed and sparkled with sun and ice.

A vague rustling now sounded from behind her, tiny feet atop a pile of dried leaves.

"Hullo." Lumpen's rough-edged voice had taken on a shyness.

As Ivy spun around, Lumpen reached into her waistcoat, fishing about in her ample padding, and produced a worn and flattened parchment.

"You're the angel," the well keeper said, pointing to the crushed scroll. "The garden angel!"

"Er." Ivy frowned. "Hardly."

Lumpen grew more insistent, tapping the page. "Only—where are your stones?"

Peering at the paper, Ivy felt her heart skip a beat.

Chapter Fourteen

The Scroll

"I t's you, all right," Lumpen decided. "Even down to that old pillowcase you're wearing."

"How—how did you know about the stones?" Ivy asked. But Lumpen had fallen into a startling curtsy, a puffy, straw-studded affair, and when she struggled again to a standing position, she loudly declared herself Ivy's servant.

"Nonsense!" Ivy's eyes were wide. "You are a well keeper. Not a servant!" And upon further reflection, "And certainly not *my* servant."

Lumpen's gaze narrowed—and for a moment Ivy wondered just what her fate might be if the odd woman changed her mind. But the moment passed into one of silence, and Ivy found herself in an uncomfortable standoff that was ended only when Ivy snatched the scroll from the well keeper's callused hands.

The parchment indeed bore a remarkable likeness to Ivy—

the image of a girl with golden hair beside a hardscrabble well astonishingly similar to Lumpen's. Gardens of lush roses and vegetation grew at her feet in abundance. In places it was blurred, having suffered for so long inclement weather and the confines of Lumpen's bosom. Cramped scratchings framed the image, and small insets contained incomprehensible images with strange writings in the old tongue. It was an unmistakable relic from Dumbcane's archive—but most astonishing was the distinctive rendering of a set of odd stones the Good King had given her in Pimcaux.

"Where did you get this?" Her voice cracked.

"Dumbkin," Lumpen Gorse confirmed. "That scoundrel paid me with it the first time he came scrounging around."

"Hemsen Dumbcane gave you this?" Ivy asked sharply. She knew the scribe's troves of valuable parchments were stolen from ancient, magical texts. "Are there others?"

Lumpen Gorse shrugged.

"I've got to go—" Ivy was suddenly, overwhelmingly worried about the safety of her stones. "I need to show this to my uncle."

Ivy looked around the hills of ice and snow, gigantic eggs beneath a blanket of spun glass. She sagged.

"How do I get to Templar?"

Lumpen thought for a long moment. It had been much time since she had departed her valley, and although she was certain she once knew the way to the capital, words were not her forte. The stricken elm tree, blackened by lightning—

63

did that still stand? Perhaps. There were old stone walls she knew to follow—but surely the paths were overgrown and desolate. The landscape had likely changed greatly while she tended her well, and any old markers were lost to time.

"I will show you," Lumpen finally decided. She propped her thin yarrow stick upon her shoulder.

"No—I hardly think that's necessary . . . ," Ivy weakly protested.

Lumpen Gorse wiped her scratchy hands upon her skirts.

"Here, miss." She offered her arm. "Come along to Lumpen."

Ivy meekly joined the stout well keeper. And it was here that Lumpen Gorse, solid arms and strong spine, hoisted Ivy Manx upon her back and, with little complaint, began trudging up the path.

As they set out, Ivy couldn't help but notice strange behavior in the dried stalks of the surrounding hills. They swayed and rolled on a day without wind, bowing and rippling in graceful arcs ever more toward them, finishing at the bristly boots of the well keeper as they walked by.

"As light as a wisp in the wind you are, miss," Lumpen scolded.

"We need to get my friend Rue on the way. She's sick. She needs water," Ivy responded meekly.

"Good thing I've got another shoulder," Lumpen said, and smiled broadly, her corncob pipe burning a pleasant scent of hay as they made their way first to Rue and then to Templar.

64

Chapter Fifteen
Explosion!

"Garden angel?" Rue tried to laugh, but fell into a distressing cough. "Never heard of them. Garden gnome, on the other hand . . ."

Ivy felt the color rise to her face. After a few meek protests, Ivy had let the name stay—for indeed, upon this, Lumpen would not be swayed. The trip back to Mrs. Mulk's well had been a warm one in the folds of Lumpen's padding, and her great strides were gentle and relaxing. Ivy had closed her eyes for a few minutes of rest.

And now before her, Rue looked anything but better.

"You do look a bit like an angel here—" Rue decided, blinking at the parchment. "Your hair is either on fire or that halo is."

Ivy gave her a warning look and would have been more fierce if Rue had not looked so completely unwell. Her lips were parched even after the restorative drink that Ivy and

Lumpen produced from Lumpen's wineskin, and deep, dark circles cradled her eyes. Her teeth, even from within the woolen shroud, were chattering uncontrollably.

"Did you rest?" Ivy asked, concerned. She felt her friend's flushed cheek for fever, pulling her hand back quickly at the touch of her blazing skin.

Rue nodded, looking into the distance. "I've been admiring the view."

The light had been too low when Ivy left Rue by the fetid well for Ivy to notice much of anything. The slight hilltop opened out onto the orphanage nearby, the brick walls bulging at unsteady angles. A plume of steam belched from a crooked chimney, but otherwise all was quiet. The dismal play yard was empty.

What worse, more dispiriting view could there be? Ivy wondered.

"Do you see the vultures?" Rue's voice was thready. "Circling the spire?"

Ivy squinted, but there was no sign of the dark city of Rocamadour.

"Rue?" she asked. The girl was shivering beneath the carpet.

"The smoke," Rue continued, more to herself than to Ivy or Lumpen. "It burns so thick, so black. Did you hear that?" Rue straightened, alert. "That voice? It's *him*. It's the voice of . . . of . . . ruin."

"Whose voice?" Ivy asked sharply.

"Why, your father's."

"Really." Ivy scowled. "And what does he have to say?"

"Once you ingest it, its darkness grows inside you—it takes up residence," Rue whispered. *"Kingmaker is now a part of you forever, Ivy. You and I are one. You will never again feel right in the shadows."*

Ivy sat down, stunned. In Irresistible Meals, when Snaith had poisoned her with scourge bracken, he had tried simply to kill her. But in some ways what she got was worse: a lifetime of battling scourge bracken's dark urges within her, a lifetime of skirting the shadow world. In Pimcaux, the alewives had told her just this. Her father was right, she thought dismally.

"Shh—" Lumpen stepped forward. She bent down and, picking up Rue, cradled her within the rug. "She's even lighter than you—" Lumpen said to Ivy, a frown deeply furrowed in her tan brow.

But before Ivy Manx could comment upon Rue's doleful vision of Rocamadour, or her friend's dwindling health, or her father's unlikely message for her, something very strange indeed occurred.

It began at Mrs. Mulk's dismal well, which groaned, gurgled, and finally belched a thin tendril of greenish fog.

A slow rumble followed this, inexplicable, as if the earth were quarreling with itself. Then, before the threesome could react to these newest of oddities, a roaring wall of scorched air hurtled over them with such force that it seemed the ensuing rain of bricks and debris that scattered all about them was doing so in utter silence.

It was an explosion, from the very bowels of the orphanage.

Stranger still, interspersed among the bricks and devastated mortar were children's valuables—a wisp of a blanket, a beloved teddy, treasured family portraits, a red ball. A particularly pricey ascot.

Completing this odd weather was a drifting rain of some sort of dark material—a black lacy moss, it seemed to Ivy at first—clumps of it landing simply everywhere, wafting through the choking air lazily, settling softly on the ground, muffled and dusty.

"My dress," Ivy gasped.

Indeed, in the old windowless laundry room, the dastardly vat and frayed, sparking cord had finally given out. With the aid of a silk scarf to the vent pipe, Mrs. Mulk's Boil Pile was no more. And, unbeknownst to them, the explosion had at least one other victim. It blew off Mrs. Mulk's carefully plucked eyebrows, before dispatching her to the place that people who are mean to orphans go when they die.

Damp Idyll No. III

"Babette," *Fifi had said. The word hung in the air like the lightest of feathers.*

How could the name strike fear in the hearts of such ancient, enchanted creatures as the Mildew Sisters? The story of Babette is the story of petty jealousy and familial betrayal. And, of course, punishment. Consider this: Fifi, Lola, and Gigi were not a mere trio. No, they were, at one time, a quartet. Together, in Pimcaux, they had a shop.

Four Sisters Tapestries of the Ancients and Royal Haberdashery

Four ancient sisters from an earlier time. The sisters were beauties, refined and elegant, and enrobed in dresses of soft, spun silk: one the color of the golden sun, the next of starlight, another of the evening sky, and the last—Babette—the pure white of a billowing cloud. They were weavers, producing magnificent works of art and draping kings and queens alike. Their creations were impossibly intricate, unpredictably magical textiles, made from the very ribbons of the Tree of Life.

The Four Sisters were weavers of such expertise that they threatened even Nature with their masterful realism. Their panels were so lifelike that an admirer faced the very real possibility of taking a wrong turn and stepping within their delicate threads, only to be trapped within the weave forever.

Because of this, the Four Sisters soon found it necessary to grant a concession.

Only Nature is capable of true perfection. And since no one would want to offend Nature, the foursome made a pledge. They promised to place an inaccuracy—an intentional mistake—in each of their otherwise perfect tapestries, thereby rendering their work suitably inferior. These inaccuracies were of the simple sort: a small patch of awkward color in the dye, an area of unappealing thinness of the weave, or perhaps a tiny knot in the silk.

Although these concessions were hardly noticeable—certainly the artistry of the works was not at all impugned—the Four Sisters soon regretted their promise. Babette, in particular, possessing indisputably the most talent for the work, quickly grew resentful.

And so, when the Good King Verdigris commissioned a series of seven panels, each more beautiful than the next, and as Babette finished the last of them, she prepared to insert some token of submission. But her hand wavered, and in the end she neglected to fulfill her pledge. She refused to make a concession. The tapestries remained pure perfection—so very lifelike that one's reflection might be spotted within the shining morning dew.

The very next morning, Lola, Gigi, and Fifi searched their small shop in vain. They upturned silver teapots, boxes of fine ribbons, and silver pins for any clue as to the whereabouts of their sister. It was only when Fifi offhandedly examined the masterpieces for King Verdigris upon the far wall did she see the truth. Calling Gigi and Lola to her side, the three remaining proprietors of the Royal Haberdashery stood in a stunned silence.

There, frozen in the weave, was Babette.

So it was that Babette was punished first by Nature herself, and then more astonishingly by her sisters, who rolled her up and delivered her to the King along with the other six tapestries. The enchanted seven were installed first in Underwood, and then, after the unfortunate rise of the Deadly Nightshades, in Queen Artilla's dining room.

Yet the remaining three sisters did not escape judgment.

While Babette's beauty was forever frozen in time, they soon found theirs abandoning them, and became the creatures we see today—the decaying, moldy hags of the Eath.

Ah, life's rich tapestry.

Currently in Axle's trestle, the Mildew Sisters braved a most dreadful predicament—their betrayed fourth sister.

"Babette!" the three sisters now said in unison. They were stooped within the trestleman's darkened study. Together, the Mildew Sisters faced a vision they had not seen in many years.

"Oh, my dearest Babette," they fretted. "But how good it is to see you!"

Part 11

Inkworks

Those Who Seek

Look to the Crows

For Crows Never Lie.

　　　　　—Prophecy, Corvid fragment

Chapter Sixteen
Rocamadour

The former scribe and calligrapher Hemsen Dumbcane was back in the business of ink-making. He had made
ink from scourge bracken but once successfully, in his small
shop on the Knox. It was a delicate mixture from a mysterious
recipe he had found in one of his pilfered papers. The ink itself was caustic, it stank, and above all it was petulant—it
needed to be coaxed into existence. Re-creating the ink here,
at the Guild, had not been easy, even though his life depended
on it.

It was therefore of no concern to Dumbcane what need
the evil Director had for the ink. He did as he was tasked, toil-
ing to produce the thick, shadowy liquid.

He wore the telltale signs of his new trade—splattered
from head to foot in dark, sticky ink, he was more shadow

than person. Whereas before, in his small shop on the Knox, he had been free to follow his own devices, establishing for himself a routine of night-working and late-sleeping, together fueled by bitter tea and burnt toast. He had lived alone, done his illicit business for the most part alone, and had to answer—in the true way of a thief—to no one.

Now he was employed. And his employer was none other than the most fearsome of all tyrants, Vidal Verjouce, the Director of the Tasters' Guild. And what of Dumbcane's wages? The currency he was paid in was an agreeable one—his life. Or rather, that he might continue to possess it.

But his was not a life of inexplicable woe—no, that distinction was saved for the small trestleman the Director had captured, and kept for his amusement in his chambers atop the tallest spire in the city. That was an existence that even the deceitful, conniving Dumbcane pitied. The small man was confined in what appeared to be a filthy birdcage beside a shattered window and was nourished—it seemed—upon nothing but frost and rime.

In through this open window came the bitter winter, its winds whipping about the evil man's offices. It was a wind from the mountains and it spared nothing—battering the small man's cage around at whim; whipping the Director's stringy hair about his head, vexing the strange, squatting creatures that hovered about him.

These creatures, Dumbcane realized—borne of scourge

bracken and black and shiny like an oil stain—were tiny monkeys. They had appeared in chittering clusters as the Director's power grew, replacing his earlier disciples, the swarm of wasps that had crowned his head. Ink monkeys, fanciful and grotesque, with small, gleaming horn buds upon their loathsome foreheads and bony spiked tails. But if Vidal Verjouce took notice of the wind, of its inconvenience to his hair and robes, or of the awful black ink monkeys that gnashed their teeth upon his shoulders, Dumbcane could not see.

Each day, Dumbcane would endure the soul-withering trudge to the evil man's chambers with a small ampoule of ink (and often a stale crust for the trestleman, which he attempted to furtively deliver; more often than not, the ink monkeys would fall upon the bread and fight viciously among themselves for the pleasure of tearing it to pieces). He produced sample after sample of the tempestuous ink, but it was never right.

His arrival always drew a gallery of jeers from these tiny monkeys and a piercing gaze—a truly dreadful one—from the eyeless Director. This blank stare, one of malice and arrogance, was made truly more horrible with the knowledge that Verjouce was *responsible for his own blindness*—having removed his own eyes so as to devote himself more fully to the sense of taste.

Each night, Dumbcane would retire to his straw pallet, where sleep for the most part eluded him. Beside his bed, a lump of charcoal and a selection of blank scrolls to occupy him—for old habits die hard.

For so many years, Dumbcane was bent before great works of art, producing perfect counterfeits. His posture was stooped, his eyes ruined with the excruciating details of his illegal pastime. To keep his forger's hands fit in Rocamadour (and without stolen manuscripts to reproduce), he had taken to scribbling, sketching, drawing anything that caught his fancy upon the page.

Just the other night, he had found himself staring blankly at the parchment before him. He had set about to sketch the mundane—his own chair, the iron claw feet of the legs grasping at perfect, glassine spheres in their long talons. . . . But in a cruel twist, the forger found his hand, quite on its own, producing the perfect likeness of Vidal Verjouce's ruthless face.

Dumbcane had felt instantly chilled and feverish.

The dark, inky pits of the Director's eye sockets pooled with shadow and, even here, seemed to be watching him.

So it was, that in returning from Lumpen Gorse's well, Dumbcane dared now to imagine the new expression—one of satisfaction—upon his employer's fearsome face. For Dumbcane's journey had been an utter success! With the water from that peculiar woman's well, Dumbcane now had his missing ingredient for his ink.

Dumbcane's entourage arrived before the massive iron-studded gates of the Tasters' Guild, where he and his party of Watchmen waited beneath the looming gargoyles.

The massive portals finally creaked and began their laborious opening. From on high, a regiment of Outriders supervised their entry—and Dumbcane's gut lurched about his rib cage fearfully. He dared not regard their harrowing visages, their shadow mouths. For they had paid the ultimate price to the Guild and its ruthless Director. They had forfeited their tongues and were left with nothing behind their wild beards, nothing but a gaping black hole and guttural, rudimentary language.

The city of Rocamadour was silent as they finally passed through, joining the Guild's frozen fountains and walking along the ash-strewn streets. The cart was unloaded, the horse dismissed. And as Calyx trudged home to the stables, Dumbcane rushed—for the first time with a hopeful heart—to his treasured inkworks.

Chapter Seventeen
The Stables

alyx knew the way by heart. There wasn't a stone beneath his feet he was not familiar with, but where once the proud warhorse was shod in silver shoes, he now made do with worn and poorly forged irons. The stables were through a shifting maze of small, winding streets that climbed ever upward and were designed with a sluice of water carved in their midst. Against the backdrop of the walled city rose the foothills of the Craggy Burls, immense jagged mountains with many buried secrets.

It was here that Calyx's stall was located, at the very end of the impressive arched corridor of the old stables of the King.

A rancid smell permeated the area, one of neglect. For Calyx, the war steed, the triumphant one, was now forced to dwell in his own filth. On good days he was brought hay, but his leather grain bucket drew nothing but mold and dust from the sodden floor.

The sound of his cushioned hooves upon the sawdust and straw stopped finally, for he had reached the end of the corral. There had been a time when many hands awaited his triumphant return from battle. His coat was immediately brushed to a high gloss, his mane braided with flowers, and his bin filled with sweet oats and honey. But there hadn't been a soul this way—save for the subrector Civer, who replaced his hay and straw begrudgingly but afforded Calyx no luxuries.

Now as Calyx advanced into his darkened stall, he suddenly spooked.

The compartment was spotless. And in it, filled to the brim, was a new, generous sack of oats and sweet barley. But that was not all! Arranged before him was an old, familiar set of garments. His war finery—his exquisite saddle, a thick, cushioned saddle blanket, and a velvet drape for his broad chest—deep and dark as the blue of the night sky. Reins embroidered with the finest silver, bells of exquisite tune for his mane.

As he reared and whinnied, a voice spoke. The voice, from long ago, the voice of his lost master.

"Calyx," Clothilde soothed. "I have returned."

She brushed him. She equipped him. Her own dress, a perfect match to his garments, like the skies above, so dark—so rich.

Clothilde's first order of business upon returning to Roca-madour had been to dispatch the subrector Civer, whose fail-ures as a stable hand Clothilde held to be a capital offense. The next stop: her vault.

Her private vault was located on the far side of the city, an area mostly reserved for maintenance needs, supply barracks, and medicines for the Infirmary, as well as a storehouse of food staples and linens. The day could be passed quite suc-cessfully here without encountering another person—only rarely did the occasional Outrider pass through—and for this reason it was a favorite spot for students wishing to avoid class without interruption. It was also, Clothilde knew—in the rows of squat stone doors, each more dreary than the next—the perfect place to hide something, should the need arise, as it had once, a very long time ago.

Through one of these very doors, at the end of a wide, dusty hall, sat a forlorn bookshelf. A winding staircase led down from the enchanted hallway to a small chamber strewn with stuff, memories of a discarded life.

Against one wall was a wardrobe of massive proportions, decorated with intricate carvings by some ancient artisan. Guardian beasts and large soaring birds intermingled, each carrying a tattered, torn scroll, a fragment of illegible wording. Within the wardrobe hung untold dresses, in every color imaginable—a few even managing to be new, undiscovered colors—intricate gowns woven from magical looms by ancient haberdashers. But Clothilde passed these by without a glance.

Against another wall, in discarded piles, were dozens of enormous leather-bound books, of the sort Axle (and Dumbcane) would consider priceless. These, her favorites, had been spared the ravishes of an evil fire. They were dust-covered and lonely, but Clothilde ignored these, too.

At the very end of the vault was a chest that sat snugly between two enormous marble urns—one of dark Rocamadour stone, the other white—relics from her grandfather's rule. Each was etched with small glyphs and scripts in the old tongue. The large trunk sprang open easily to her touch, and, gripping it on both sides, Clothilde peered inside.

Soon she was rifling through the chest's contents—jewels and amulets, a crown. Her silvery hair fell forward, and, annoyed, she paused to secure it—a flash of her gleaming hairpin. At the bottom of the chest, she found what she was looking for—a shrouded package.

It was wrapped carefully in rich fabric, which she unfolded and allowed to fall to the floor. In her hands now, a saddle of exquisite beauty, to match the darkest blue sky and bejeweled with the very stars themselves. The saddle of her warhorse, Calyx.

Smiling her particular unhappy smile, she wrapped the saddle again carefully, and the glowing stars were extinguished briefly beneath the weaving. In a corner, she retrieved her spear and a long coil of leather—her whip.

The Tasters' Guild, by all outward appearances, did not possess any weaknesses. But Clothilde knew better. Somewhere, she was sure, there was a crack in the mortar.

Now, though, in the stables with her beloved stallion, as she spoke her gentle words, curiously, a small light—that of a golden star—pierced the blue velvet of her hem. It twinkled and glowed at the reunion of the two warriors. Its beam shone upon the bony ankles of the stallion, blinked against the dust motes and the rock wall. As she braided his mane and combed the knots from his long tail, a few more glowing pinpricks appeared on her gown, in the shape of one of Caux's many constellations. From afar, the old stall twinkled and shone as Clothilde readied her steed.

Here also, at the lonely end of the stables, lay a small, forgotten door. Its existence was unknown to nearly all but Clothilde—she had lived in Rocamadour and was privileged to the city's many secrets.

The trestleman Peps was not.

Chapter Eighteen
Peps's Escape

f entering the dark gates of Rocamadour uninvited
was an impossibility, departing them without permission was
an exercise in futility. Still, what choice did Peps D. Roux
have? When Ivy and Rowan had left him for Pimcaux, in the
depths of the catacombs beneath the city, he straightened his
spine, flung back his stout shoulders, and set his tiny feet on
the path to rescue his brother. Axle was imprisoned by the
tyrannical Vidal Verjouce, and Peps needed urgently to get
word to Cecil Manx.

How was he to leave Rocamadour?

Built by the Good King Verdigris, and intended as a place
for apotheopathic learning, Rocamadour possessed defenses
both vast and intimidating. The city itself sat against the
Craggy Burls, and before it, like a long jagged carpet, were the

ancient spiked hawthorns that made up a thick—and enchanted—forest. The city wall was wide enough to host a dozen Outriders in their maneuvers as they patrolled deftly, silently atop its heights. Guards perched on fortified outposts that perforated the barricade, examining all who dared to bring business below. Beneath the city, in the sewers—once a clandestine entry point—shadowy patrols lurked in every tunnel. Nor was nighttime an advantage for the uninvited, for Outriders—feared servants of the Guild—were at home in the dark, their vision having adapted with their loss of taste.

So, Peps reasoned, if there were to be a means of escape, it would have to be an overlooked one. And, above all, it would have to avoid the forest of hawthorns—for he had sworn never again to enter the dark and treacherous wood.

As the city of Rocamadour became the city of the Tasters' Guild, horses—lively, majestic beings of the Good King—fell out of favor. Where once the stables were attended by several dozen hands, the most enterprising of whom was given the highest honor of attending to the King's warhorses, now the job fell to that single, dejected soul, Civer. In this way, the small door beside an unused tack stall at the very end of the stables was overlooked—dismissed as storage, and soon succumbing to the cloak of inevitable straw and grain dust a stable brings.

Still, there were those who had not forgotten the secret

door. Professor Breaux and the dejected Librarian Malapert had handed Peps a bag of sugar candies for the lone remaining horse and showed him the way to the stables. But it was Peps's own inexplicable courage that in the end allowed him to slip away, unnoticed by the Outriders. He traveled deep beneath the mountains, through the empty bettle storehouses within the Craggy Burls, on his way to find Cecil.

And Peps would indeed arrive in Templar, a glint in his eye, the taste of sugar upon his tongue—bristling for revenge.

Chapter Nineteen
Snaith

he subrector Snaith stood in the blaring heat of the arched doorway—his face orange and flickering with fire, his hunched and ruined back side deep in shadow. He was horrendous to behold. Disfigured from battling the dark wasps that swarmed about the Director before the arrival of the ink monkeys, his skin was lumpy and mottled with scars. The cat Six had torn off an earlobe, and it hadn't bothered to heal; it had the appearance of a cauliflower and was perpetually weeping. In that fateful encounter his tongue, too, had not emerged unscathed. It had endured a gruesome tear and was now slit very much like a snake's, resulting in a profound lisp.

But these disfigurements bothered Snaith not in the slightest—he had others, after all. Nothing bothered Snaith about that final encounter in the Director's chambers—where he fell prey to the swarm of stinging insects and the Director's feral beast. Nothing bothered Snaith, that is, but the memory of the girl called Ivy Manx, the girl who somehow had gotten the better of him in the spire. She had escaped.

His life's work was pleasing his master, Vidal Verjouce, which meant first producing the proper formulation of the ink.

Then he would get the girl.

But while Snaith's face was illuminated by the scorching production line before him of Dumbcane's inkworks, it was the path behind him that was of most interest to the Watchman. For Snaith was returning from the depths of the catacombs beneath the city, a place so sinister and fearsome that great courage or great conviction was required to successfully navigate it. The catacombs contained the years of the Guild's dead—and more. The bowels of Rocamadour were better left to the beings of fire that inhabit shadow, a dwelling place of thankless air and pressing earth; it was a suspect world that did not welcome tourists. For Rocamadour was indeed an ancient city, built by an ancient and magical King, and where the dead left off no one knew for sure what lurked beyond.

Not Snaith—who, for a subrector with teaching duties, had been spending an awful lot of time beneath the ground. Not Malapert—the disgraced Librarian who tossed the flame that consumed all the ancient books in his care, burning the many magical testaments and works of a dying king. Not even the horrendous Vidal Verjouce, who wandered the maze of crypts without the need of a torch (for what blind man needs light?).

Perhaps the only beings who knew the nature of the underworld were the Outriders, who inhabited the darkest regions of the catacombs. Yet they would not speak of such things—they could not speak of such things. They were without their tongues.

No, the subrector Snaith had been spending a lot of time beneath the city because it was there—in the hallowed ground of a decrepit crypt—that the weed called scourge bracken grew.

Snaith watched now as the forger Dumbcane returned to his production line with a vessel of Lumpen's water. Procuring a sample with a long ladle, the scribe scurried to a side workstation. He wore thick leather gloves against the caustic ink, which reached above his elbows, nearly meeting his stained smock. But these he eagerly tore off, shedding them haphazardly at his feet.

In a small series of practiced steps, Dumbcane strained and poured, sniffed and swirled, and admired the blue-black vial. The ink had been so refined, the scourge bracken made so potent, it was no longer a mere liquid. It was thick, gelatinous—sneaky, even. It moved unhurriedly, leaving a trail of slime in its wake within the small tube.

Squinting, he carefully tapped the vial with a chipped and

blackened fingernail. He peered in, closer, a beleaguered smile across his cracked lips. There was but one final test. With a shaking hand, he coaxed a single bead into the thinnest of glass pipettes and allowed it to pool at the tip—reflecting a thousandfold the fires that burned behind him. Finally, the droplet oozed into his cupped palm.

The searing pain and resulting acrid smoke were indeed the most welcome events in the scribe's life. He stifled a cry.

Perfection!

Lumpen's water had indeed been the missing ingredient. So viscous, it was like liquid shadow. Barely ink any longer, it was fuel for an empire. It was a weapon of tyrannical rule—the ultimate poison. One capable of blotting out the very sun.

Exalted, he raised the vial in the ashen air of the Warming Room—and then, in a moment of temptation, he lowered it, clutching it to his breast secretively, peering about him. The scourge bracken called out to him even now. Wiping his brow with the back of his hand, he contemplated his options. His eyes darted for the arched door. The calligrapher conspired privately—as the scourge bracken ink tore his conscience in two—until a hand gloved in red leather made its acquaintance with his frail shoulder.

There ended any hope Dumbcane had of delivering his personal achievement to the blind Director, for Snaith had arrived to claim the sample, and the credit.

Chapter Twenty

The Message

The blind Director did not take any notice of the shards of icy glass that were all that remained of the diamond-shaped window in his chambers, for buoyed by scourge bracken, the Director was impervious to the cold.

The trestleman writer was not as fortunate.

Axlerod D. Roux lay in his cramped cage, shivering, drifting in and out of consciousness. His prison was beside the shattered opening, and his view was of the distant city below, the twisting cobbled streets and Guild offices, the shuttered shops, the towering wall.

He was vaguely aware of a scarlet-clad visitor—not that turncoat Dumbcane, as usual. He recognized Snaith's crablike scurrying, his soft slippers scraping against the stone floor. There were murmurings, a few sharp words.

The trestleman took this all in—the delivery of a small ampoule, the intense agitation of the ink monkeys, the shadowy look of triumph upon the stained face of Vidal Verjouce. And then he felt a cloying sleep wash over him, the sleep of one so cold that in it are only dreams of fire.

Before he slipped away again, however, there was one other arrival.

At the window—at first the small man thought it was another of those awful monkeys come to jeer at him—was a winged creature of the glossiest black. The crow cawed softly to the trestleman, and while the remainder of the room was distracted by ink, Shoo flew to the trestleman's side and delivered the following message:

Great enchantments are soon to be broken.

And since Axle knew quite well that crows never lie, he was bolstered, determined to survive. He would begin with the dark, long night ahead.

Damp Idyll No. 10

Axle's study was suddenly quite crowded. It was home normally to the remnants of Caux's finest literary achievements—what few books survived the awful fire ordered by Vidal Verjouce, a vast and messy desk, the trappings of a reclusive writer. But it was abandoned, and this showed distinctly in the disorder and chaos—as if the place had been turned upside down and shaken. Yet its intricate pulley system remained and crisscrossed the entire room along the low ceiling, and currently Lola, Fifi, and Gigi were forced to stoop to avoid it.

And now, with the arrival of their lost sister, Babette, the room had taken on a rather dramatic silence. Beneath the trestle, the frozen Marcel cracked harmonically, like the string of a cello, a hollowish noise of some distinction.

That Babette—the Mildew Sisters could not have failed to notice—had not experienced the ravages that they themselves had endured was a curiosity. And upon this very topic Lola could not help but comment.

"I say, Babette, how incredibly well *you look!"*

Babette did *look well. Especially before the current company. Her eyes sparkled, reflecting the prisms of dew that seemed to coat her cloud-spun ball gown. Her skin was pink in all the right places and her posture the picture of grace and purpose. But Babette's face was unreadable, and it was this alone that gave Lola pause.*

"And who is this—your companion at the window?" Lola indicated the small transom, where, quite silently, a large black crow perched, unblinking.

A moment passed in silence.

"Do say something, sister," Lola urged nervously.

Babette coughed once, daintily, into her hand—a dry cough, that of coarse wool. And then she spoke.

"Look at you three," Babette declared, to which the Mildew Sisters dropped their eyes to the floor miserably. "I thought perhaps to punish you for your treachery, but it seems that you have managed quite well on your own. I suppose being cursed by Nature, abandoned by one's sisters, and rolled up and delivered to the king has its advantages after all."

The crow cawed and shook out his wings, shedding a few frayed black threads as he did.

"I'd say, in the end, you've gotten the better of the deal," Lola managed to point out to a chorus of agreements by the other two. "Preserved in that tapestry for these long years."

On this Babette concurred. She then turned her attention to the room, the discarded pamphlets and disorderly stacks of manuscripts. It was a place steeped in sadness, a trestleman's abandoned desk.

Approaching a hefty tome, Babette ran her otherwise delicate finger—the tip of which was wizened and rough from her years of tapestry-making—along the book's spine. But when Babette opened the ancient book, a puff of soft insects fluttered about languidly, an event that was followed with great gasps and horrified expressions from the four trespassers.

"M-moths!" Fifi stammered.

"Oh, get them away—horrid creatures!" Gigi complained.

"Well, of all things!" Lola attempted to quell her shaky voice. "There appears to be one upon my shoulder. . . ."

"Oh!"

"Here—oh, someone, do something before the thing does damage!" Gigi shrieked.

Babette clapped the book closed and came to the aid of Lola, brushing the moth aside with a brave flick of her finger. She then turned to the hovering gray cloud that remained, and, glancing about Axle's cluttered desktop, she found what she needed: an old specimen jar in which the trestleman had stored a few broken pencils, a pearl button. Into this Babette coaxed the majority of the fluttering creatures, sealing the jar, which she then pocketed.

The Mildew Sisters spent a further few uncomfortable minutes cowering as the few remaining moths dissipated, and then looked at their sister appreciatively.

"They're gone," Babette reported.

Babette wrote something now on a scrap of paper. Rolling it, and tying it with a ribbon from her hair, she presented it to the crow. "For the apotheopath," she instructed.

Turning back to her treacherous sisters, Babette frowned.

"Show me your hands," she ordered.

The three held out their gnarled hands for inspection, a fine display of calluses. Large knuckles bulged within wrinkled skin. Veins ran ladders over discolored liver spots, and the deep ridges of the sisters' palms were maps of uncharted lands. Babette nodded appreciatively, and the room relaxed.

"Ladies, the time has come again for us to weave!" Babette announced.

Part III

The Creatures of the Air

From pitch and swill

A savage weed blossoms

Everything is extinguished.

—Prophecy, Chimney Swift fragment

Chapter Twenty-one

Rowan

he city of Templar, the ancient walled capital of Caux and once the seat of power for the Good King Verdigris before the Deadly Nightshades assumed power, was a pleasant mix of eclectic buildings, twisting streets, and a formidable bridge upon which most of the city's commerce was conducted, the Knox. For years, under the tyranny of the Tasters' Guild, the city languished. It became a favorite for scoundrels and urchins, and most of the respectable storefronts and shops were shuttered or reborn into the poison trade. Spectacles of debauchery were common; the Cauvians of the time were conniving, plotting, and expert at poisoning. And even the annual Festival of the Winds—a celebration under the tranquil rule of King Verdigris—was hijacked into a distasteful occasion for executions.

The last such public execution was to be a heretic apotheopath, under the truly awful charge of quacksalvery.

At one time, before the Deadly Nightshades and the Tasters' Guild, apotheopathy was a revered and sacred form of medicine, harnessing the forest for its healing properties. Its study took many long years, and the memorization of many arcane charts and tables, but its results could be astounding.

But the execution of this apotheopathic heretic was interrupted, a very fortunate event for the prisoner, a man named Cecil Manx. It was interrupted by his niece, Ivy Manx, and some very potent and ancient words the apotheopath spoke, awakening a set of ancient tapestries.

This very apotheopath heretic was currently crushing a few dried leaves and berries in a mortar and pestle with uncharacteristic impatience. Cecil Manx was mixing a potion he hoped would both alleviate the grogginess from a potent sleeping draught and jog the memory of his current companion. He turned his attention to a shelf of odd bottles, but since few seemed to be labeled, he soon gave up. His long, graceful fingers paused beside a plain box labeled *staunchweed* and stiffened. The lid lifted easily enough, and inside, Cecil inspected the finely crumbled leaves. He sniffed carefully at it, but just as quickly flipped the lid closed and continued his search.

"How my niece finds anything in this mess, I'll never know," he grumbled. "It's chaos. Pure carelessness."

Rowan opened his mouth to inform the apotheopath that Ivy had often commented on Cecil's own apparent lack of order—his disorganized shelves and penchant for hiding things even from himself—but thought better of it. Instead, he stifled a yawn.

"She has her staunchweed here—of all places! Devastating, if used improperly. Can ruin a whole day's work."

"Then it should fit right in with all her other herbs." Rowan sighed. Staunchweed, Rowan knew from Botanicals, a dreary class for first years, did have its uses—mostly custodial—none of which would help relieve his grogginess.

Cecil had settled into a moody silence. He had found what appeared to be parsley root, a universal antidote, and was mincing it carefully. Quite wisely, Rowan dismissed Cecil's foul temper to be what it was: an uncle's worry for his missing niece. He struggled in the silence to gather his thoughts.

He and Cecil were in Ivy's workshop in Templar, where, inexplicably, the taster had found himself the previous day—asleep on the stoop of the Apothecary. One minute he was in Underwood, with Ivy, after emerging through the Thorn Door. They stared with wonder at the series of famous tapestries that had escaped their silken boundaries and come alive.

Next thing he knew, he was here in Templar, his head heavy—a crick in his neck from spending the night on the frozen stone stoop.

He had the uncomfortable feeling that he was a great

disappointment to the apotheopath, who had grilled him hopefully on Ivy's whereabouts (Rowan had no idea) and their accomplishments (no idea, again) in Pimcaux.

All he had to show for himself, it seemed, was the acorn.

"Yes, this acorn of yours is quite remarkable." Cecil followed Rowan's gaze, and paused his potion-making to examine the knob of silver on the table beside him.

The taster nodded absently. His hand rested upon a large clump of spiky white bristle and tusk—the sleeping form of his dear old friend, the bettle boar Poppy. Periodic snorts and low growls escaped her long snout as she dreamed of icicles and mountain passes, the frigid terrain she was meant to inhabit. Out the window was an open, cobbled square, and the citizens of Templar were busy upon it. Beyond, the river Marcel had frozen over.

"Solid silver, it appears," Cecil murmured. The apotheopath paused to examine the smooth shell, holding it up to the light. "To think—this grew upon a tree!"

"It—and the thousands like it—nearly killed us," the taster explained. He and Ivy had been pelted by them in a windstorm of oaks on their way to find the King in Pimcaux.

Cecil's eyes narrowed as he thought.

"Acorn"—Cecil was pensive—"means *eternal life.*"

"Or *imminent death*," Rowan added glumly.

The apotheopath and taster were referring to an arcane and ancient communication based on botany, called Flower Code.

Page 746 of Axlerod D. Roux's famed *Field Guide to the Poisons of Caux* (titled "The Secret Language of Flowers") begins a long treatise of various meanings assigned to Caux's rich plant population. While the origin of the coded meanings remains unclear, Flower Code was said to come from a time when plants behaved in their true natures, and their names illustrated these natures variously. Axle maintained that with the help of his book, it was entirely possible to carry on a secret conversation *in complete silence* while enjoying one of Caux's many gardens or woods, or by simply fashioning and delivering the appropriate bouquet. The Code had delivered them to the doorway to Pimcaux.

"Ah, it seems you are learning that much of what's important in life comes with a range of meanings—some agonizingly contradictive. And that includes the Prophecy," Cecil said pointedly. Straining his mixture through a fine cloth, he held out his hand, a small chipped glass within.

"Drink this." Cecil's tone was kind. The glass contained a pale green misty syrup. "It should do the trick."

Rowan did—it was tart and sweet and not at all bad—and then slipped into silence.

"Perhaps, when spring finally comes," Cecil mused, "we shall plant this acorn with Ivy, and see what it might bring."

If spring comes, Rowan thought.

If Ivy *comes.*

The window seat upon which he sat was crowded with

Ivy's potted plants, and their earthy presence reminded him of her. His stomach sank.

Where is she?

The Prophecy hung over the room like a deadweight. It was troubling in many ways, but mostly because it was secretive and vague, and seemed to occupy the arcane realm of adults. Rowan knew that much of what was predicted long ago was lost to the ages. But what was known was this: a child of noble birth was destined to save the kingdom—and to do this, · she must cure the ailing king. This child was Ivy Manx—Rowan's friend—and currently, the future of Caux was not looking so hopeful.

Rowan's eyes fell upon the square below, and the Marcel beyond. A few children were skating upon the river's surface, playing some sort of game. Rowan watched them idly as another skater approached the children from upriver—an adult, and one lacking the children's confidence and grace.

Cecil had returned his attention to exploring Ivy's medicines—disorganized unguents, powders, snuffs, and gargles of which he could make little sense. Rowan leaned in further to inspect this new arrival.

He saw the stranger—a ragtag salesman—race into the midst of the skating children, unapologetically knocking several down. The stranger then turned to snicker as he kept for the shore. After a moment, he alighted upon the quay of the capital and bent to remove his blades.

The man was dirty, which was hardly unusual. His skates were tied with crooked knots to a pair of misshapen boots and a rope secured his pants where a belt might normally be found. On his back was an unusual contraption, a skin of sorts, with a brass spigot on the bottom; Rowan had seen his type before—he was a lowly wine merchant.

Yet before Rowan could contemplate the vagabond further, the door to the workshop opened and the apotheopath and the former taster were joined by a very welcome sight.

Chapter Twenty-two

Grim News

"Ah, if it's not Master Peps D. Roux," Cecil greeted the tiny man who stood before him. "How they packed so much bravery into such a small package, I'll never know. A trestleman, surely, who will be the subject of many a ballad before our time is over." Cecil winked.

Peps flushed generously at the compliment.

Indeed, Peps had just completed a journey worthy of an epic poem—with helping hands he had been directed through a secret passage behind a neglected stables, through dismal, twisting tunnels and hidden empty vaults. Yet he managed to bring word from inside the Tasters' Guild.

"And Grig. Welcome," Cecil greeted Peps's companion.

Rowan smiled at Peps, but rose eagerly at the sight of the trestleman Grig, upending a pot of snapdragons.

"Master Truax!" Peps greeted the former taster with enthusiasm. "A welcome sight, you are!"

"Peps!" Rowan gasped. The last time he had seen this particular trestleman was in the dark crypts beneath the city of the Tasters' Guild, and Peps's escape—and return to the land of the living—was in itself remarkable. Rowan made a point to quiz his friend as soon as he could, but a bitter look had overtaken Peps's face as he turned to Cecil, and Rowan knew that now was not the time.

"Have you further news of my brother, Cecil?"

"I have dispatched three very worthy associates," Cecil replied. "We shall find something of assistance at his trestle."

"These three, are they swift-footed and trustworthy?" Peps demanded.

Grig cleared his throat loudly at the impertinence of the question.

The apotheopath paused. "They are long in my debt. They do as they are tasked."

An anxious look hardened Peps's face, and for a moment he seemed as if he had something further to say, but the moment passed.

"And Grig!" Cecil turned to the other guest. "My weatherman."

Grig smiled; his gray hair was wiry and defied gravity at his temples, where it stuck out like a set of whiskers. Grig was known, like many of his kin, as a fine inventor. He specialized in weather-themed inventions, but was equally adept at tinkering with fabric and wire. These small packets, when loosed, released tensed coils of canvas into incredible—and useful—creations called springforms.

Cecil continued. "I had that book you requested placed with your belongings. In the meantime, do you have everything you need? Is your new shop satisfactory?"

"I do, and it is," Grig replied.

Only then did Peps relax, a small smile debuting—a peek of gold shining from his prized tooth.

"I should be able to equip our army with a few tricks. But first—" Grig continued.

"First, we need an army," Cecil interrupted, squinting out the window at the sky as if one might materialize from thin air. The winter sun chose this moment to barge its way between the mullioned windows and find the apotheopath's face. Cecil Manx looked at once pained and older.

"What news is there from Rocamadour?" Rowan asked, worried.

Peps glanced at Cecil quickly, who gave an imperceptible nod. "The news is grim, Rowan. They have discovered scourge bracken in the crypt beneath the city. I suppose it was only a matter of time."

Rowan nodded gloomily. He knew the place. He and Ivy had seen it, too.

It was Cecil who now spoke. "Hemsen Dumbcane has

taken the worst elements of the weed and concentrated it a thousandfold. But Verjouce is perfecting it—and fueling his empire with it. He will stop at nothing, exhaust all resources. Until all that is left are burnt and smoldering fields, blighted and crumbling forests, and the rivers run poisonous and black."

"We should have put a stop to the weasely scribe when we had the chance," Peps growled. Turning to Rowan, he asked, "And of Ivy, is there any news?"

Rowan shook his head dismally, his thoughts drifting off to the gloomy city of Rocamadour, the place of his schooling for so many years. Anguish surged through the former taster. There were students and professors—*friends*—who remained there.

The group continued to talk in low voices, and again Rowan found his attention drawn outside, this time to the square. He spotted the vagabond again: he had now slunk into the shadows by a few sparse tables of a small outdoor restaurant. Those who had chosen to dine there huddled protectively over their fragrant stews as the vagabond neared.

The untidy fellow was joined by a companion. Mr. Sangfroid was his name, and he was a curious mixture of nastiness and petty grievances—a trait that lent itself well to his reputation in town as an overbearing complainer. His face bore a pinched look of permanent dissatisfaction.

Together, they made an unlikely pair—the dirty stranger

and a man of some means, dressed in the finery of the day, a gold chain even making an appearance from a waistcoat pocket. But there was an undeniable familiarity between the two. They chatted easily, and as Rowan watched, Mr. Sangfroid periodically would crane his neck about the open square and sink lower in his seat.

If the vagabond was aware of his companion's ill ease, he did not show it, for he seemed to match the man's discomfort by raising his voice and gesturing wildly. Behind him on an abandoned table, the remnants of a chicken were piled upon a greasy plate, waiting to be cleared. The stranger reached for these, and hungrily crunched upon a thighbone.

Rowan looked closer at the man's untidy face, but it was eclipsed by the brim of his filthy cap. There was a stain of a mustache on his upper lip and the beginnings of an unkempt beard—a scant and patchy one. Finishing his stolen meal, the man scanned the remaining tables, but the restaurant was a proper one, and little else remained to eat. He dug his fists into his pockets, his head cocked to one side, relaxing in the winter sun. It was here that Rowan managed to get his first good look at the vagrant's face. And as he did, two things happened.

First, Rowan saw that the man's skin possessed a distinct yellowish cast.

Then Rowan's blood went cold.

Chapter Twenty-three

The Vagabond

he vagabond in the square below the Apothecary's workshop was draining the dregs of an abandoned goblet when several guards materialized by his side. As he tilted his head back, greedily finishing someone else's brandy, he was taken into custody.

"Sorrel Flux, you are hereby arrested by decree of the Steward of Caux."

"What's this? On what charge?" Flux demanded as two powerful hands clamped down upon his bony shoulders. He looked around, confounded. "That wine was going to waste!" He indicated the empty glass. When no reaction was ensuing, the vagabond took a different tack.

"Surely some *agreement* is possible...? My associate here—" But Mr. Sangfroid had wisely vanished, and Flux's protests ceased abruptly. Despairing, he tried one final time to reason with the sentries.

"I demand to see the—the Steward. What's his name? Cecil Manx, I believe. Yes, I'm quite certain that is what he calls himself."

Flux need not have protested a moment further, for before him the imposing figure of Cecil Manx now materialized, his long silver cloak flashing.

Flux blinked. "And you are . . . ?" Before him was a man of some impressive stature, not the malnourished tavern keeper he once knew.

"The Steward," Cecil hissed at the yellowish man, the former assistant to Vidal Verjouce. He towered over him.

"There must be some mistake—" Flux assessed the man confusedly, craning his long neck to see if anyone lurked behind this imposter. Cecil Manx, he knew from memory, was a broken man, beaten down by a year in the Nightshade dungeons. This purported Steward was well fed and dangerous-looking, and Flux did not like the glint in the man's eye.

"Sorrel Flux," Cecil continued, his voice as cold as ice. "It appears Mr. Sangfroid has abandoned you. You should choose your friends more carefully."

"I don't know who you mean," Flux sniffed. His lumpy throat bobbled. He peered at his interrogator.

Rowan stepped forward, and Flux arched a brow. The boy he most certainly recognized. Something large and white, with tusks and teeth, was growling at him by the boy's side.

Flux jumped backward, but Poppy was upon him, hackles raised.

"Where's Ivy?" Rowan glowered at Flux.

"Call off your beast!" Flux squawked. He never did like that swine—and should have cooked her in a stewpot when he had the chance. But a small and unfriendly smile soon appeared beneath the stray hairs upon his lip. He appeared lost in thought. "Ivy." Flux shook his head. "So sad."

Cecil's face was rigid. He stepped forward, closer. "I am quickly losing both patience and interest in you," he warned.

Flux paused, looking about the ancient square. He relished such moments. He opened his pasty mouth to deliver some bad news.

Chapter Twenty-four

Flux's News

Sorrel Flux was about to do one of his most favorite things. Over the years he had, in fact, been called upon to deliver much unwanted information, factual or not, dispensing it heedlessly and with giddy authority, much in the same way he sprinkled arsenic in a rival's soup. This was a true perk of his former employment, with his previous master Vidal Verjouce, to make so many miserable so much of the time—but nothing could compare with today's tidbit. He was finding himself slightly light-headed and for a brief moment wondered if he might ruin the delivery by rushing his words.

"Ivy, you ask?"

A look of alarm crept over Rowan's face, and Verjouce's former servant savored it. Poppy stood tensed and unblinking, trained on Flux, but he ignored her.

"I am afraid, my kind sir, I have news of the direst sort." Flux pulled at his unimpressive wrists, in an attempt to loosen the rope and return what little circulation he had to his hands (although it would be better directed at his heart).

Rowan's stomach was cold with fear.

"So you say. Be quick about it or I'll instruct the guards to bind you tighter next time." Cecil glowered.

The ropes only seemed to be getting tighter the more he struggled, so Sorrel Flux ceased his wriggling and peered out from beneath his tattered hat. His yellowed eyes met those of Ivy's uncle—with the pretext of grief. But his expression darkened, Flux's own pleasure pouring forth. Like him, his news was simple, and utterly appalling. He spoke in the voice of a street caller, addressing the crowd.

"The one they call the Noble Child, Ivy Manx, is . . . dead."

The entire square fell silent (indeed, it was as if the entire city of Templar was still). And then, at once, the noise returned—to Rowan's ears, deafeningly so—as Flux continued with his horrid tale.

"There was . . . an explosion at the safe house her mother entrusted her to—"

"Her mother?" Cecil snarled. "Where? How have you come upon this news?"

But Flux was quiet, a self-satisfied look upon his face despite all efforts to the contrary.

"Speak, you weasel," Cecil growled, "or I will give you something to make you talk."

Flux merely blinked his heavy eyelids. He knew a bit about this apotheopath. "I suspect you want to very much—but you couldn't. I know of your *oath*—you are bound by it. To do no harm."

Rowan watched a strange look pass over the Steward's face, an indecipherable expression that was soon lost to rage.

"To the dungeons!" Cecil uttered horribly, in a voice thick with fury. He turned on his heel so quickly he nearly knocked Rowan over.

It was the word *dungeons* that, in the end, had the intended effect upon the yellowish man, as it would most any soul. The dungeons in Templar were notorious—more so than perhaps any other. Cecil Manx knew this personally, having spent an entire year there when the Deadly Nightshades ruled the land (while Sorrel Flux was enjoying the comforts of Cecil's millhouse and neglecting his niece).

"Let's not be hasty!" Flux squeaked. He began urgently resisting his binds, even as he was marched across the uneven cobbles by the battalion of guards who stepped forward.

"Wait!" came another muffled cry from the prisoner, but it was lost to the chaos in the square. He wrenched his arms and dragged his feet, attempting to grasp something in his pack. Again the condemned man called, this time with all his voice, and it was Rowan who finally heard what it was that Flux spoke.

"Stop!" Rowan shouted to the guards—to Cecil. Rowan ran to the apotheopath's side, breathless. "He has something of Ivy's!"

Chapter Twenty-five

The Stones

orrel Flux was a genius at one thing: staying alive. If there is an art to saving one's skin, he was its master craftsman. Throughout the years of his miserable life, the world had repeatedly offered up precarious—even treacherous— situations in which other, less ingenious people might have suffered, surrendered, or even perished. His unremarkable childhood was spent honing his craft against fevers and bullies. His later youth saw him learn the true virtues of patience, an evil sort of patience—one concerned only with retribution. He learned to lie in wait. Then his skills were completed at the Tasters' Guild, under the evil tutelage of Vidal Verjouce—but even the Director could not keep Sorrel Flux in servitude.

"I found this in the wreckage," Flux lied. He brandished a small box. It was dented and battered, but—to Rowan—cloyingly familiar.

"I have journeyed here, at great personal and physical expense, to simply give it to you in your time of need. And should you feel it appropriate to attach a small reward to its return—" Flux paused, examining the thing closer.

It was a small opaline box, a blue or silvery gray—really, the color of tears.

Flux continued, his courage returning. "I know not what's inside, for it was not my place to open it." He gave the thing an anguished shake, holding it to his ear, listening. The box showed signs of having recently met with a large rock.

Cecil snatched it away. "Whatever it is, it's locked," he said.

"That it is," Flux muttered.

With a jolt, Rowan realized he recognized it. "It's empty." Rowan's voice was hoarse. He swallowed hard.

"Hardly," Flux scoffed.

Rowan ignored him, looking at Cecil. Flashes of his brief encounter with Ivy in Underwood were returning to him now, as if the box were freeing a few jumbled memories. "The box is Ivy's. The Good King gave it to her, in Pimcaux. Inside was a set of stones, or pits, from some sort of fruit. The King told her to plant them only in Caux—saying that Ivy would know where when the time came," Rowan spoke.

A strange look passed over Cecil's face, and Rowan flushed.

"I, too, am familiar with the . . . stones," Flux sniffed. He looked around. "And here it seems like we have come to an interesting juncture. Because unlike the boy—or, for that matter, the dead girl—I know exactly where these, shall we say, *stones* belong."

"An interesting juncture indeed." Rowan nodded, retrieving a closed fist from his pocket. The one thing he remembered about his return from Pimcaux was that Ivy had asked a very important favor of him.

"For you may very well know where the stones go"—Rowan opened his palm—"but Ivy gave them to me."

•

Chapter Twenty-six
The Field Guide

As the dust settled at the Wayward Home for Indigent Orphans and Invalid Hotel, a chilling silence had set in—one punctuated only by the hissing of a broken steam fitting and the perpetual dripping of water from the rusted sprinkler system. Ivy stood, examining the scrapes on her hands and knees from where she had met the ground, and was amazed to see that Lumpen was still standing.

The well keeper had about her a more scorched appearance, her corncob pipe was blackened at the base, and the ends of her hair were nothing but wisps of ash. But the sturdy woman still cradled Rue, and had not let her fall.

"Storm's a-comin'," Lumpen said matter-of-factly.

"Uh." Ivy squinted through the aftermath of the explosion. "I think it's come and gone, Lumpen."

Ivy scrambled over the hardscrabble hillside to the fetid well. There, in the gritty breeze, Ivy spotted something. A book lay perched precariously on the well's rim, wobbling and threatening to pitch over and into the dank hole. Ivy's hand closed around the thick leather-bound cover just in time. It was wet from its trip from the Boil Pile and lay dejected and soggy—yet still with a certain dignity. It was Axle's master-work, *The Field Guide to the Poisons of Caux,* and it was indeed a welcome sight. It lay open, the inner cover inscribed in perfect penmanship.

All appeared to be in good order: the gilt edges were only slightly singed—a few of the thumb tabs were missing—and the binding was, for the most part, intact. But the book bulged with knowledge. Ivy knew—because she had helped Axle write it—that the remarkable book contained, among many things, recipes for various restorative tonics, and suggestions and uses for ash (in particular, it makes a good ink). A section compiled reliable weather-forecasting tools, and another de-tailed the Cauvian night sky. There were remarkably thor-ough diagrams and sketches of all sorts of botanical finds—including tactics for negotiating the purchase of various herbal and flower remedies should you be unable to forage for your own. Within the numerous appendices, the eager reader could decipher all matter of enigmas (including, but not limited to, the meanings of a secret language known as Flower Code). There were entire chapters devoted to birdcalls and to dowsing for water (yarrow sticks made the best divining rods).

Ivy snatched up the *Guide*. Its familiar weight, the feel of the worn leather in her hands, was a great comfort. Her own copy, ringed with failed potions and splattered with her experiments, had been left behind in Rocamadour.

"Now, Lumpen." Ivy clutched the thick book to her chest. Suddenly the path ahead—with Axle's fine reference work in hand—seemed much less daunting. She thought of her uncle, of the well keeper's parchment. "If you would be so kind as to show us the way to Templar, I would be most grateful."

The silence that had followed the explosion of Mrs. Mulk's laundry room had faded away in increments. As Ivy's hearing returned properly, the first sound she heard was of a soft wind, muffled by the powdery layer of ash and dust that coated the immediate area—but as the threesome made their way off the hill, and the quality of the air improved, there was a distinct—and unnerving—rustling.

Ivy looked to Lumpen's vast skirts and straw stuffing within her patchwork smocks, but that was not the source. There was just the well keeper's noisy breath, for she carried the sleeping form of Rue, wrapped for warmth within the dark carpet. The rustling was almost coy, coming from all around them, matching their speed and progress, the sound of dry leaves and straw bales. It grew steadier and stronger, ever elusive, as they walked along. At Ivy's insistence, Lumpen ceased her march for a moment, but—maddeningly—the rustling stopped as well. It seemed to be matching their pace.

And then in the silence, the most chilling sound of all—a hoarse howl of a wolf.

As they resumed their march, this time quicker, Lumpen shook her head, dismissing the strange rustle. But she pointed out one very particular thing.

"Nor do I hear a single bird, miss. Not one—and not for some time. Even in the heart of winter I can usually hear the little chickadees, the hoot of a grouse. And that, I say, is highly irregular."

It was as if each and every bird had vanished.

Chapter Twenty-seven
Teasel

There was, nevertheless, one bird—but he made not a peep.

He bobbed and weaved in the aftermath of the explosion at the orphanage, concentrating very much on the task of flying, for it had been quite some time since he had spread his wings. He was missing a tail feather, and his balance was impaired.

Over an open, windswept, dreary moor a fox chased him, and he flew recklessly and with all his might until he reached the safety of a dense hedge. But he did not rest long. The old stone walls would lead him to the ancient meeting place.

Mrs. Mulk's caged warbler, whose name was Teasel, soon returned to the skies, for he knew—as only the caged can—the preciousness of freedom. He also knew something else. He knew that a caucus had been called, and that his presence, like every bird's, was required.

On page 973 of *The Field Guide to the Poisons of Caux*, in a chapter devoted to the migratory habits of Caux's bird and butterfly populations, the author deviates a moment. He abandons his charts and seaside attractions and mentions in brief an event of such rarity that little more than its name can be confirmed.

The event is called a caucus.

Its location is secret. Its origins are murky. It is a rare and powerful phenomenon.

Here is what the *Field Guide* says:

Under certain mysterious circumstances, birds may choose to lay down their mutual distrust and various barriers to cooperation, and caucus. This meeting is extremely rare and, in the history of Caux, is known to have happened but once, the events of which have been mostly lost to history. There is one surviving tale—unconfirmed folklore—of a duck hunter having the misfortune of wandering into a valley of some vastness and overgrowth and coming upon a veil of green ivy, through which he could just glimpse what seemed to be the sky. Parting the growth eagerly, he realized only too late that he had stumbled upon not the sky at all, but the entire population of it. He awoke some days later—if the growth of his beard and his fingernails were any gauge—in a distant town, his huntsman's attire plucked and pulled in such a way as to indicate a thousand beaks had lifted him aloft and carried him, depositing him three days' journey from home. The man lived in perpetual fear of birds from then on, and his weapons grew rusted and dusty. He never did hunt again.

Tiny Teasel, with his chipped beak and ragged form, felt the calling of the caucus deep within him and another welcome feeling—a shiver of great anticipation.

Chapter Twenty-eight

Wolfsbane

They moved through a lifeless wintry wood, Ivy and Lumpen Gorse, with Rue slung over her generous shoulder. Ahead lay nothing but hoarfrost, slackened pasture, and open moor. But in their wake, there grew a small splash of color— as if Ivy trailed the very arrival of spring.

Before her the cold was apparent—in the form of icicles on the bald trees, in the mist from her mouth as she exhaled. But she could not feel it in her fingers or toes, no prickling goose bumps; in fact, winter did not seem to attend to Ivy at all. This, she knew, was the scourge bracken inside her.

And still, she could not shake the eerie feeling of being followed.

Several times, over her shoulder, Ivy had thought she'd

spied the drifting shapes of skulking wolves, weaving in and about the gaps in the crumbling stone walls. These creatures were hideous and hungry, stooped, their noses pinned to the ground in search of a scent. But they never drew close. Something was keeping them at bay—this invisible escort, this rustling that accompanied Ivy and her friends as they drew closer to Templar.

Lumpen took them along the path of tall, stone walls— evidence of ancient, ruined kingdoms. To either side were ghostly fields and farmland. Ivy tried to walk as best she could in the open sun, for when she stepped within the shadows of the hulking, crumbling stones, her vision betrayed her with frightening images of glittery, glowing eyes and repellent dark growth—a mossy blight like black velvet that grew in heaving clumps. This was the domain of scourge bracken: the crevices between the rock, dim and obscure. In it, Ivy knew, could be found the voice of her father, Vidal Verjouce, his evil inflection reminding her that she would never again be right in the shadows.

When the stacks of stones or the orientation of the sun above prevented Ivy from avoiding these dark places, the visions would resume. The world would ripple like a tapestry, a confounding apparition. She would see her father's awful garden—his Mind Garden, dreary, morose—as if a transparent veil upon the snowy pastures of Caux. She would walk not the path that Lumpen Gorse plowed on ahead, but the ambling rows of her father's ruined vines—ravaged by scourge bracken. The slate-colored sky of the Mind Garden punctured holes in the clear afternoon of Caux's; the turf turned hostile and murky. She walked between these two worlds, neither one quite real, a hostage to both.

For comfort, Ivy clutched Axle's book. She stumbled as her father's ravaged whisper returned to her ear—a slight song, in the tune of insanity—the sound of gnashing teeth. Unbeknownst to Ivy, it was a contribution not from Axle, but from the book's owner, Rue, that was to prove to be invaluable to their journey. Something slipped from the pages of Rue's *Guide* then, and drifted for a minute in the open air before settling on the snowy ground.

Blinking, Ivy stooped to examine the object—a plant, a pressed clipping that Rue had preserved between the pages of Axle's enormous and heavy book. A prime specimen, it was. A small cutting of aconite, its rousing color faded to a brown, the delicate blue flowers now nearly transparent upon its stem. Rue had spread it attractively before flattening it, and Ivy held it in her opened palm, admiring it.

Aconite, Ivy knew, was known by another name. Wolfsbane. Its dark shiny leaves were keeping the wolves at bay.

A shadow fell over her; she felt the sun's glow glide away.

Ivy—came a voice on the bitter wind; in the new darkness it was ready, waiting. Her father's.

She closed her hand around the specimen as she sank to her knees. Lumpen's scratchy arms were about her then—for it had been merely Lumpen's expansive shadow Ivy had sensed—and she felt herself hoisted upon a sturdy broad shoulder.

Chapter Twenty-nine

Jalousie

he crumbling walls of fieldstone gradually tapered off, and through a meager copse of young pin oak, they vanished entirely, converging quite suddenly upon a house of some worth—as evidenced by its size, if not its upkeep.

"Here we go," the well keeper announced. "This is the place."

But the estate of Lumpen Gorse's memory was now destitute, shutters rusted and hanging at odd angles, and doors rotted or missing entirely. What remained of the windows was wondrous, however: great towering panels of interlaced colors, peaked archways of stained glass, and, above the entrance, a circular rose window of some great magnificence. Vandals had managed to mar its perfection with the toss of a few well-placed stones, but the windows had survived their years sufficiently. Within their deep cobalt blues and drenching reds, still wrapped by veins of lead, one word was written.

JALOUSIE

"What is this place?" Ivy asked.

"A place as good as any other to rest for the night—unless you want to be walking in the dark, miss."

Ivy didn't.

And for the first time since their journey from the orphanage, Ivy realized she had found a landmark of sorts—and she eagerly opened Axle's *Guide*, hoping to learn anything about their whereabouts.

After searching the extensive index for the word *Jalousie*, she found it under the broader category Estates, Fortresses, and Palaces and flipped quickly to page 1421, section 4. Under the heading of Noble Manors, Ivy read:

JALOUSIE: Once a bustling and impressive manor belonging to a former nobleman of Requiem, the Marquis of Furze, whose foolishness led him to commission a series of magnificent windows in irresistible hues. He soon fell under their spell, and began rejecting all visitors, preferring instead the company of his stained-glass companions. Each was more

spectacular than the last—some that predate the current regime
and are quite notable in their depictions (see Specimens,
Botanical, and Contraband, Nightshade). His addled brain
came to the conclusion that he, too, was made entirely of
colored glass. Through the long windows, the sun transformed
both his own pale skin and the marble of the floors into slashes
of the color spectrum, until one day he was simply never seen
again. With no descendants, the upkeep of the home was left to
the various field mice and voles that inhabit this lonesome part
of Caux's northeastern front, where the traveler should be well
advised on the ruin that madness can bring.

Ivy's heart sank. No wonder everything was so unfamiliar—Requiem was a lonely outpost to the north, an area where the land holds up the sky with its ghostly stone walls. From here, she knew, it was several days' journey to Templar—if they were lucky. With Rue barely able to lift her head, even this seemed unlikely.

In the gathering gloom, Ivy could just make out Jalousie's small, untended graveyard. Amid the toppled graves, and a dilapidated vault, there were a few unmistakable shadows. The wolves were gathering for the coming of the night.

The great doors complained bitterly as the threesome entered the manor, and Lumpen was forced to lean on them with her substantial backside to shut them again. Together, the travelers lowered a wooden hasp in place, barring the way. The yelping of the wolves was closer now.

"Nothing's getting in that way," Lumpen insisted.

Ivy heard the skittering of some animal in the ceiling above her. The neglected floor was scattered with dead leaves and made an unsettling noise as they passed over it. Piles of brush had migrated to the corners and seemed to house a variety of rodents.

Lumpen made her way casually up a set of servants' stairs to the upper floor, which to Ivy's great relief was a more open space, and together the airiness and large windows formed a chamber that at one time must have been the home's proudest. A set of louvered doors clacked against an unfastened railing—Ivy could see a small, lonesome balcony off one wall.

An old iron bed was thrust against one wall haphazardly, and its rotting canopy was a spectacle of dust. The thing disintegrated entirely as Lumpen moved it aside, placing the sleeping form of Rue upon the pallet. The old woolen carpet had somehow survived Ivy's journey to the orphanage and currently wrapped Rue against the night chill, her pale moon face emerging from within its dark weave.

"Now, miss, I think you best tend to your friend," Lumpen whispered.

Ivy knelt unsteadily beside Rue, who was dreaming, muttering protests in her uneasy sleep.

"Lumpen—" Ivy began, her voice failing.

"Isn't that what they say about you? You're the healing child?" Lumpen crossed her arms over her broad chest, the ashen thumbprint left by the scribe a deep-set shadow in the center of her forehead.

"Yes," Ivy allowed meekly.

"Well, here's a good use of your talents."

"I—can't."

"You don't know how?"

"No—it's not that. It's—I'll enter *his* realm." Ivy's voice was low and anxious.

"Whose realm?" Lumpen asked patiently.

"If I perform a cure, my father will know it. I fall under my father's control—he will find me. I cannot risk it." Ivy felt terrible. Here was the very real truth—if she attempted to heal Rue, Ivy would find herself in the dismal and appalling world of her father, in Vidal Verjouce's insidious Mind Garden. She didn't know if she could return.

"Then your friend will die," Lumpen declared.

Ivy looked around desperately for a sign.

Night was coming on, but the last remnants of the day are sometimes the brightest, and their fleeting moments often offer surprising revelation. The setting sun cast its eye upon the magnificent windows of the madman's estate, illuminating them spectacularly.

The room had once been decorated with a botanical theme—wallpaper, now yellowed, peeling, and water-stained, depicted stylized patterns of foliage. The neglected bedclothes beneath Rue were a swath of ferns and palm fronds; the iron posts of the bed were capped with pineapples. And the windows, too, were dedicated to that which grows of the earth. Brilliant variants of the color green—a shocking emerald, a pale spring sap—coursed throughout the display. The plants were all labeled stylistically in the old tongue, and here and there the stained glass held ivory-colored cartouches— miniature billowing scrolls in which some small descriptive text was written.

The Army of Flowers

Ivy knew this phrase. It was said that King Verdigris led with an army of flowers, a reference to his mighty alliance with Nature. The *Field Guide* had mentioned these windows, too, and Ivy realized they must be quite old. She examined them with more interest.

The center panel was a ruin, a lost city. Ivy could just make out a tall spire beneath the mounds of greenery that shrouded the place like a living blanket, orphaned columns emerging from the deep thicket. A place no longer touched by men— the forest had emerged and taken over. Ivy marveled at it—it was as peaceful-looking as it was mysterious.

The baying of the wolves outside the windows was closer now, more desperate. Ivy wrenched her eyes away from the panorama and realized something was in her hand. She still held the pressed wolfsbane from Rue's book.

Ivy opened her fist.

A final slice of sunlight slipped in from the balcony, shearing the room in two, and it alighted upon Ivy's open palm. The dried and lifeless flower had vanished. Just as in Professor Breaux's moonlit garden, the ruined plant was now in full bloom, flourishing inexplicably, drenching the stale air of Jalousie in golden summer.

Ivy placed the deep blue flowers beside Rue's pale cheek and readied herself to meet her father.

Chapter Thirty

The Mind Garden

vy's first dramatic healing, on board the *Trindletrip*, seemed like a lifetime ago. Now she sat beside the ailing Rue, and, as with the trestleman Peps upon the houseboat, Ivy cleared her mind, allowing the world to drop away. And it was here that Ivy's more practical abilities with herbs and potions left off and a more miraculous, a more *inexplicable* talent made itself manifest.

There are those that run through life with great determination, while others meander aimlessly along a course not of their own design. It is left to the great sages—Axle is one of them—to debate the merits of each. But then, there exists the rare few who are somehow destined for greatness, and operate with enviable ease, as they are not subjected to the same rules as others.

This was Ivy Manx.

And as the world lurched and seemingly tore itself apart at the seams, only to reweave itself together in a vapid, dismal incarnation of a ruined garden, Ivy wondered—not at all for the first time—why it was she could not just inhabit a world where much less was expected of her.

She entered her father's Mind Garden as only she knew how—at his insistence. Gone were Jalousie, the wolves, the ailing Rue. Before her, a veil of drifting shadows fell away.

The first thing Ivy noticed about the Mind Garden this time was its size. It had grown with Verjouce's power, the ruined earth stretching as far as her eye could see, a festering plot of velvety scourge bracken growing in Vidal Verjouce's imagination. The folly—a small circular building with a peaked roof, at one time meant for doves—still stood to one side, but it had the decrepit air of the lost and abandoned. To the other side now stretched a lonely sea, calm and gray, a mirrored pool of the roiling sky. A slight wave lapped at the slick shore.

The Garden was silent, muffled, save for an occasional dripping and the buzz of some insect in the distance. Yet it was an oppressive sound, somehow overripe and objectionable. Gnats descended upon her, swarming her face and arms, and a chill ran up Ivy's neck. A loud droning followed, the clicking of millions of glassine wings. The air around her was now filled with shimmering, flying creatures.

Bettles, Ivy realized.

Recently in Caux, bettles had been prized as talismans to ward off poison, before they all hatched when the Deadly Nightshades were overthrown. She had had one of the rare creatures, a red one—a thing of beauty. But these things before her now, they were shades of morose grays and browns, dull and stupid—colliding in midair like drunken flies.

Like everything in the ever-changing Mind Garden, these bettles were the product of her father's twisted mind.

She gathered her courage.

The last time she found herself here was on a detour to Pimcaux; her father had interrupted the journey and she had been separated from Rowan. Verjouce had been a horrible specter to behold: limited only by his own imagination, he had refashioned his eyes, and Ivy saw at once that they were *her* eyes, too, a family resemblance. Her father had hoped to lure her to his side, offering Ivy the power that came along with the despicable weed. He would not give up.

Ivy could see just to what extent her father's powers had grown. Her heart sank at the endless, bleak lake that mirrored the foul clouds. It was new, and infinite. The waves left an unpleasant foam on the dark shore, and staring out, she could see nothing at all—a vague and distant place where sea met sky.

Turning, Ivy noticed some activity unfolding behind the folly.

A gardener was tending to something in the dirt, in uneven rows. She approached on a path of jagged slats, avoiding the eerie folly as best she could. A topiary rose off to her right, great hedges rearing, fashioned to grow into the shapes of beastly creatures.

Ivy peered closer at the gardener's project. He was on his knees now, piling the sludgy earth up around a small hill by hand. From the center grew a thin, bald stalk that thrashed uncooperatively when the man attempted to water it. Something about the plant made Ivy shiver, and in a moment she was to know why.

The gardener felt his way to the next hill and stood above it with a long shovel. The man turned over the earth unceremoniously, even roughly, and reached down and gave a harsh yank. An unearthly screeching filled the air and Ivy gasped—the gardener was appraising a handful of black fur. Ivy stared, and then a wave of revulsion overtook her. In his hand he held a small, chittering monkey—as black as ink with small horn buds growing at its temples. The thing swung about angrily from the gardener's fist, upside down. When it turned to her with its yellow eyes, Ivy found herself running blindly.

The menacing topiary reared upon her, the path switchbacking between one macabre beast after the next. Horrid, hissing vultures with beaks of thornbush jutting from the earth. Impossibly large salamanders with forked tongues curled about winged serpents—suddenly alive, each and every one of them—but made of twig and leaf. Lurid half creatures strained as Ivy rushed by, pulling at their roots in a vain attempt to grasp the girl. Again Ivy felt the world ripple, as if the fabric of life were unraveling.

She continued to run—a brief flash of something catching her eye ahead. The swish of a tail—the matted, dingy tail of a creature she knew at once: Six, the cat, a familiar friend from her travels to Rocamadour. Could it be? He had come with her to her father's Mind Garden once before. She chased the vision until she realized he was gone.

Ahead—a dead end.

But something was there, on the ground. Ivy frantically swept her hair from her face and peered down.

It was Rue's *Field Guide*! Ivy saw a few of the flattened botanical specimens jutting from its pages, springtime blooms: a pale wisp of an early violet, some wake-robin. But as she leaned to pick up the book, clutching the welcome sight to her chest, the distant chittering of the tiny monkey grew louder, its voice one of many now, overwhelming her. Axle's book slipped from her fingers and fell to the ground, the pages fanning out, open. A dank wind off the lake played about them, turning them quickly.

The book was blank.

Gone were Axle's reassuring script, his carefully assembled advice, his comforting and informative charts and illustrations.

In their place on every page, a new message. A raised seal, the unmistakable image of a skull and crossbones. And one word.

POISON

Ivy sank to her knees beside the book.

She felt her father before she heard him.

Your beloved book! Vidal Verjouce cackled, his voice rough and dry from the depths of his throat. *When you need it most, it fails you.*

Chapter Thirty-one

The Carpet

vy stood back in the upper floor of Jalousie, blinking in the dim light. Lumpen Gorse greeted her at first with a great look of confusion upon her sturdy features, followed by a wash of relief at Ivy's appearance.

"That was somethin'." Lumpen wiped her brow. "There you were, plain as day. And then . . . gone! This happen often? Next time, I could use a warnin'."

Ivy nodded, struggling against the murkiness of the Mind Garden that had followed her here. She was shivering uncharacteristically with cold.

Rue was lying still, very much as Ivy left her, and it seemed that she had been gone but for a minute on her awful trip. But the carpet that enshrouded Rue suddenly begged to be admired, and Ivy's eyes fell upon it as if for the first time. The smell of mildew was overpowering. It was as old as the hills, this tattered thing, but where it was not frayed or threadbare, it still possessed a surprising amount of intricate detail to its weave. It had been well made by expert hands, and depicted some sort of scenery, Ivy could see. She smoothed its bumps and ridges as best she could, trying to make sense of the dark palette of wool.

"Lumpen," Ivy called. "Help me unwrap Rue."

Ivy was pulling at the carpet, while trying not to disturb her friend.

"No, child! She'll chill."

"Please, just do it—" With growing concern, Ivy moved quickly. Images of her return from Pimcaux through the thorn door were swimming before her eyes, and a new, terrible realization was forming. Before waking at Mrs. Mulk's, Ivy had been standing in Underwood with her friend Rowan, admiring the transformation of the underground retreat.

What Ivy had mistaken for a mere carpet around Rue was in fact a *tapestry*—a very famous, and very dangerous, tapestry. One in league with her father. The last time she had seen it, it was hanging in Underwood with its less lethal counterparts.

It was one of seven, made by four beauties for a lone king, the darkest of the garden sequence, a nightscape. Made of threads cast from the blackest ash, the thickest tar, the deepest moonless night. The woolen clouds swirled about the sky in an unfriendly manner, and the entire copse was surrounded by a very ornate, very imposing wrought-iron fence. One that was utterly familiar, choked with weeds.

And now, standing before it, Ivy finally recognized it.

It was of a dark and twisted garden scene, an eerie lake, fanciful hedgerows. A folly. She had, in fact, just returned from there.

Her father's Mind Garden.

As they ripped the tapestry from Rue's body and pulled her free, a throaty cackle, the rasp of flint striking deadwood, filled the air. It was her father's laugh—and it grew stronger, rattling the old windows. The well keeper hauled Rue away from the iron bed.

Lumpen had been right: Rue was just a wisp of a thing. But her eyes fluttered open, and, seeing Ivy, Rue managed a smile.

The tapestry lay discarded in a pile upon the floor, and Ivy and Rue—shielded by Lumpen's generous figure—retreated to the back wall, watching the muddle of wool, for it was bulging and heaving. It ballooned, a bloated tangle of weave. It collapsed upon itself, flat, and then resumed its strange behavior. There was a disgruntled scratching from beneath its folds, and then again another attempted exit. A deep, unearthly growl.

"What *is* that?" Rue gasped.

Ivy shook her head, unwilling to guess at what further horrors her father was capable of.

And then, the inevitable.

Whatever it was beneath the Mind Garden tapestry was now free, and hurtled into the low light of Jalousie with a tremendous *yowl*. It arrived with such fury that it seemed as if the creature were ejected from its hiding spot by some force greater than its own. The thing was giant and matted, a flash of dirty fangs. A filthy specimen.

It looked hungry.

"Six!" Ivy shrieked at the enormous cat. "Six—it's me, Ivy! Here, kitty, kitty . . . ," she called.

Alas, Six was not the only curiosity hidden beneath the ancient tapestry. For as Six shook his mane in an attempt to recover some dignity, the tapestry bulged and quivered again, this time with genuine ferocity. Six abandoned his preening and, in a truly alarming display of savagery, the cat turned—his tail electrified, his spine arched, hissing fiercely.

From the depths of the discarded clump of wool poured forth an army of black, iridescent scorpions, clicking their pincers and turning the stone floor into a dark and seething sea. But the scorpions were not the last of Vidal Verjouce's gifts. For emerging now with their gleaming yellow eyes and high-pitched chatter were his inky disciples—teams of tiny monkeys. They easily climbed the mantel, skittering up the peeling walls, swinging wildly on the chandelier. Several bounced wildly on the old iron bed. The room was filled with their un-earthly screeching.

Ivy was backed against the wall, watching with horror as the monkeys ravaged everything within their path—tearing at the curtains and gleefully shredding the ancient tapestry. They charged each other with their horn buds and whipped the air with their bald tails. They enjoyed themselves immensely at the expense of Jalousie.

And then Ivy felt it—a cool knob just behind her.

The unlikely group—Ivy, Rue, the sturdy well keeper, and the enormous cat—retreated through the double doors of the nobleman's house to the small balcony beyond as the ink monkeys pounded their tiny fists and bared their awful teeth at them through the glass—the famous windows of Jalousie holding strong.

Chapter Thirty-two

The Caucus

The sky was an anemic yellow, the winter sun having already set between the distant ridges. Pools of frozen water along the open fields reflected the heavens, small fragments of the sunset torn from above and left dying below—an effect that gave the spectator the unreal sensation that the broken earth had been mended by a madman.

Upon a small outcrop of winterthorn sat Teasel, waiting.

Here the stone walls converged, and the small bird knew it would not be long. His little bones, light and airy, tingled in anticipation. All was wintry and desolation. ·

And then, on the horizon—there it came!

What, to the uninitiated, appeared to be an immense storm—a whirlwind of specks, a roiling brew of a cloud—was overtaking the sky. A swirling thunderhead, full of lightning and mischief.

From the balcony of Jalousie, Ivy saw it, too.

Lumpen paused, and whistled.

Behind them, the ink monkeys were rattling the doors, but as this new weather phenomenon grew closer, they shrieked, abandoning their pursuit. And then, from the silence devoid of birdsong, the world erupted. The swirling mass of air was upon them; Ivy's golden hair was a tempest in its own right, stinging her eyes, blinding her.

The group huddled against one corner where the balcony met the exterior wall as Ivy's eyes strained upward to the rebellious sky. A shattering sound reverberated around them as the earth welcomed the birds of Caux to their caucus, and indeed, every available space was soon inhabited by a winged creature. The bare branches hung low with their weight; the open moor was a blanket of feathers.

There were birds of all sizes, birds of all temperaments. Sharp-eyed hawks perched beside trilling bluebirds. Waterfowl rested comfortably on the hardened fields beside ridge-dwelling falcons. Downy snow geese tolerated the showy parrot's vanity in the interest of fraternity. All differences were laid down—forgotten—for all bird quarrels were abandoned to their one joint cause.

There was an air of expectation in the chatter. In a slight rise, where the crumbling stone walls parted into a stricken

gateway, a lone signpost stood, its lettering long erased by wind and rain. It was upon this that a large crow alighted, surveying the caucus he had called.

At Jalousie, Ivy did not see her crow, Shoo, for she and her friends huddled fearfully, fretting at the sky above—this strange, unearthly event. So many birds in one place was not only unnatural, it was incomprehensible. To Ivy, it was all noise and agitation. The language of the birds was a difficult one for anybody to master, but the dialect of the caucus was a formal, arcane one full of rules and diplomacy, and, above all, it was deafening.

Then, a final pair of arrivals. Two simply enormous birds were directly above, their graceful arc of wing gliding them lower and lower from—seemingly—the heavens.

Rocamadour vultures, Ivy thought desperately. *They have come for me.*

In the twilight, she braced as the pair of shadows found them easily, alighting on the balcony's rail.

Part IV

The Army of Flowers

Long lament, take wing

Whosoever speaks to the Trees

Speaks to the King.

—Prophecy, Moorhen fragment

Chapter Thirty-three

The Hairpin

His first inclination had not been to arrive in Templar loosely disguised as a wine merchant, whispering about for the location of his old comrade Sangfroid—or for anyone who might point him in the right direction of the Knox scribe called Dumbcane.

No, plans had changed.

Specifically, his plans had changed when he saw a silver flash as Clothilde had been toying with her hair. They had together departed Mrs. Mulk's orphanage and had stopped at her suggestion at a roadside tavern. Clothilde had removed her silver hairpin from its place in the knot behind her head, and Flux had been distracted by her lush length of moonlight hair, its sheen reflecting the flickering candle. And then, another flash of light as the hairpin had arced across the darkened corner booth, piercing his neck like a viper.

"But . . ." was all he had managed before his lips went cold, the rest of his face numbing quickly after. He blinked at his would-be assassin.

"Change of plans." She shrugged, securing her perfect silver hair again in a bun. Clothilde rose, her evening-sky dress a crisp sound of frost and leaves, already thinking of the journey ahead. "You didn't really think I would ever help you, now did you, Sorrel?"

Flux slumped in his high-backed wooden chair, a slight gurgle escaping his lips. She stepped away into the shadows, and would be gone forever in a moment. What Flux's paralyzed mouth could not say was a small pip of a sentence—an undignified thought, he would realize later, when it became obvious he was not to die.

Why me? he wondered pathetically.

He realized too late, he should not have trusted Clothilde, that no one could ever trust such a woman. But in the verdure of Underwood, he had approached her while Ivy and Rowan were admiring the transformation brought on by the tapestries, and a plan was hatched.

The former taster was left alone to ponder his wicked existence, his body immobile.

Ah, but she was returning now—he saw by the tavern's dim lights. His frozen heart soared. Surely she was back with the antidote; if only his treacherous lips might move, he would but beg.

She advanced again into the low light of the candle on the table, her hair glittering like armor.

"That was for Pimcaux," Clothilde whispered in his cold, helpless ear.

And then she was gone.

But die he didn't. He came to, in a hovel by the side of the road—and soon he thought of his associate in Templar. Mr. Sangfroid was just the man to help him. In a small piece of fortune, there had been a rusting pair of skates in the hut, which, while too big, he'd lashed to his feet and, following the river Marcel, he had made his way to Templar.

Chapter Thirty-four

Sangfroid

t was said that Mr. Sangfroid was a self-made wid-
ower, after the introduction of a dose of antimony into his
wife's porridge. In Mr. Sangfroid, Sorrel Flux had chosen a
friend quite well.

Flux felt Mr. Sangfroid was, in fact, perfectly poised to assist him, as the man was stubborn and resistant and wanted
more than anything for the return of the old ways. These old
ways, it should be noted, are not the same old ways that such
ancients as Axle and his brethren wished for, and that were
foretold in the Prophecy. No, Mr. Sangfroid wished every moment of his living day—when his devious eyes opened at the
leisurely hour of those unaccustomed to children in the house
to the minute he extinguished his lamp at night—for the return of the Deadly Nightshades. (This was a time when, it

must be said, he had enjoyed a particular, addictive notoriety.) And to this end, he was willing to devote all his resources to mounting a campaign to discredit the Noble Child, who he believed should be but a footnote in the history books.

He had some powerful friends.

As he decried the ancient Prophecy through gritted teeth, he could be seen often at a printshop upon the Knox, conspiring to produce pamphlets and posters to this end, which he then paid young urchins to distribute throughout the town. A selection of the headlines that clung to the lampposts with a thick layer of wheat paste:

PROPHECIES ARE FOR FOOLS AND DREAMERS
POISON IVY—BROKEN PROMISES AND
A BAD RASH
CHILDREN ARE BETTER SEEN, NOT HEARD
IVY MANX—FRAVD OR HERETIC?*

(*This last one was his particular favorite, as he had spent the extra minims to commission an artist's rendering of the young girl with untamable hair and a devilish smile.)

Under the Deadly Nightshades, Mr. Sangfroid had held the position of unofficial curate of Templar. For those who enjoy titles, this was a nice one, although a curate was a person of no particular importance in society. As curate, Mr. Sangfroid comforted those in need: the sick and the aging—particularly the ladies of Templar, the widows. He was a staple at every burial, a practiced mourner and occasional confidant. A reliable dinner companion, with a proven (and discreet) taster. If he gleaned, through his years, the occasional tidbit of information that might prove valuable, he would sell it to the highest bidder. From his entourage of widows, he would not decline the incidental gift of art, a rare and ancient book, a box of jewels. Mrs. Leatherstocking, his dear, dear friend, had been persuaded to change her will to benefit the curate and had thereafter met with an unfortunate turnip-and-hemlock supper. Mrs. Leatherstocking's neighbor, Mrs. Tattle, fell ill only after donating the inventory of her departed husband's rare coin collection to Mr. Sangfroid (and toasting the event with a bitter-tasting cocktail of brandy and oleander).

It was only natural that two like-minded souls such as Flux and Mr. Sangfroid would strike up an acquaintance.

Yes, Flux's association with Mr. Sangfroid was quite an opportune one, contrary to what Cecil Manx believed. While agreeing with Mr. Sangfroid about the days of old, Flux harbored one notable difference of opinion. He did not wish for the return of the Nightshades—he wished nothing of the sort. Sorrel Flux wished Caux all for himself.

Achieving this end would be the easiest of things.

He just needed to pay his former master a visit.

Chapter Thirty-five

Time Is Wasting

t was Flux's good fortune that Cecil Manx had decided to keep him close by—the better to keep an eye on him. Nothing was worse than a stay in the terrible Nightshade dungeons. Well, perhaps there was one thing. The monstrous boar that was trained on him, guarding his every move, might be deemed a fair runner-up. Still, the pig was preferable to the rusted bars and stench of the nightmarish cells beneath the palace. A bettle boar must sleep sometime. A bettle boar must eat.

Flux watched Cecil from his corner of the workshop. The tiresome man was bent over an old parchment of some sort, a mortar and pestle and various other workshop essentials weighing down the curling corners. Two tiny men on tiptoe examined the thing alongside. Flux yawned as he listened to their mutterings. It seemed that the apotheopath was attempting to wage a little war.

"We need an army," Peps growled.

"For that, we need Ivy."

The room was quiet.

"Well, where is she?" Peps glared in Flux's direction. "Cecil, you rely on the words of a scoundrel! His foul breath is laced with ill will and lies."

"Patience, Peps. Soon we will have word." Cecil's voice was kindly.

"We cannot simply abandon my brother to his doom," the trestleman muttered bitterly.

"Perhaps I might be of some assistance?" Flux called from his perch across the room. "I hardly see the benefit of keeping me idle. I hear you need an army. I do know a few things about tyranny."

Cecil moved so his back was to Flux and lowered his voice further. Vague words drifted over to Flux, who caught a few fragments before thoroughly losing interest.

"There is one way—you know it, Cecil. Hawthorns . . ."

"The forest is cursed. Simply too dangerous to attempt . . ."

"Under other circumstances I would agree, but what choice do we have?"

"Treacherous . . . Imprisoned souls . . ."

"I've been there, don't forget. . . . Slashing barbs, fetid streams. And worst: the feeling of always being watched . . . the trees. The malevolent trees."

166

Flux rolled his eyes. The whole thing seemed quite point-less. The Steward must be desperate—or mad—to consult with such tiny men, no bigger than children. Anytime now, they'd be wanting a nap.

"Yoo-hoo? Hullo? Might I trouble you gentlemen for a drink?" Flux called across the room—as Poppy jumped up, alert eyes on him, mouth in a perpetual snarl.

He was again ignored.

"I—er—I am quite parched over here, you see. A little something to wet my whistle, if you please?"

Cecil waved his hand at a nearby guard dismissively. "Get the prisoner some water."

"Water?" Flux was astonished. "Surely you can do better than that. I personally make it a point never to drink the foul stuff. It runs along the gutters, through the alleyways—I can't imagine what people see in it. Of all things, *fish* live in it!"

He was getting no response.

"Perhaps a nice wine?" Flux tried again. "A vintage brandy?"

As no one seemed to care about his distress, he refused the water with a limp hand and returned to glumly staring at his shoes—which, he now noted, were in need of a shine.

"I say, the service has really declined in these parts," he sighed.

Time is wasting, the former assistant to Vidal Verjouce thought. He must get to Rocamadour. He eyed his porcine guard uncivilly, reaching for a wicked vial in his tattered waist-coat, the one he kept for just these sorts of situations.

167

Damp Idyll No. V

Across from Axle's trestle stretched the thick and foreboding Southern Wood, an ancient forest, the type that swallows curious children—respectably disorienting and dangerous. But for certain beings—ancient, enchanted, capable of great works of weave—it was just the place to invigorate and enthrall. The Four Sisters swept along at a steady clip, breathing deep the night air, sniffing the various woody delights, for they were made of these woods, they were at home. They searched, stopping for nothing until it was before them.

Here was a tree, like any other, giant and towering. But this one had long ago formed a partnership with a small cottage, which protruded from the base of the trunk.

Lola dusted her brown skirts where she had picked up a few stray twigs. "Ah—the King's Cottage," she murmured, sniffing the air.

Around the kingdom of Caux, in sheltered coves or forgotten woods, sat a series of small cottages, waiting out the poisonous regimes for the day the Good King would return. Each was like the next, in that they all had a generous table, set with two plates, two candles, and an earthen jug. They shared another similarity. They were also all gateways to the King's lonesome retreat, a palace beneath the ground, fashioned from the living roots of the trees above.

Lola inspected the small door before them. All appeared in order. Through the frosty windows, a table was set. An impressive fireplace was beyond, the chimney jutting cozily out one side of the tree.

The sturdy front door was not locked for long—Babette's rough hand held a ring of golden keys, and almost immediately the door swung open and the Four Sisters entered the gateway to Underwood.

Lola was first down the stone steps hidden behind the fireplace—and she was first to emerge into the greenery of the underground royal retreat. What she saw there surprised her. The series of magnificent tapestries had emerged from their weave, and their growth had overrun the cavernous main chamber.

Turning to the other three and batting a stray branch out of her way, she scowled. "Look at this mess!" she cried.

"Naughty behavior indeed!" agreed Fifi.

"The tapestries have been shockingly disobedient," Gigi admonished.

For a moment the foursome stood, taking in the disarray.

"Well, ladies." Babette now spoke. "I told you there was work to be done."

Chapter Thirty-six
Caucus

he Field Guide to the Poisons of Caux, on page 988, proclaims the nightingale to have the most mournful and most beautiful voice of all birds—but what Axle's book does not say (a forgivable omission) is that the nightingale's song also serves a cherished position in the hierarchy of birds. Its call brings all meetings to order. But bird etiquette was unknown to Ivy, Lumpen, and Rue (Six, however, knew much of birds—including their particular digestibilities).

So it was that when, from the darkness, a nightingale burst forth in its powerful song, none of the travelers knew that the caucus was about to begin.

Ivy, while still clutching Rue's copy of the *Field Guide,* had little hope of consulting it. They were cornered, trapped on one side by chittering, cackling ink monkeys and on the other by the shadowy form of two massive birds. Six let loose a low, throaty growl that, while scaring no one, did much to betray his own growing discomfort.

A few words about birds.

Like people, birds come in all shapes and sizes, and correspondingly possess varying personalities that should not be generalized. That said, robins can be relied upon to regularly argue and nitpick—they are intelligent creatures prone to disagreement. On the other hand, kestrels, respected warriors, are silent and aloof. Tiny sapsuckers are surprisingly fearless, while certain species of duck have an astonishing affinity for problem-solving. But it was an old friend of Ivy's from Pimcaux, an albatross, that had once told her, "If you want something done, ask a crow."

Appropriately, after the nightingale had finished its last lonesome trill—a particularly lovely one, it congratulated itself, for it was not without vanity—Shoo got down to business. Because, in the hierarchy of birds, it is the crow who wears the crown.

On the balcony of Jalousie, Ivy cowered in the shadows of the two great birds.

Ivy—came the voice of one, a voice of the salt air, of sea spray and empty sky.

At first, Ivy shuddered, thinking her visions and whispers

of her father had returned. A fear welled up inside her, nearly overpowering her, and it was at these moments that the scourge bracken within her sensed her weakness, and its own power grew.

Child—came a second voice, a finer one, although also of the sea.

She dared peek through laced fingers, and what she saw took a moment to grasp. These were not Rocamadour vultures at all! The last time she had seen these two great winged creatures, she was in Pimcaux.

"Klair! Lofft!" she shrieked. "Oh, is it really you?"

The albatross pair shifted their weight where they grasped the railing, lowering their heads in a humble greeting.

"It is us, child."

"But how—?"

"Shh," Klair advised. "The birds are caucusing."

"A caucus?" Ivy asked, astonished.

"A very important one," Lofft explained in a low voice.

The albatrosses regarded the large cat coolly and turned back to Ivy. "Your presence is requested."

Chapter Thirty-seven
Shoo

he fact that no one without wings had ever before attended a caucus in the history of Caux—let alone been the guest of honor—was a fact unappreciated by both Ivy and Rue. The girls were too busy holding on to the silken bridles that harnessed the giant seabirds as they careered through the crisp winter air.

Ivy had flown on Lofft's back in Pimcaux.

There she had the distraction of being in Pimcaux—the beloved sister land to Caux, one whose mention peppered the lullabies and nursery rhymes of her childhood. And she flew through the Pimcauvian nighttime sky—one filled with silvery, winking stars in unfamiliar constellations. Further, her mind had been on her very real errand—to find the King—and her companion, a capable and glamorous alewife, was a welcome diversion.

Here the flight had a more urgent feel. The seabirds gained altitude in a series of dramatic wing flaps that nearly knocked Rue—whose health was returning, but who was a true novice at flying—off Klair's back. Then, quite quickly, they were very high up, with a startling view of the gathering below, as the last wisps of evening were swept away by the tidy hand of night.

"Ivy!" Rue called, stretching her arms out in a bountiful gesture of flight that matched perfectly Ivy's own exhilaration. Ivy was happy, too, to see a healthy flush in her friend's cheeks. She turned her attention to the ground far below.

They had left Lumpen and Six on the balcony of Jalousie, with assurances from the well keeper that she would wait out the caucus in safety. Apart from the mansard roof and lonesome grounds of the manor house, Ivy saw nothing but feathers, gleaming, downy, bristling, and showy, in an endless tapestry of textures and colors. The bare trees that bordered the open moor were heavy with dark birds—and still, below them, more arrived. There was a low murmur. In the slight gray mist that had crept in, a symphony of musical voices hummed as all of Caux's birds were speaking as one.

And then, a moment of pure silence as the albatrosses simply soared, where it seemed they were hanging in the air without effort—as if gravity itself had excused them from its conventions. But too quickly, Klair and Lofft started their descent—elegant wide circles—and Ivy and Rue were forced to grip their harnesses tightly while squeezing closed their eyes, for the view below was approaching swiftly and dizzyingly.

The bumpy transition from air to land was tempered by Ivy's extreme pleasure at being among so many birds. A small strip had been cleared for their arrival, and as she stepped off Lofft's back unsteadily, nothing could have prepared her for the peculiar sensation of hundreds of thousands of their alert, button eyes upon her.

The albatrosses cried a long, lonely greeting to the endless caucus and stepped away, leaving Ivy in the forefront. And where there was silence in the moor, there now erupted a thunderous racket of such magnitude Ivy covered her ears before she realized what she was doing. Lofft and Klair had settled in behind the girls, in a ruffle of feathers, as they sat upon the earth with an expression of silent scrutiny. A minute passed, and some semblance of order was achieved.

A familiar, raspy call rose above the rest, and, in the dimness, Ivy saw a haphazard signpost that rose at an angle from the old stone wall beside her. A rusted nail loosely held a directional sign in place, and upon the weathered arrow sat a jagged silhouette of sleek spikes and proud tail feathers—which now flew silently to the young girl's shoulder.

"Shoo," Ivy whispered. Her crow—her longtime companion and confidant, her guide. He had escaped his tapestry, where he was trapped alongside a mysterious woman in white.

But the last time Ivy had held him was on Axle's trestle, when her adventures were just beginning. Shoo had saved her from capture by an Outrider and suffered horribly in the process. With her elixir, she had cured him, but she had left him behind.

A surge of emotion caught her by surprise, and the tears finally came.

Chapter Thirty-eight

Keepers of the Prophecy

Should you be so inclined, you might, on a nice spring evening, remove yourself to the outdoors and listen. With very little effort, you are sure to hear music. The songs might even fill the air. Birds are nothing if not precise, and were you to speak the language of the birds, you would find it quite complex—with many words, for instance, for describing food, and intricate directions for arriving at it. But also—and more interestingly—words that resist translation entirely.

Ivy did not speak Bird.

Klair and Lofft *did* speak Ivy's language, however, and but for this bit of fortune Ivy and Rue would have been entirely in the dark while the caucus continued on deep into the night. A yellow moon was perched in the hills in the distance, and although Ivy could not be sure, she felt certain that was the direction of Templar, of Cecil.

The old crow Shoo began to speak. "Welcome, creatures of the air."

The clucking, trilling, lilting, and whistling all ceased as a profound respect for the caucus's leader set in.

"There is a bitter wind that blows through Caux. Our skies have grown dangerous," Shoo cawed as Klair translated for Ivy and Rue. "Great burning fires and billowing black fog menace the air above the city of Rocamadour. The traitorous vultures grow daring; I have heard unspeakable whispers that they make grotesque alliances."

Shoo paused for a twitter of disapproval for the unwelcome beasts.

"Our own migration routes are threatened by drifting smoke and ash—vile emissions from the Tasters' Guild. I have called each and every one of you here on wing to report, and to remedy what we can—if indeed it is not too late. It is therefore time for us to lay down our various conflicts, and assemble the fragments in our possession. The fragments, my dear friends, of the Prophecy."

And then, according to long-standing protocol and the caucus's set of arcane rules, Shoo began the lengthy process of welcoming the delegates. The crow named each and every one in attendance, neglecting not a soul.

Birds of the Southwind he greeted first, from the south lands of Kruxt, their colorful feathers and vocal songs jaunty and vain. Shoo thanked them for enduring the frozen winter for the caucus. He turned then to the sharp-eyed, hook-beaked arctic birds of the Northwind, past the mountains. He was thoughtful about their long journey, and excited to hear their news from beyond the borders of the Craggy Burls. He hailed the wisdom and patience of the seabirds of the Westwind, calling on their knowledge of the tides and innate partnerships with the surf and sea. The birds of the Eastwind— the ground-dwelling, dancing birds of the prairies—he greeted as old friends. He congratulated each and every bird before him for the simple fact that their wings had held them aloft, and for answering his call. And then he turned to the albatrosses from Pimcaux.

"The doors are slowly opening again," Shoo said. "May someday Caux and Pimcaux's borders dissolve completely. It is my great pleasure to welcome the seabirds—emissaries from our sister land Pimcaux."

And after much hooting and whistling, Shoo called the caucus to session.

Because a great many things had unfolded in their land since their last gathering, the old crow began with a history lesson. The History of the Birds is a long affair, and one occasionally open to interpretation, as most birds are generally opportunists and favor exaggeration. Crows, who never lie, are for this reason ideal keepers of the past.

But the History of the Birds does not concern us here and, indeed, is quite their own to tell.

There is one point in the history of the creatures of the air that intersects quite squarely with that of the people of the earth, and it is on this small footnote that Shoo eventually spoke. It was a sad end, an end to a life—in particular, the beloved Princess Violet.

Princess Violet had the distinction of being the daughter of the Good King Verdigris, and her death was a tragedy to everyone except the traitorous advisor to the King, Vidal Verjouce, and the subsequent rulers, the Deadly Nightshades. Indeed, Violet's mysterious poisoning was Caux's very first poisoning, and her death brought upon darkness—a suspicion that blanketed the land—and the people of Caux began to forage deeper into the ancient forests and use herbs to poison and kill. The Tasters' Guild was born as the need for reliable tasters soon followed the Nightshades' poisoned policies. Violet's death remained unsolved as her father slipped deeper into misery.

Another death occurred that day—of special concern to the caucus—and this was the demise of the barnacle goose Fern.

Fern, in her time a plump mother of thirty-seven goslings, was inadvertently and unfairly the cause of the Princess's tragic end, for Fern had been roasted by the cook and served—poisoned—to the princess. (At Shoo's mention of Princess Violet and Fern, a kerfuffle broke out in the geese section, which took some time to settle. Barnacle geese, to this very day, are known to be quite disagreeable: being the unwitting cause of a princess's death will make anyone irritable.)

Ivy and Rue began to see that the caucus was going to be a long affair. The events of the day—Ivy's grueling visit to the Mind Garden, Rue's draining illness—had begun to take their toll. The caucus was large and, therefore, tended toward disorganization. Scattered flocks were still arriving, coasting in to land on cupped wings. Small disruptions would pop up as the tardy delegates settled in, or, as in the case of the geese, in reaction to Shoo's narrative. A vast restlessness was thick in the air. The field of arrivals stretched on into the darkness, and although the excitement was palpable, it was tempered by a solemnity—a respect for the unusual proceedings and, even more astonishing, the presence of two human girls.

Despite the activity, Ivy was finding it impossible to stay awake against Klair's warmth. Her eyes were shutting on their own accord, and Klair had ceased her whispered translations as a result. But Ivy sat up suddenly to search for both the well keeper and Six, wondering suddenly if the pair had made it away from the balcony at Jalousie. From her spot, she could make out the abandoned estate, but it was shrouded in night. She saw no one.

Klair and Lofft were speaking quietly to each other, their voices a pleasant windsong. Together, they had decided something.

"We are needed here in a moment," Lofft spoke. "But now we will take you somewhere to rest."

This is how Ivy and Rue came to miss a small warbler—an earnest fellow, full of pride and trembling with enthusiasm—give the very first speech.

Chapter Thirty-nine
The Shepherd of Weeds

easel took to the signpost and began to tell his story.
His little legs hopped with some nervousness from point to
point along the faded wooden sign, but he raised his head
bravely and began to speak.

He began with the tale of Ivy's arrival.

Teasel's small, pure voice reported on the orphanage. He
took some time to describe how it was that he lived there, his
cage, and Mrs. Mulk. (The word *captivity* is an awful one between birds—there is arguably only one worse. *Captivity* is
used only in the most serious of situations—and poor Teasel
was loath to offend such a vast gathering.) He faltered, searching for the appropriate words for such an important occasion,
but finally, after much inner debate, he did say it—*captivity*—
and was heartened when the crowd erupted in sympathy and
dismay.

He continued.

A scrawny man appeared at the door late at night, Teasel explained. This was in itself unusual—but even stranger was he had the coloring of a canary. (At this, several of the canary faction cheeped disagreeably.) The man had with him a package wrapped in something unpleasant. Teasel did not have a word for *tapestry*, but he knew that it was to be avoided, much in the way he would stay clear of a net.

The package, Teasel soon came to understand, contained a girl, and the girl was placed down in the dark room below. The warbler shivered at the memory. (In general, birds do not inhabit dwellings beneath the ground, as this is the realm of other, shadowy beings.) But the deliveryman remained in the parlor, and for most of the night, Teasel was positioned to hear their conversation. Here the sparrow faltered, and Shoo kindly urged him to continue.

It seemed to the sparrow that the human pair had a long history, Teasel reported. They discussed confusing names and events that came before Teasel had been tricked into the rusty cage.

(Again, a brief uproar.)

The topic seemed to involve a steady stream of lost and forgotten human children being shipped to Mrs. Mulk's, both by the current visitor and through others arranged by him and the Tasters' Guild. He approved pricey stipends for their care—although this arrangement had suffered of late. Mrs.

Mulk complained much on this topic, and the yellowish abductor pretended to soothe her, but to Teasel, he seemed more interested in refilling his small glass with something the man called sherry.

When Mrs. Mulk asked for a stipend with which to care for the newest arrival, complaining greatly about the costs involved, the man paused. Teasel had been forced to wait as the man poured more sherry down his bobbing craw. Finally, he shook his head—there was no stipend. Mrs. Mulk had sagged. But, the yellowed man continued, there was something better. Much better. The word he used was one unfamiliar to Teasel, but he dutifully reported it: the word was *ransom*. Teasel explained that the word must be a cheerful one, for Mrs. Mulk clapped her hands in a display of glee. After many more of these sherries, and much prodding by his impatient hostess, the visitor confided in Mrs. Mulk about the identity of this orphan he had delivered.

"The girl is the . . ." Teasel paused. He was about to use a very ancient phrase among birds.

"The Shepherd of Weeds."

Chapter Forty
Aster

At the mention of the Shepherd of Weeds, a thrill passed through the crowd, a wave of alert feathers rising and falling like the sea.

Here, a few more words on the nature of the birds.

Birds, while quite happy to fly and hunt, forage and eat—and, of course, sing—are guardians of the forests and fields. By nature, they are alarmists, and in their numbers they make a watchful bunch. But more importantly, birds have long been entrusted with carrying the vital news of the day from sea to cliff. They take themselves quite seriously, as any novice bird-watcher might see. Why is this?

Because birds are keepers of the Prophecy.

The Prophecy. It was a messy, arcane thing that predicts in unclear metaphor what was to come. It was a hopeful morass on torn, crumbling parchment, written by an ancient hand, whose whereabouts were unknown. In this case, it concerned a child of noble birth and the reunion of nature with man. Who better than a bird, then, to guard the knowledge contained in its fragments?

Long ago, those who foresaw the events of the Prophecy inscribed it carefully upon parchment. But because parchment—as everything—eventually grows old and unreliable, they took steps to ensure the message's survival. They whispered it to the wind, and the Winds of Caux, in turn, carried the message to the birds. The Prophecy was broken into fragments, and the families of various houses were each entrusted with a piece. While the minds of men were subject to age and distraction, the birds have never forgotten it.

In fact, wise men such as Axle and Cecil, and wise women such as Clothilde and the alewives, have never possessed the knowledge of the Prophecy *in full.* Axle was privy to most of the ancient knowledge, but even he did not know the entire, and far-reaching and at times contradictory, predictions it entailed.

Now, as the birds came forth, a single delegate at a time, they reassembled the ancient prediction. And what a song it was—rich, complex, sorrowful, and inspiring. And finally, when it was complete and the very last note had faded into the night, the poor, suffering widow of the hummingbird eaten by Lumpen flew forward.

It was her turn to speak.

Her name was Aster, this poor, suffering hummingbird, and she was hardly bigger than a bee. Her wings fluttered so quickly they seemed to disappear, and she flitted about Shoo's head for several moments in indecision. (Hummingbirds are not as nervous as they appear, but Aster, having been dealt this unkindness by Lumpen, found herself unusually wary.)

Aster and her mate had been traveling from Templar when tragedy struck beside Lumpen's well, and she began by informing the caucus of this very event. For her loss, she received the appropriate amount of sympathy and outrage from the audience, and she continued. But hers was a mission of neither sympathy nor outrage. Aster wished instead to sow the seeds of doubt.

"In Templar," Aster said as she flitted along the length of the weathered board, "they do not believe in the Prophecy."

A low grumbling of disapproval met this news, but Aster stood firm. "They denounce Ivy Manx as a heretic," she continued, wings humming earnestly now. "They say she hears voices. Sees visions."

This piece of news was not as dramatic as one might think. Birds are unimpressed with madness in general, inhabiting a world where visions and voices are very much the norm.

(Enchantments and magic of all kinds are like lightning—they are great forces assembled in the sky.) But Aster, having made the acquaintance of Mr. Sangfroid's hummingbird feeder in Templar, received along with sugary water a differing outlook on the future of Caux were Ivy Manx to succeed. Beware what secrets are shared beside an open window!

Aster continued, taking a different tack. If the caucus was not receptive to her disparaging tone, she would speak, then, of one thing they were sure to agree upon: the Shepherd of Weeds' current choice of company.

"Friends and neighbors." She alighted again, wings still. "Look who she chooses to align herself with. Two bird killers! One, a hideous specter of a lady who eats birds for breakfast, and the other—the other, a horrible, malingering *cat*."

(*Cat* is the only word more disliked by birds than *captivity*, and here Aster received the reaction she was hoping for.)

The hummingbird paused, dramatically turning to Shoo. "Tell me, where is it foretold that the Shepherd of Weeds travels with our enemies?"

Chapter Forty-one

The Rookery

vy and Rue were becoming accustomed to being airborne, as this flight was a longer one, but the heights brought along a great chill. There was a side-slashing frozen rain within the night clouds, and while the scourge bracken within Ivy made her impervious to cold, Rue was frozen to the bone. When asked where they were headed, Klair and Lofft did not reply, so the pair were left to fly on, huddling down against the broad backs of the seabirds.

Soon it was evident that they were very far up—either that, or the weather had changed significantly. The clouds that obscured the skies had vanished, and the stars that made up the intriguing Cauvian constellations shone brightly. As Ivy fixed her gaze on Vitis—a rare treat, for the constellation was far too north for her to usually see—she felt the voyage come to an end beneath the lowest star. Ahead, great pines rose from the side of a rock face.

At the top of the highest one, the girls struggled to gain their balance against the knee-high moss beneath their feet. They had alighted within some sort of bowl-shaped terrace, the sides of which were well-woven dark branches and mud, basket-like. There was the sound of wind, but none gained entry.

"What's this?" Ivy asked, cupping a handful of the dried moss and playing it about her fingers.

"A rookery," Lofft replied.

Ivy dropped the soft lining.

"A nest?" Ivy was incredulous. "How high up are we?"

"It's quite safe." Klair smiled, anticipating her next question.

"And secret," Lofft inserted.

"And cozy!" Rue enthused as she slid down into the fluff, feeling the warmth return to her hands.

"My only worry is what to feed you two," Klair fretted. "We have nothing of the sorts of foods consumed by humans."

"What's wrong with raw fish?" Lofft demanded. "There's nothing like a herring slipping down your throat, still wriggling!"

"Ugh." Ivy frowned. "I mean—I'm sure it's quite tasty to you, but I prefer my fish cooked, thank you."

"There might be some seed around, and we're sure to find

a cache of worms. . . ." The pair of albatrosses looked concerned. "Or perhaps some juicy grubs? The barn owls might be able to drum up a mouse or two. . . ."

"We'll be fine," Ivy said brightly, clutching Rue's *Field Guide* to her chest. "I've got something else in mind."

"All right. Well, we'll be back for you in the morning, so until then, Ivy and Rue, eat, sleep, and rest your wings. There are hard winds ahead."

Ivy sat down beside Rue in the soft moss lining of the giant bird's nest. It was warm and safe feeling, and there was a pleasant swaying that reminded Ivy of her stay aboard the *Trindletrip.*

"What's on the menu, then?" Rue asked. Her appetite had returned.

"Let's see." Ivy held the *Guide,* propping it on her lap. Rue's botanical specimens poked out from in between the hefty pages. Ivy randomly opened the large reference book.

"Blisterbush?"

"I should think not," Rue demurred.

"Sicklerod? Saberweed? How about some beardedtongue?"

"After the wolfsbane, I was hoping for something a little more . . . edible." Rue smiled.

"You tell me. They're your specimens," Ivy teased. "Hmm, I know. I'll surprise you."

She flipped through the pages eagerly, finding eventually a dried, flattened leaf and tiny, delicate white flower. "Perfect," she said, holding it carefully in her closed hand, as she had done in Professor Breaux's night garden and in Jalousie. Soon there was a pleasant tingling and warmth, and a quite promising smell—delicate, fruity.

Rue's eyes opened wide—there was no mistaking the scent. "Strawberries!" she cried, delighted. "Grandfather told me about your . . . abilities. But, Ivy, this is amazing!"

Ivy nodded happily, clearing away a small area of the moss beside her and Rue. She carefully placed the unfurling shoot upon the mud-laden underlayer of the nest, and quite quickly, and to the girls' utter delight, the plant began to flourish. Soon there were wild strawberries nestled beneath the small green leaves of the plant, and although there were at first only a few (of which Ivy insisted Rue eat), soon there were more than either of the two might desire, the greenery overtaking most of the nest. They fell asleep happily, smudges of crimson upon their chins and staining their fingertips—which was a fortunate thing in more ways than one. For in the open moors far beneath the rookery, where the birds of Caux met to discuss what it was they might do to help Ivy's undertaking, a small hummingbird was plotting her revenge.

Where are the seeds of betrayal sown? For it cannot be said that Aster was born bad, or even brought up poorly. No, little

Aster was neither. What happened to Aster was this: she suffered a great loss, which somehow curdled her instincts for kindness and sent her down the very path that many before her have passed (even royals are not immune to grief's ravages, which, as it did with the Good King, can turn the tides against an entire nation). But it's what you do with grief—not what it does to you—that matters.

Grief can be a mark, or a stain, that slowly creeps over you, subtly changing you in its wake. Or—and this is much harder—it can pass through you, eventually leaving you stronger and wiser.

Aster had succumbed to the first variety, and her little heart was now a hardened pellet. She remained at the caucus, however, for there was much in the world of birds—beings of air and wind—to discuss. She dutifully participated in the varying forums and events, all the while watching, noticing, dreams of vengeance and retribution growing like a stain within her chest.

Chapter Forty-two

One Condition

n the early sun of the next morning—a shocking red glow to the eastern edge, with grays and purples awaiting their turn—Klair and Lofft returned for the girls. Strawberries draped luxuriously off the edge of the giant nest, nearly everywhere, and Ivy and Rue looked sheepish at the lavish abundance they had caused.

But the albatrosses seemed tired and sad, and the excuse that Ivy was formulating stalled on her lips.

"The caucus has finished," Klair began. "The fragments of the Prophecy were reassembled, recited, spoken aloud to the wind. The words are inarguable. The Shepherd of Weeds will lead us into battle."

Ivy and Rue looked at each other.

"The Shepherd of Weeds?" Ivy asked Klair when it became clear that the great birds were not commenting further. "What is that?"

"It is an ancient and powerful name in the language of the birds."

"A name for what?"

"The Child of the Prophecy. For you, Ivy."

"For me? Why do they call me the Shepherd of Weeds?"

"The true nature of plants is awakening. You are their Shepherd."

Ivy and Rue, sitting in the lushness of the giant crow's nest, with the richness of strawberries growing in undeniable abundance, could not find a reason to disagree.

"We are of the air, we birds," Lofft continued now. "Air is but one element. There are beings of water—the alewives—and those of fire and shadow, though these are neither helpful nor reliable. You, Ivy, you are the Shepherd of Weeds. You are of the earth," Lofft explained.

"The caucus requires you to gather your forces of the earth," Lofft went on. "You must ask the forest for help. It is time to assemble your army of flowers."

"Army of flowers?" Ivy asked, alarmed.

Breathlessly Rue turned to Ivy. "A favorite poem of my grandfather's! *The Ballad of King Verdigris!*" she said. "'*The air brimmed with sunlight and dew/His enemy lay vanquished/Behind him, an Army of Flowers.*'"

Ivy's mind raced. How was she to gather an army, here, in

this desolate corner of Caux? She had no talent for this. "Surely this can wait until we get to Templar? My uncle—he will know."

"Enough time has been wasted already," Lofft said. "Call forth your allies, my Shepherd. On this, the birds are absolute." Lofft shook his elegant head. And"—he looked down sadly—"there is something else."

"What is it, Lofft?" Ivy's heart sank.

"There is one other condition the caucus has put forth."

Klair and Lofft were silent, and when Lofft finally spoke, his deep sadness had returned. "The birds will not align themselves with a cat."

"Cats have for eons been, at best, disrespectful nuisances," Klair elaborated.

"Six?" Ivy swallowed hard. The cat had been her traveling companion, and some measure of comfort on her journey to Pimcaux, and while he was smelly and unlovely to the eye, his loyalties were no longer suspect.

Klair and Lofft exchanged a meaningful look, and then Lofft spoke again, softly. "They were very clear on this point. The birds will wage war in the name of the Shepherd of Weeds, as it has been long foretold. But they will not align themselves with a cat."

"What am I to do?" Ivy asked.

"You must make him go. There are those within the caucus who wanted a much stiffer resolution."

"I see," Ivy said meekly. How was she ever to make a cat to do anything other than what a cat wanted to do? She felt again the dark throbbing in her head and hoped her father's voice would not awaken from its slumbers. "Lofft, Klair, can you take me to find my friend Lumpen?"

Chapter Forty-three

Lumpen's Flock

How many millions of eyes regarded Ivy and Rue as they alighted again off the backs of the beautiful Pimcauvian seabirds? Surely it was a number unfathomable. With the caucus drawing to a close, the air was charged with a different feel, and as Ivy stepped upon the open moor, Shoo joined her, flapping solidly to her shoulder. The winter morning was arriving, and a thick coating of hoarfrost clung to the far trees; the facade of Jalousie was draped in white lace.

Ivy stroked Shoo beneath his beak. His feathers were as chilled as the air. She was dreading the sight of Six, for how was she to explain?

"Oh, Shoo," Ivy whispered. "What I would give to be back with you at the Hollow Bettle, with Uncle Cecil! In the back room, my workshop—before any of this. Just me and you, my experiments—and Axle! How unfair this all seems."

The crow moved in closer on her shoulder.

From the east, the sun soothed ruffled feathers and glazed frost into polished prisms. Shoo's own feathers were the deepest black, a blue-black, and their shine—his beauty—now bolstered Ivy. She walked with him to the very edge of the vast field where the young wood began.

These were hemlock trees, evergreens, and little grew in earnest beneath their low branches. Still, there was a soft, padded forest floor, one made of discarded pine needles, and the sensation of walking upon this was a pleasant one.

"Lumpen?" Ivy called into the soft wood. From the moors, the audience of bird eyes keenly watched her every move.

After a minute, Ivy noticed that there again was the undercurrent of rustling that she had heard nearly her entire journey from the orphanage—the rustling that had been following her since she met the well keeper. It came now from all corners of the hemlocks, indeterminate, the sound of distant brooms upon an earthen floor. She wondered if she should be scared.

At first, Ivy saw nothing in the dimness but a glowing red ember, which flared to bright orange and then seemed to snuff itself out. Then Lumpen stepped forward, her corncob pipe clamped between her lips.

Ivy's heart surged to see her. If possible, Lumpen appeared wilder than before, the straw stuffing within her threadbare casings growing untamed, poking through the inevitable holes like whiskers. It was difficult to discern where it left off and her own bushy hair began. The appalling inky smudge from Hemsen Dumbcane stood out starkly upon Lumpen's thick brow. Her ruddy cheeks seemed strikingly red—a pair of berry stains upon the canvas of her face—and her yarrow stick was thrown over her wide shoulder.

In the filtered light of the hemlock trees, it seemed to Ivy that Lumpen *was* a scarecrow. And further: she was not alone. Behind her vast skirts and wide bodice, a silent crowd, clothed in grit and burlap, stepped forward. A flock of scarecrows— big ones, tiny ones, those with painted faces, or button eyes and pitched hats, and some with no face at all—emerged silently to stand beside the trees. And with them, the riddle of the rustling was solved. Curious field mice, a few chipmunks, and a small red squirrel peeped out from their pockets.

"At your service, miss," Lumpen announced. "The true nature of plants is awakening, miss." Lumpen pointed to the creatures made of hay, of weeds, of flowers.

Shoo flapped his wings and coasted over to the shoulder of a nearby scarecrow, cawing loudly. To Ivy's astonishment, she recognized it at once. It was her own stricken scarecrow from the walled garden beside the Hollow Bettle—still wearing the work shirt her uncle had unknowingly donated, and sporting the dented pocket watch Cecil had discovered on a dead tavern guest.

"Jimson!" Ivy called out at the sight of him.

"You are our shepherd, miss. The Shepherd of Weeds. We are your flock. We are the Army of Flowers." Lumpen curtsied.

Ivy looked around at the vast crowd of unlikely soldiers. Their numbers stretched as far as the eye could see. The scarecrows had made the particular rustling Ivy had heard along her journey.

All were standing still, as if they were propped there by an invisible farmer, their faces a study in blankness. Wildflowers grew from their pockets and rough seams. Blooms sprouted from top hats and buttonholes. The colors of their wind-worn clothing were muted, a spectacle of patchwork, of life's rich tapestry.

Chapter Forty-four
To Catch a Cat

But where was the cat Six? Ivy wondered, looking through the spindling hemlocks and the worn cloaks of the scarecrows. Within her fist was another of Rue's dried specimens, and Ivy crumpled this now and sprinkled it on the wintry pine floor. In the *Field Guide,* she had found it beside the entry for *Nepeta cataria,* and Axle had listed a few of its common names: catswort, hangman's courage.

But Ivy knew it as catnip.

"Kitty, kitty," Ivy called. She felt like a traitor of the worst order, but the birds had given her no other alternative. She was conscious of a dull wish within her: that the cat would come quickly—or not at all.

Within the stand of scarecrows—motionless, eerie—Ivy saw something move, and her heart sank. For Six now emerged, rubbing his tatty fur upon the faded dungarees of a nearby scarecrow, rearing slightly as he did so, and then treating Lumpen to the same.

The cat, true to form, was filthy. His passage through the Mind Garden had supplied him with streaks of sludge that greased his haunches and tail, while here in Caux he had quickly found himself a patch of burrs. He was covered with them—a fact that seemed to please him to no end. He purred a deep, raspy growl at the sight of Ivy and, in his own time, approached.

While the scarecrows had no effect upon the sea of birds (a fact any farmer would do well to note), the appearance of a cat caused a nervous twittering, which grew in strength, tinged in outrage.

"Oh, Six," Ivy whispered.

Shoo had not left his perch upon her shoulder. Six and Shoo eyed each other for a length of time. Ivy watched as Six's eyes eventually narrowed, finishing in a slow blink. From here on, he would diplomatically ignore the bird. The cat continued to approach, and Ivy looked nervously to Shoo, whose gaze had not left the beast, and then to Rue, who stood some distance behind.

Six reached Ivy, and he greeted her with a raspy meow and a dry, scratchy nose against her hand. He somehow managed to appear both indifferent and enthusiastic at the reunion, twining about her legs—his arched back and long unkempt mane easily reaching her waist, his weight causing her to stumble backward.

Ivy felt the caucus behind her growing impatient, and her nervousness grew.

She leaned down, scratching a torn ear, his chin. "Six, somewhere there's a nice bowl of milk and a fish waiting for you, but that's not here—not now. But I promise you this—the next time we meet, I'll have them ready for you."

Six was unimpressed.

"The birds insist you go," Ivy pleaded.

Mid-nuzzle, the cat paused, suddenly alert to the acres of birds that carpeted the field behind them. His cheeks—pincushions of whiskers—tensed. A few of the more ornery birds, grackles and jays, began to taunt him with catcalls and cackles, shrill high-pitched whistles.

The cat crouched down, tail whipping back and forth, but Rue's specimen of catnip beckoned for now.

Ivy reached down and stroked Six, pulling at a large clump of knotted fur behind one ear, whispering. She found another tangle and worked her fingers patiently through it as well. Shoo flapped to a nearby scarecrow, settling on its jaunty head, his tail levering for balance. Ivy held open her small hand, and the cat plowed his pointed chin into it, nuzzling himself against her with great delight. He rolled to the ground, on the carpet of carelessly torn leaves, indifferent to the squawking caucus. Six stretched out fully, his impressive length gilded by his glinting claws.

It was now that the birds attacked. Ivy felt the wind of

their wings upon her cheeks and stood, taking several steps away from the cat.

"I'm sorry." Ivy choked back tears.

The smaller birds buzzed him, and Six swatted at them in surprise, springing up hastily. But he was far outnumbered, and swarms of them dived and jeered as he crouched to the ground. Ivy saw him look at her, puzzled, a low growl escaping his bared teeth. Shoo, too, flew from his scarecrow perch and charged at him, a small thundercloud of black feathers and talons.

Several emotions betrayed themselves now upon Six's haughty face, beginning with confusion, and ending finally in a rueful look, his ears turned down in disgrace.

Ivy stood still, unable to help as the birds shamed Six farther into retreat—he fell upon himself, a rare stumble for the sure-footed cat, his humiliation complete. Picking himself up, he paused as Ivy stared back at him, tears running down her face.

And then, to both Ivy's immense relief and great sorrow, the cat Six turned, and was gone.

Damp Idyll No. VI

The Field Guide to the Poisons of Caux, *in an early chapter on the home and hearth, offers several pertinent pieces of advice. On page 311, under the subhead "Caring for Your Tapestry," Axle tenders this:*

A tapestry, should you be lucky enough to possess such an item, wants to avoid such things as dust and sunshine—both for the damaging effects they wreak upon the fibers of the weave. But by all means display it—storage poses untold problems. It is all quite well and good to dust the surface on a regular occasion, inspecting it routinely, but under no circumstances should the tapestry ever encounter its most dreaded enemy: the moth.

So it was when the Four Sisters emerged into Underwood from the chimney-side passage and surveyed the mess their tapestries had caused, they realized that indeed only one dramatic option remained.

"All of our hard work!" Fifi complained.

"Who is responsible?" Lola demanded.

"Of all the exasperating, terribly disobedient things I've ever witnessed . . . ," Gigi proclaimed, and lapsed into silence.

The scene before them was one indeed of utter natural chaos. What remained of the series of tapestries was little more than a few colored and frayed strings upon the cavern's walls, a tattered, colorless canvas backing visible in places. Here and there a noticeable patch of weave persevered—a splash of brilliance—as did the silken edging that framed them all. But the scenery—once so thrilling and the picture of perfection—was missing. Or rather, displaced, for one need only to look about the vast great room of King Verdigris's underworld palace to uncover the whereabouts of the tapestries' contents.

A dewy patch of irises sent their voluptuous scent into the air beside the Four Sisters, and its very tempestuousness angered Lola so that she kicked the stalks cruelly aside. A heaving pear tree dropped a bushel of smooth, ripe fruit, but this, too, was received as an affront by the Sisters. Everywhere—nothing but unmanageable fertility!

A patch of colorful toadstools punctuated the carpet of rolling moss. A pure white rabbit, unaware of the visitors, paused to nibble grass beside an arched garden gateway, through which the careful observer might see a mere blur of falling stars or catch the occasional smell of sea air, for this was the thorn door by which Ivy and Rowan had returned from Pimcaux.

208

"Start the fire," Lola whispered to Gigi.

Lola, who had been thinking it was high time for some tea, had also remarked that nothing does a tea justice as well as roasted rabbit—and she began making her way toward the unsuspecting creature. This was not at all easy; the lushness of the reawakened plant world made a silent hunt impossible. She cursed the rustling beneath her feet as she flattened a patch of sicklepod, trampled a growth of fiddleheads.

The rabbit, meanwhile, tempted by a clump of cloudberry, had loped forward beneath the thorny archway, and, as Lola watched, he took one ambling stride on two large back feet, and then another—and vanished through the thorn gate.

"What?" Lola accused. "Where the—?" Lola turned impatiently to the others, but was greeted with little sympathy.

"We must start from scratch," Babette decided, indicating the obvious need for replacements.

They quickly reviewed their options.

"Indeed," concurred Gigi, who was busy discouraging a snail from taking up residence on her greenery shawl.

"We have no choice," Fifi echoed.

"So be it." Babette removed from her gown the specimen jar she had taken from the trestleman's study.

"Oh!" Gigi cried, trembling. It was all the Mildew Sisters could do to steel themselves against what was to come.

Babette unscrewed the jar's lid and, with a grim look of determination, released the cloud of moths into the air.

Chapter Forty-five

The Fountain I

As the sun did its business throughout the land, dragging day along by the ear, it did so with little regard to the natures of those below—whether they be good or evil. But consider this: along with light comes shadow, for darkness cannot exist without the sun.

On this morning, the sun shone down on the barren fields beside Jalousie—the birds had vanished, leaving behind a collection of feathers and trampled snow. Wispy bird tracks remained everywhere, waiting to be deciphered like an undiscovered language. The sun shone a little ways away upon a dejected creature—a cat, who crept along the outskirts of a small weald, hungry and tired, alert to creatures larger than even he.

The sun rose upon the enchanted and forlorn Hawthorn Wood, whose canopy of interlaced barbs knitted a foreboding blanket of darkness over its mysteries and secrets—all safe for the time being. It drenched Templar in day as Cecil—who had yet to see his bed—busied himself in the workshop over a hastily scrawled parchment from Babette and the Mildew Sisters, and with plans of war.

And it rose equally over the dark city of Rocamadour, where the black stones and dead moss shrugged off illumination, preferring night's embrace. Yet within the ancient city, a single spear of light defied the inviolable walls, moving diligently along a narrow alley, across the ancient cobbles of a fabled square, vanishing into the recess of a darkened doorway, only to reappear upon the stricken figures of a disgraced fountain.

Beside the fountain crouched the figure of Hemsen Dumbcane, sketchbook and pen and ink in hand, ignoring the silhouettes of the roosting vultures and their stench. The scribe had timed his visit, awakening before dawn, trundling blindly through the small, twisted alleys to this very spot, where many of the school's larger lecture halls could be found. The fountain beckoned him, the way an old memory would, for he was certain he had seen it somewhere before—perhaps in one of his pilfered magic scrolls.

In a greedy attempt to keep his forging talents alive, the calligrapher often found himself sketching, using his hands in the manner that had once brought him such fortune. (But in the end, they had only led him here, to desolation.)

Dumbcane now waited in the darkness for the sunrise. As it approached, its golden beam slicing through the floating dust and ash, the calligrapher urged his hand quicker along the paper, agonizing over the exact angle of the stone sylph's wings, the majesty of the dazzling statues before him now gloriously illuminated. But his fingers failed the exercise. The sunbeam vanished. He had not been quick enough.

Cursing, the scribe vowed to return again the next morning—every morning, if need be—until the sketch no longer eluded him, for it was in this activity that his sanity was ensured.

A clattering on the cobbles in the dim square alerted him to another's presence, and he expertly slipped back into the shadows. It was in this way that the scribe saw a hunched Watchman—the ruined silhouette could be only one man, he knew—arrive with several hulking Outriders. The group had with them a cart, the contents of which were giving the Outriders much difficulty. A set of wooden planks was arranged; a bale of straw was opened and spread over them. Finally, a large blackened cauldron was pushed along the entire contrivance, making its heaving debut upon the doorstep to Snaith's own lecture hall, beneath the peculiar image of an ox head, a swarm of bees flying forth from its mouth—the dreaded home of the infamous course in Irresistible Meals.

Dumbcane, against all instinct, peered farther into the square, his curiosity piqued. He knew Snaith little, if at all—but he did know this: the subrector was to be avoided at all costs. While Vidal Verjouce's evilness was the burning pyre of destruction, Snaith's was worse, in Dumbcane's view. Snaith's villainy was the fickle spark that fanned the Director's flame—darting, caustic, and completely unpredictable. He was an unapologetic assassin. He seemed to be everywhere at once, his feet at home in Dumbcane's inkworks as well as the Director's chambers. His bulbous features and missing ear cast horrid shadows from the fire in the Warming Room, and Dumbcane was happy to relinquish all his small triumphs to Snaith, allowing the Watchman to claim them as his own. His soft-slippered feet and crablike gait seemed to be forever in the shadows—behind him, always behind him.

He was bent on vengeance, Snaith was. Dumbcane knew this; he could sense it. Snaith's devotion to the Guild was complete, but for one thing. A girl had escaped him—an eleven-year-old girl, and it was during this unlikely event that Snaith had succumbed to the wounds of the giant cat, the fearsome wasps.

So here it was: the uncommon solidarity between the two, the calligrapher and the assassin. For Hemsen Dumbcane, too, could not rest until revenge was his. Revenge upon the errant taster call Truax, Rowan Truax, whose pitiful existence had been the source of his own downfall, and who, he had heard Snaith grumble, traveled with the girl called Ivy.

Dumbcane peered closer at the early-morning operation playing out before him. The Outriders were encountering some difficulty with their burden, and it seemed of some interest to the scribe that they were forced frequently to step back, shielding their faces, gasping with their dark mouths for lungfuls of air.

His parchment escaped his hands, the delicate tip of his quill broke off as it hit the dusty cobbles, but Dumbcane hardly cared.

The giant charred vat was distinctly familiar.

The subrector Snaith had somehow procured a vat of ink—the potent ink made in Dumbcane's Warming Room from the destructive scourge bracken weed—and was hiding it away in his lecture hall for his own secretive purposes.

Part V

Poisoned Pen

All things written can be unwritten.

—Prophecy, Kingfisher fragment

Chapter Forty-six

Grig's Workshop

he trestleman Grig had arrived in Templar with an overloaded cart, several of his most trusted assistants, and a desperate need for a workshop. Cecil Manx quickly obliged, handpicking the venue: it was centrally located, and a convenient walk to the palace. And it was vacant. It was also a place familiar to the apotheopath—and Ivy and Rowan, for that matter—for, until quite recently, it had been occupied by a tenant of some infamy, the calligrapher Dumbcane. The scribe's oversized quill, advertising his trade, still hung above the doorway, and in the window, the ghostly remnants of the Nightshades' seal could just be made out.

Grig had wasted no time in establishing himself in the scribe's old storefront. The place was soon unrecognizable. In fact, to the casual observer, Dumbcane's old shop might now be mistaken for a junkyard. The single window let in no light, since it served not as a window but as an appendage to the ledge below it, upon which Grig had stacked various grease-smeared boxes, vigorous fabrics, and machine parts. About the only thing in its proper place was the front door—which had a naughty tendency to disappear when ignored.

The inventor Grig considered this to be a temporary operation, and for his assignment he had brought with him from home merely the necessities of his tinkering profession: a sturdy oak table, his collection of tools, and what he called—when apologizing to Rowan for the general disorder—"a few odds and ends."

"Not at all," Rowan had responded. "I can see everything has its, er—place."

"Indeed!" Grig agreed with some enthusiasm, and as if to illustrate this very point, he began turning in a small circle (for beneath his feet was the only clear patch in which he might perform this act) earnestly looking for something or other. His efforts provided him with a small coil of copper tubing, and this he brandished triumphantly.

"Aha!" His eyes twinkled. "Yes, this is exactly what I was looking for, you see. And now I've found it. How wonderful! Let's see, where should I put it so I don't forget . . ."

"I'll take it, if you wish." Rowan looked worriedly about the workshop—he feared if Grig put the tubing down, it might never be found again.

They had been discussing Grig's incessant preoccupation: the weather. Grig's presence in Templar could mean only one thing: that he and Cecil were conspiring together on some weather-themed invention, and, judging by the immense book atop precariously stacked crates of cogs and spokes—and what appeared to be giant clock mechanisms—Rowan was right. The book's gleaming gold title caught the taster's eye.

Dewes, Mysts, and Vapours

Grig, like nearly all trestlemen, was a masterful inventor of sorts, and his area of expertise was exceptionally wide. Over his long years he had experimented with various contraptions—most weather-related, some more successful than others. His snow twirler, for instance, performed as promised, and his sleet beater was renowned throughout the land. He even had mastered a small metal box that would every so often produce a heavy ball of snow—a clever invention indeed, until he was asked to what purpose such a snowball might serve. Having no answer at first, he soon improvised. He used milk (rather than water) and served the result to his critics for dessert, topped with flavored syrup. This improvisation brought him great wealth and afforded him the leisure of his more eccentric pursuits.

These eccentric pursuits were familiar to both Ivy and Rowan from their recent journeys. They were small, coiled packets of canvas and strapping, called springforms, that when released—usually with a surprising amount of force—would transform into objects of varying usefulness. In this way, something the size of your palm might suddenly become a kitchen sink (it's surprising how watertight waxed canvas can be), or—Axle's favorite—a weather balloon.

"Great, thank you! Very helpful of you." Grig handed his discovery to Rowan. "It's the final piece for my current device, and it wouldn't do to misplace it. So there we are!" The trestle-man looked at Rowan, his rosy cheeks like two small, shiny crab apples. "Now—what was it again that you wanted from me?"

Rowan cleared his throat uncomfortably. Hemsen Dumb-cane's storefront held disagreeable memories, and although there was no visible remnant of the forger's business, Rowan couldn't help but wonder if the dark, cramped corners contained something dangerous.

"The springforms, sir."

"Oh yes! Of course! Don't you worry, young man—I have hardly forgotten. I must congratulate you for testing them! No one, er, ever wanted to actually *use* them." A cloud passed over the trestleman's face. "It's a good thing—for you especially—that they performed as expected. Shall I bring them to you, then, in the morning at the palace? They are in tip-top shape—just a few adjustments needed."

Rowan smiled, relieved. "Yes—and thank you! Oh"—he handed the coil of copper back to Grig—"here you go."

Rowan's enthusiasm for departing the cramped shop now got the better of him, and his shoulder met with a stack of blueprints. What began as a small disruption to the hastily piled scrolls soon became an avalanche, and as the taster and inventor moved to staunch the cascade of papers, for their effort they were soon covered high in them.

Flushed and embarrassed, Rowan began to apologize, but the words stalled on his lips.

The stack of mechanical drawings had been propped against a wall, and now, with their absence, Rowan was treated to a view of what lay behind. Tacked to the chipped plaster were a few of Dumbcane's sketches, an attempt at an ornate alphabet—Rowan remembered these from his last visit to the calligrapher's shop. They had been fanciful and grotesque, and one even appeared to have the image of Ivy upon it. He had had enough of the forger's treachery for a lifetime.

It would be another several minutes before either he or Grig could find the exit, the process of which involved a good amount of trestleman ingenuity and patience. Alas for Grig, for in somehow finding the door, he managed to lose the tubing.

Chapter Forty-seven

Peps

Rowan had hardly emerged from the scribe's old storefront when he collided with another former inhabitant of the Knox Bridge.

"Peps!" Rowan gasped. "I didn't see you! Are you okay?"

The trestleman muttered as he dusted himself off, his face reddening.

"What were you doing there by the door?" Rowan suddenly wondered.

Behind Peps was a group of several dozen townsfolk. Rowan recognized a few in the forefront as the hardened street urchins Peps sometimes kept company with.

"Just out for my usual constitutional," Peps explained casually.

"With forty of your good friends?" Rowan joked uneasily.

Peps shrugged this observation off, preferring instead to glower at the large quill dangling above the taster's head in the twilight. Rowan followed his gaze.

"Someone should see to that," Rowan decided. The less he had to think about the scribe, the better.

"Hardly." Peps's jaw was set. "Let it serve as a reminder of our enemies. Yours, above all."

"Mine?" Rowan was shocked.

"Master Truax"—Peps stared at him intently—"surely you haven't forgotten that the calligrapher has sworn vengeance on you? He blames you, rightly so or not, for his current predicament. When Axle and I saw him in his cell in the catacombs, he was mad with rage. The one name he repeated over and over? Yours. He had been on his way to obscurity when he was visited by the Taxuses—who held a lien on you for the death of your charge. Now Dumbcane is captive—a slave to Verjouce's desire for ink."

Rowan sagged. His first commission after graduating from the Tasters' Guild—and he had killed the man. Rowan had taken an oath to stay by his charge, Turner Taxus, but instead he had run. A stolen scroll from Dumbcane's shop had inadvertently been turned over to the Taxus clan, along with Rowan's Guild papers, and, indeed, caused Dumbcane's arrest.

It was beginning to dawn on Rowan the seriousness of his predicament. He looked nervously from Peps to the crowd behind him. Peps softened.

"But if we have our way, there will be nothing left of the weasely cheat but this quill over the door," Peps said.

"But what does the Director mean to do with all of Dumbcane's ink?"

"You don't know?" Peps scowled. "He's going to unwrite the Prophecy."

Chapter Forty-eight
The Prophecy

Peps was right, Rowan realized as he trudged to the palace—and to his cold room. He thought about what the trestleman had told him as he moved him aside to speak with Grig about weapons. The Prophecy, as Rowan had come to know it, was ancient—before even the time of the Good King. It was what bound him and Ivy together on their adventures— in search of Pimcaux, it brought them to the darkest regions of the Tasters' Guild, and was therefore the reason Axle was imprisoned. The Prophecy rallied them, was the reason Cecil was plotting the assault on Rocamadour.

But what do I really know of the Prophecy? Rowan wondered. Certainly he had never been privy to it—nor did he ever pay it much attention. It was not spoken of in the teachings at the Guild. And those wise men who knew of it only

225

knew *pieces* of it, not the thing in its entirety, for it existed only in fragments. If Verjouce was successful—if he could somehow change the Prophecy—*or erase it altogether*—what would become of them, of Caux? With scourge bracken, Peps had said, there would be nothing left but razed fields and rubble.

Rowan's next thought chilled him to the bone. *What of the child of the Prophecy? What would become of Ivy?*

Back in his cold bedroom with a thin moon rising through his window, Rowan was restless. In Templar, he felt out of place and unwanted in the bigger world of adults, and he had found himself spending many hours in this very room, usually at his window, thinking about Ivy. He was drawn to the window, for he felt (although he didn't know why) that something big was brewing. The skies, and the short moments he had spent in them aloft, beckoned him. Until there was news—any news of Ivy—he would wait here with a cold pit of dread in his stomach.

Now he wanted nothing more than to speak with Cecil. Cecil had potent allegiances of his own, Rowan knew. The master apotheopath had served with King Verdigris, his powers were vast and indisputable, and for him the Prophecy was not some mysterious tangle of riddles. But Ivy's uncle had been extraordinarily busy and uncharacteristically bad-tempered, and had little time for Rowan's questions. And Flux—that despicable turncoat of a former servant to Vidal

Verjouce—he might be bound and guarded by Poppy, but his mouth was quite free and seemed ever ready with a snide quip or sneering aside at Rowan's expense.

Rowan turned from his perch at the window, agitated. Since arriving at Templar, he had had the unsettling feeling that he was being watched. Even here, alone in his room, he could not unwind. His eyes drifted to the side table, where he had placed Ivy's stones.

They had not fared well in his care.

When Ivy had slipped them into his hands in Underwood, they were a glistening gray tinged with pink (like gristle, Rowan thought). Now they had shriveled and had taken on a decidedly unhealthy brownish coloring. Thinking that perhaps they required air, he had removed them from his pocket and placed them on his table beside his silver acorn from Pimcaux, but with their new surroundings they seemed—if anything—worse.

He stared at them dismally. He should just throw them in the ground and be done with them. He did not enjoy being their guardian, and a new thought had occurred to him— one that made a dull ache appear at his temples. If Ivy was really gone, as Sorrel Flux maintained, then it fell to him to complete the Good King's task.

Plant them, the King had told Ivy. *You will see when it is time.*

Impulsively Rowan reached for the stones, but as he

touched them, he was at once filled with such a feeling of dread, of utter revulsion, that he quickly let them drop. His heart was pounding, and just for a moment, he thought he had heard something gurgling.

He threw open the heavy wooden door to his chambers, thinking perhaps the noise came from the impressive hall, but nothing was there. The small stone step up to his room was just as he'd left it an hour ago: empty. Grig had yet to deliver the springforms.

Returning miserably to his bed, he threw himself under the covers and awaited morning.

As it turned out, there were great forces bent on destruction. But tonight, as Rowan slept, it was a small one—a tiny one—that moved about Templar. A hummingbird, no bigger than a bee, was darting through the square below him, keeping to the shadows, making haste on her own vengeful errand.

Chapter Forty-nine
Aster's Errand

ster had remained at the caucus, even after it became painfully clear to her that the consensus was not with her. She had argued strenuously against entering into battle with the girl, but in the end the crow had outranked her. Her anger grew inside her; it burned with a cold glare. The Shepherd of Weeds traveled with the very one responsible for her mate's demise! She vowed vengeance against Ivy, Prophecy or not, as she flew ahead of the caucus, her wings a spray of translucent gray, her tiny soul capable of great destruction.

Aster buzzed about the city of Templar looking for the man called Sangfroid, knowing that somehow in his proximity a plan would hatch. But Sangfroid was not at home, and he had neglected his bird feeder—an unforgivable oversight. She alighted on a bare flagpole upon the Knox Bridge and thought through her options.

At first, she thought she might just have a look at the curious canary-colored man that the warbler Teasel had sung of. Flux, he was called. He seemed of similar temperament to Sangfroid, she reasoned, and perhaps with his aid she might mete out some real vengeance. But where might he be? The warbler Teasel had not said.

She flitted about, finally settling upon a pulley (that routed a pail from street level to the upper floors) in an open square. Here, she noticed, was an Apothecary, flanked by many brightly colored flags, wind-shorn in the winter air. Above, a bank of steamy windows—one cracked open to let in the cold.

There seemed to be a great deal of activity inside. And there! Languishing to one side, a yellowish man. He was reclining on a chaise with one elbow propped beneath his head, a bored expression upon his face. There were others with him (much less yellow), but they attended to some business on the other side of the workshop, and Flux seemed uninvited and petulant. What a partnership might be like between a hummingbird and human, Aster did not ask: she was simply drawn by the driving need to warn someone—anyone—of the caucus's decision.

A small creature such as Aster would have no problem squeezing through the opened window, and indeed this event went as planned. She alighted on a bookshelf, then upon a darkened brass lantern, and finally—after gathering great courage—she raced to Flux. Only too late did she see that at the former taster's feet lay a mountain of white fur, a massive prickly bulge of bristles. As she flew above it, it gathered itself into the shape of a boar—a wild, grimacing boar—who snapped at her, teeth and tusk very nearly ending her mission of betrayal.

Poppy snapped at the treacherous hummingbird, but Aster got away—darting for the window in the nick of time, and with the resolution that a new plan was called for.

But alas, Aster had not failed entirely. Her visit had provided the distraction for which Flux had been waiting. The bored captive saw the pig playing with a bumblebee. Glancing quickly across the workshop, Flux casually reached into his waistcoat, finding the vial within its secret pocket. He then administered a deadly dose of its contents to the boar's water bowl; the only evidence of his deed was a small, unlovely smile that played about his thin lips.

Outside, Aster's heart beat even more rapidly than usual. She would need to rethink her plans—and quickly. Birds from the caucus had started appearing, dropping down from the sky, first a few, then several—and Aster knew that soon the air would be thick with wingbeats as the convention arrived.

The hummingbird decided to make for the Guild, for Rocamadour, ahead of the battle. Surely someone there would take interest in her warning.

Chapter Fifty

Winged Boy

he morning found Rowan again at his windowside vigil. He had slept fitfully, waking often, and with the sense of dread and disorientation that comes from being watched by unknown eyes.

Today, though, Rowan's wait was to be rewarded—and more so than he could have ever imagined. For as he stared glumly out the palace window, the sky fell in. Or, more precisely, bits of it began raining down. Small, floating, feathered bits—blotting out the weak sun.

Where in one moment there was a pale blue satin sky, in the very next it seemed that dark holes occurred throughout, riddling its perfection—tearing at the very fabric of the firmament. The sky appeared a boiling black and was accompanied by a noise like that of a screeching train—a hundred screeching trains—and Rowan's panic was followed by the very real need to cover his ears.

The former taster's heart sank, as he had been treated once to such a vision—an awful one, when dark, stinking vultures arrived to spy on him and Ivy upon the Knox. But Rowan quickly saw that these birds before him now were not vultures; they were in fact everything *but* vultures—birds of all shapes and sizes, fowl from all parts of Caux (and beyond!). More birds than he ever thought possible.

When he had recovered from his shock, he realized that all of the chatter had stopped at once, and he peeled his hands gingerly from the sides of his head.

The city below him was utterly, completely quiet.

A few brave citizens were beginning to peek their heads out of shuttered windows. A street sweeper, caught out at the onset and soon overwhelmed with birds himself, shook his broom free of a flock of sparrows and was tiptoeing to safety. An unlucky laundry line sagged beneath a colorful string of parakeets and clothespins. Signposts, streetlamps, lead gutters all sagged with the arrivals.

In the distance, Rowan could just make out Cecil, accompanied by several sentries and a small trestleman—Peps, he guessed. They had emerged from the workshop above the Apothecary to investigate.

Rowan ran for the door himself—nearly tripping over the small package from Grig that now awaited him. Congratulating himself on his good fortune, he grabbed the packet eagerly, feeling as if he had been reunited with an old friend. Turning not to the street, but in the other direction, he ran away from the palace doors, up—through the nearest set of stairs that he knew would take him to the roof.

The stairs let out on a landing, and before him was a small, wooden door. Heart beating, head a mixture of both heavy and light, he wrenched open the wooden beam that secured the exit. He was treated next to a spectacular view of the great capital city. Templar stretched out before him, beneath its blanket of birds. Above, the satin-blue sky was restored.

He was on a small platform, low ramparts flanking him on three sides. The bird cover stretched as far as the eye could see. With his arrival, they held their perches, shifting their weight from foot to foot, thousands of wings patiently folded.

Rowan inspected the sky again. High above, there were two specks. These gently coasted, soaring on wide wings in ever-smaller circles.

The utter silence was broken only as Rowan opened his small canvas satchel from Grig and, with a familiar *whoosh*, released the tensed coils of wire and canvas that were his beloved springform wings.

Those of us who are made to walk the earth cast our eyes skyward, envy stirring in our hearts. For who among us has not dreamed of soaring effortlessly beside the clouds? But only creatures of the air are gifted with flight.

234

Rowan pushed this thought aside as he stood balancing on the low rampart, wings spread wide and glorious. He did not look down as he jumped. Instead, chin high, he let his feet depart the castle wall in a demonstration of utmost faith in Grig's invention.

Air surged by his ears in a giddy rush, but soon—quite soon—it did not. It met resistance in the small, oiled scales of the wing's partitions, and miraculously, Rowan found that he was rising with each flap of his arms. Soon he was high above the old palace, high above even the tallest flagpole on the towers. A feeling coursed through him—one of utter and complete fulfillment.

The springform wings had brought him safely to Ivy's side in Rocamadour. And they would not fail again as he soared high above the city, the vision of two enormous albatrosses approaching, the reunion with his lost friend stirring in his heart.

"Rowan!" came a rejoicing shout upon the wind. "Rowan—is that really you? Why, look—you've got your wings!"

"Ivy!" Rowan banked sharply, a wonderful feeling of control as he steadied himself beside her. "Flux said you were dead!"

"Nonsense. Never felt better!" She smiled happily at her friend.

Rowan turned his head into the winter sun, so close now, the pale light overwhelmed his vision in a shock of force. After

a disorienting moment, he could see properly. He gasped.
There was another girl atop the second seabird. "R-Rue?" In
his surprise, for a horrid moment he felt his momentum stall,
but some innate knowledge soon righted his balance. Rue
smiled, waving.

"Rue! Why, look at you! I don't know whether to laugh
or cry!"

Rue, while her health was restored, was still clothed in
Mrs. Mulk's preferred orphan attire, and her hair was inele-
gantly chopped about her face. But her smile was the same—
the one he remembered from the Guild's dark lecture halls and
her grandfather's garden. Captivating.

Together, the three friends flew graceful circles, lower and
lower, cutting through the light clouds and feeling their cool

caress as they descended. Rowan weaved happy figure eights between the two girls.

Klair and Lofft, wise old seabirds that they were, merely cocked their heads to examine the most unusual sight: a winged boy.

"Astral trespasser!" Klair called. "How does a boy grow wings?"

"You fly well, son," Lofft decided. "Not like you fell from the nest too early. Who was your tutor?"

"Um, well. No one, sir," Rowan admitted. He smiled as he gently cupped his wings inward to ease his landing, catching the air in a perfectly natural way, as if he'd been flying his entire life.

"And to think—landing is the hardest part." Klair was admiring.

And here it was that Rowan thought it was some measure of his surprising day that he was conversing with a pair of giant albatrosses—and this was the least of his momentous experiences.

Chapter Fifty-one
The Rustling

Ivy and her windswept group descended into the central square before Cecil's Apothecary. A surge of excitement coursed through Ivy's body as she watched her beloved city of Templar from this new vantage point. She could just make out the shock of gray hair that marked her uncle's pate as he rushed to join the throng in the square. And was that Peps beside him? Had he really managed to escape Rocamadour?

But as she alighted from the back of the giant seabird with a bright smile for her uncle and the trestleman, she got nothing in return. Cecil Manx stood stock-still, a dazed look upon his face, and it was a point of question as to whether he had even acknowledged his niece's arrival at all.

For this wisest of men was being treated to a very unusual sight.

This was not the hundreds of thousands of caucus members who fluttered and flapped, and draped the city in a curtain of feathers—although they were wonderment enough. No, what shocked the Master Apotheopath was another, even more astonishing arrival.

Lumpen Gorse stood before him, legs wide, determined chin held high, her yarrow stick thrown over one shoulder. A slight wind played about her burlap frocks.

And she was not alone.

Impossibly, she was accompanied by an endless array of scarecrows who crowded the Knox behind her. They had appeared silently, announced only with a vague rustling—like wind through grass. They settled into rows on the cobblestones as the birds fluttered to make room, and when they had exhausted the cobbles, they stood upon lampposts, flagpoles, rooftops—wherever space would have them. The scarecrows carried pitchforks and pointed sticks; a few had homemade bows slung over their shoulders. Their silent forms draped over the railings of the Knox, congregated in taverns, were propped against storefront windows and entranceways.

An eerie quiet washed over the city.

Ivy saw Jimson, her own scarecrow from the Hollow Bettle, nearby. Shoo was upon his shoulder. Squawking, the crow flapped noisily over to Ivy's.

"Long live the Shepherd of Weeds!" Lumpen cried, raising her yarrow stick in the air.

The scarecrows stood silently, the wind their only reply.

But the silence ended there as the caucus erupted in their own welcome—and with that, Cecil blinked, and realized his niece stood smiling before him.

Looking around at the chaos, Cecil turned to the trestle-man, bending down. "Well, Peps. Looks like we've got our army."

"Indeed." Peps's eyes sparkled.

Cecil appraised the scarecrow throng. Hay, wild caraway, and clover buds burst from their overstuffed clothing.

The apotheopath was no stranger to the ancient ballads.

"An Army of Flowers, no less." He smiled.

Chapter Fifty-two

Staunchweed

"How many are you?" Cecil asked Lumpen as she made her way forward to deliver the scroll from the folds of her dress.

"Five hundred strong, sir." She curtsied awkwardly, adding, "And five hundred more await me at the Lower Moors."

Ivy hugged her uncle and Peps and pushed past them eagerly, leaving them to discuss further details with the well keeper.

Back at the Hollow Bettle, Ivy—when she was meant to be studying her apotheopathic texts—would find herself instead in happier pursuits: boiling, or distilling, or crushing some dried leaf into powder and pressing it into a pill and selling it to her ragtag group of regular clients. She would sift and bake and coax her herbs into greasy balms, or biting gargles, or fine and noxious powders. The hours slipped away as she experimented with her particular alchemy.

With Shoo by her side, she had created a truly remarkable elixir, one that was capable of curing any illness—it had been recklessly lost, but not before both Shoo and Rowan had been helped by it.

The simple workshop was hidden behind the tavern's blackboard menu, and she and her crow Shoo might spend the entire afternoon combining a strange, lumpy fungus with a few potent berries in hopes of inventing a new, terrible tonic—running back and forth from her small but dangerous garden for inspiration. But it was Ivy's accidental abilities with elixirs of the curative sort that had brought her here, to Templar, and to this new—and much more impressive—workshop above the Apothecary.

Ivy now raced to this workshop, up the regal steps leading from the crowded square. She was elated by the day's events and the reunion with her uncle, Rowan, and Peps, but she ached for a quiet moment with her old alembic vessels and little alcohol stove. Bursting into the wide and open room, she was greeted by her well-tended plant cuttings, all straining for the weak sunlight at the large windows, as well as that lovely smell, a twinge of burnt charcoal and a sharp note of distillate, that accompanied her experiments.

All of her most favorite things lay within this room—which is why the voice she heard next was so unpleasant. It had the tone of a rotted turnip, oozing and sulfurous.

"Ah, if it's not the little poisoner," it said.

Ivy reeled, looking about the room.

"Imagine my surprise! I guess my preparations for your funeral were premature."

The voice was coming from an unfamiliar chaise in a far corner. There, her former taster and would-be executioner Sorrel Flux reclined, a smug look upon his face, his hands bound behind him, the large bettle boar Poppy guarding him vigilantly. With the exception of his polished shoes, he was quite an untidy spectacle. "And to think, I was assured of your untimely death."

"Seems you can't get that one right," Ivy replied.

"Practice makes perfect, I'm sure you'll agree."

Ivy toyed with the idea of approaching—she ached to hug Poppy again—but she was already as close as she ever wanted to be to her former taster.

"How did you get here?" Ivy asked the reasonable question.

"Same as you—by way of your mother's treachery."

Ivy spied a small, waxy plant upon the windowsill. She considered administering the blisterbush to her former taster—just one small dose would do—and allowed herself a moment to imagine his face covered in painful boils. Her fingers twitched for her poison kit.

Flux continued. "Your mother and I had agreed to assist each other in our mutual pursuit of great power. She spent many years at the Guild with your father—she knows all its crevices. But I lived there, too. And I know them better," he bragged. "She's gone off, in search of scourge bracken. Apparently, she's not good at sharing."

"And you are?" A more unlikely partnership Ivy couldn't imagine.

"Well. That remained to be seen, didn't it? But you're right. She got to me first—with that silver hairpin of hers. Her only mistake was leaving me alive."

"That can be remedied," Ivy replied brightly.

Behind her the group from the square was arriving, and Cecil moved quickly to distract his niece from her former taster.

"Ivy," Cecil called sternly. "A moment, please." He held the scroll from Lumpen and moved to the table, unfurling it. "It seems Ms. Gorse's parchment will tell us everything we need to know about those stones of yours."

"Yes, do go!" Flux eyed her evilly. "Make haste with your battalion of wastrels before they molder in the rain or are beset by vermin. Men of weeds! A more fearsome army I cannot imagine. Why, they can't even scare a crow!"

Ivy turned on her heel, but not before plucking a small flower from a cluster on her window seat.

"A boutonniere." She smiled, presenting it to Flux. The taster's eyes widened in recognition and his body grew stiff as he struggled. Ignoring his protests, Ivy pinned the showy bloom in his ragged buttonhole, scratching Poppy behind the ear and exchanging a loving hello when she was done.

"What was that?" Rowan whispered as she joined him and Rue beside her uncle with a satisfied look upon her face.

"Staunchweed." Ivy smiled, exchanging a private look with her uncle.

"Wow, that's powerful stuff." Rowan nodded, understanding.

"It has an insatiable thirst. Dries up any moisture it encounters—it acts on the salivary glands. Even the scent of its bloom is enough to make your mouth dry as sand—making speech impossible." She winked. "And the root, when pulverized, can make an entire lake congeal."

The three watched as Flux's face became pinched and his cheeks grew hollow, and although his mouth was open and he appeared to be speaking, not a sound came forth.

"I can't believe I didn't think of that," Cecil muttered.

They turned back to the weathered paper and to the sound of Poppy, who had begun a loud drink from her water bowl.

Chapter Fifty-three

Lumpen's Scroll

At night, when the city slept, it did so to a lullaby
of the dry winds. The people of Templar dreamed of parched
lands and unquenchable thirst—and not because of staunchweed.

The scarecrows, their dry countenances and eerie rustling, made everyone think of dust. The citizens of Templar
found them to be quiet, ominous guests. It seemed that the
strawmen were profoundly shy of human contact. The majority of the flock kept to the frozen river, huddled in a pack
beside Lumpen. But a fair few wandered into forgotten
broom closets, for brooms, made of straw, comforted them
greatly. Servants began refusing to sweep, as the fright of
opening a broom closet with a scarecrow inside was too much
to bear.

Lumpen made camp by the water, assuming guard, her corncob pipe glowing reds and oranges, while Cecil busied himself translating her scroll. The work was made more difficult by various interruptions in their war-making effort, as well as Flux's irrepressible croaking.

Cecil was finding the work maddeningly elusive; the tiny script seemed to dim at the exact place he chose to inspect it, only to reconstitute after he moved on to a new passage. The whorls and flourishes of the lettering gathered themselves into impenetrable knots. After an entire evening, with river stones weighing down the four corners of the document and a huge gold-rimmed magnifying glass in hand, he had translated only one small cartouche—a caption beneath one of the images that appeared to be his niece.

And in his folly—let him be sure to see.

He stood, pulling on his beard absently.

He tried the phrase out thoughtfully to himself several times, hoping to get at the obscure meaning. His days at the Good King's side were long ago, but that sort of learning is never forgotten. Before the great fire—the wretched point in Caux's history marking the end of the reign of the Good King Verdigris and the beginning of the new regime, that of the

Deadly Nightshades—there would have been cloistered scribes available to translate this very document. When Rocamadour was an academy for apotheopaths—before Vidal Verjouce distorted the King's teachings and built the Tasters' Guild on his corrupt ideals—Cecil had helped to amass the great collections that could be found in the Library at Rocamadour. A library that at one time contained nearly all of Caux's valuable scrolls, a vast storehouse of ancient magical know-how available to anyone who so wanted it.

"And in his folly—let him be sure to see," he said thoughtfully.

A strange sound from the other side of the workshop startled the apotheopath. A dry, raspy croak. Flux had been listening, Cecil realized. The parched man was laughing a staunched, choking laugh, the sound of a saw meeting dead timber.

Adventure in Botany

It was not long after her reunion with Cecil that Ivy found herself whisked away to a quiet area of the Good King's old palace and into a steaming bath filled with fragrant lavender and lemon balm. Rue, too, was being treated to a restorative soak, and after some time, the two girls—wrapped in thick robes and cheeks flushed with warmth—convened in Ivy's room over Rue's bloated copy of the *Field Guide*.

A plate of sugar-dusted cakes sat between them, but it was gone quite quickly, and the creams and jellies that filled each pastry dotted the girls' chins, crumbs collected in the *Guide*'s sturdy binding.

With sugary fingers, Ivy pored over Axle's masterwork.

"What are you thinking?" Rue asked.

"Well, while Cecil's busy figuring out what to do with the

King's stones, I reckon I'll give some thought to our own plan of attack."

"With the *Guide*?"

Ivy nodded, eyes alive. "With your specimens, Rue."

Rue's eyes grew wide. "Being with you, Ivy, is an adventure in botany," she declared.

"Rue—you're a complete genius! Without your meticulous collecting we'd be lost. Axle's book has rescued me many times—and it's full of surprises. But this time, it's not what Axle wrote—it's your contribution that's saved the day!"

Ivy gathered a few cuttings of sunflower and thistle and ran to the tall window.

"What are you doing?" Rue wondered.

"The birds must be hungry," she called over her shoulder to Rue.

Throwing open the mullioned windows, Ivy waited. Soon Shoo alighted upon the stone sill, and the pair shared a short moment of hushed conversation. Finally, after rubbing his sleek feathers, she held out her other hand, and the crow pecked at her open palm—and flew off noisily into the dark.

Turning back to her friend, she settled in to read a chapter on invasive weeds.

"There's a whole footnote here on warring plants," Ivy pointed out. "Would you help me take an inventory? I see you have a cutting of saberweed—good! I wonder how sharp it is. How about crampbark or slippery elm? Whipweed? Gagroot?

Ah—here's some bearded tongue, an old favorite—although it would be useless against the Outriders."

The girls worked intently, cataloging their defenses.

Outside, Shoo had spread her gift in a sparse field beside the quays as night settled in. The only light shining in the square was that of a small lantern, sheltered from the gusting wind by pasty fingers—creeping forward between the still figures of the scarecrows and roosting birds. The small light cast long shadows upon the shifting strawmen—and a strange sheen upon the bearer's highly polished shoes.

As Flux pattered across the cobbles, he blended in perfectly, for Sangfroid had enabled Flux with a means by which to escape. He produced a disguise of such cleverness that the former taster—not one for praise of another—congratulated his friend wholeheartedly before dispatching him to the hereafter with a sprinkling of the antimony Sangfroid had so favored. Then, in a surprising display of strength (for Flux possessed very little muscle, and was mostly sinew—and as a meal he would be deeply unsatisfying), he managed to jettison his accomplice Sangfroid into the old castle moat, where, after a few worrying moments, the man finally began to sink.

Alas, however, Sorrel Flux's treachery was not complete.

He left behind another victim. In Ivy's workshop, Flux had found it impossible to move the body of the enormous bettle boar—the pig had died quite quietly, curled in a ball on the floor, beside her tainted water bowl. Flux had been too exhausted from his exercise with Sangfroid to see to the creature's disposal, and besides, he was already consumed with his new freedom—for, as Teasel would attest, there is nothing like captivity to make you appreciate hard-won liberty.

Chapter Fifty-five
Alarm

n the morning, a field of sunflower and thistle had grown up where the Knox deposited itself on the far bank of the river—huge, round disks of gold facing the sun, interlaced with wiry purple spikes. Birds dived and soared above the feast Ivy had provided. A loud affair it was—it nearly drowned out the clanging of Templar's many bells.

Sorrel Flux's escape had been discovered.

Ivy and Rue awoke to the birdsong interspersed with the alarm—Ivy had been dreaming of dark, overgrown passages filled with ghostly plants and hidden, shifting shadows—and at first she was quite relieved to climb from her bed. Groggily, Rue emerged from under a heavy down comforter, and together the pair stared at each other.

The stone floor was cold on their bare feet, and they

quickly threw on some thick woolens that the cobbler Gudgeon had provided in a generous pair of trunks, bursting with clothing.

"What do you suppose . . . ?" Rue asked Ivy as they made for the door.

Ivy's face was still creased from her pillow, and she gave Rue a look of worry.

Outside, they raced through the congregating scarecrows, Ivy's uneasiness growing with each toll of the bells. Guards and sentries fanned out around them on some urgent errand.

In the workshop, the worst was confirmed.

A group was gathered there—everyone, that is, but Sorrel Flux.

At once Ivy noticed the long chaise that Flux had occupied was empty—his binds were severed and abandoned—and the only reminder of his stay was a slight wisp of an impression that his scrawny body made upon the soft velvet. Upon the tasseled pillow, his boutonniere of staunchweed.

"Flux!" Ivy snarled.

"That man was like a poisoned well—no good to anyone, and impossible to mend," Lumpen muttered.

"How did this happen?" A cold fear swept over Ivy now as she noticed another absence.

"Where is . . . Poppy?" she hardly dared to ask.

Cecil, his back to her, lowered his head.

"Where is she?" Ivy pleaded. "Please, Uncle!"

Cecil spun around, his long cloak fanning out.

Ivy had never seen her uncle so enraged. A dark, mad anger washed over his features, pale where his teeth clenched, flushed at his brow, hair a wild mane. But his eyes—his eyes were unlike anything she had ever before seen. Glimmering, vicious daggers—eyes belonging not at all to her uncle Cecil but to a stranger. A murderous stranger. They flashed, searing the room with their ferocious power, and then, just as suddenly, their fire was gone.

"It's not too late! I—I can heal her. . . ." Ivy's voice faded in her throat. The image of the awful, stagnant Mind Garden swam before her eyes, and she willed it away.

"You cannot heal the dead," Cecil replied quietly.

Behind her, Rue gasped.

Poppy was curled in the corner, as if asleep.

Ivy sat beside the mountain of white fur and bristle, tears in her eyes. Reaching, she felt the haunch of the enormous boar that was her friend and traveling companion—and pulled her arm away. Poppy was cold to the touch, and somehow her fur felt unreal.

"Where's Rowan?" Ivy asked suddenly. She knew Rowan adored the boar perhaps more than anyone else did. "Does he know?"

"He has flown out in search of Flux," Cecil said.

"Against my advice," the trestleman Grig faltered. "The wings are imperfect, highly mechanical. They are, after all, canvas and wire. I expressly warned him that after each flight, they would need adjustments, and I haven't seen them since his last flight."

The exuberant look upon Rowan's face returned to Ivy suddenly, as he soared to meet them in the sky, his oiled wings reflecting back a thousand little suns.

"And Flux—where was he going?" Ivy wondered, dreading the answer.

"Where else?" Peps replied. "Where we all are headed. To Rocamadour—drawn to scourge weed like a moth to a flame."

Damp Idyll No. VII

The cloud of gray moths had made quick business of the remnants of the remaining six magical tapestries in Underwood—the great pieces were no more. Lola, sitting on an enormous toadstool, picked her teeth absently and threw some bones upon a small fire, where they crackled pleasantly.

"Are you thoroughly done?" Babette demanded.

Lola nodded and stood, throwing a white rabbit skin over her shoulder.

There, before the Four Sisters, was a loom of enormous proportions. It was made of a silvery gray wood and seemed somehow both sturdy and transparent. And after a quick spot of tea, and a toast to their reunion, the sisters were now ready to weave. Their gnarled, crooked fingers coursed with creativity; snaggle-tipped nails and tea-stained fingers flexed and stretched. Hearts beat with a contentment only found when doing one's true desire.

They gathered before the loom, as they had done so many times.

"Well." Lola sighed, looking each of her three sisters in the eye. "Here we go again!"

"One more time." Gigi giggled.

"Yes." Fifi's head bobbed adorably. "One more time."

"One last, final time," Babette clarified.

Four sets of fingers flexed, followed by a symphony of knuckles cracking. Hands on sinewy wrists whirled, mottled skin a congregation of liver spots. The threads eased, and then strained.

The weave began, bewildering the eye.

For their palette, the Four Sisters had chosen hundreds of spools of thread spun from the ribbons from an ancient tree in Pimcaux— the Tree of Life. With names such as Faded Whimsy, Faint Star, Bygone Tragedy, and Boneset, all the threads were of varying shades of white.

As the Four Sisters wove their fabric, a calm spread about the vast chamber of Underwood. A slight, melodious tune could be heard—just barely, as if rising from the very earth and settling down as dew. For the Four Sisters were weaving the very fabric of life, and as they did so, their transformation began.

A small mouse, at home in the hem of Lola's skirt, peeped out, alert to something magical. A parade of wood lice crawled along Gigi's eyebrows. The dark fuzz that lined Fifi's upper lip sprang to life—a woolly caterpillar—and crawled away.

"You're shedding, dear." Fifi motioned to Gigi, for indeed clumps of green and brown were beginning to drift from her oak moss shawl.

Chapter Fifty-six
The Fountain II

In Rocamadour, Hemsen Dumbcane kneaded his eraser—a pleasing soft putty made from boiled sap, which captured the scribe's fingerprints, raised whorls and ridges particular to him alone. Here he was again—at the disgraced fountain before sunrise. What was it, he wondered, about the broken plumbing, cracked drains, and decrepit statues that brought him back, morning after morning? For indeed, he seemed drawn here. Certainly there were other fountains, other subjects with which to pass the time, to practice his forging talents and keep his hands supple, his mind clear.

Now was his chance for a glimpse of sunlight.

He toiled all his waking hours over vats of thick, caustic ink, black as pitch and darker than night. It sapped his soul. He craved the radiance of the sun—he'd settle for even the flickering gas lamp above his drafting table back on the Knox.

His former profession, forger, calligrapher extraordinaire, required perfection—as did ink-making. But it also required light. And nothing in Rocamadour needed the sun. Dumbcane had come to realize the city was built of moisture, mildew, and nightmares.

Here it comes, he realized.

The small beam of sunlight slid through the mossy square, illuminating dust motes in a spray of effervescence. It bumped along the dreary cobbles and tiptoed over the rim of the once-great fountain, finding the gloomy vultures in hapless clusters, bald heads hidden beneath their wings.

The very center of the fountain featured an enormous horse and rider drenched and half submerged in filthy water as they toiled in eternity to reach the safety of some imagined shore. The rider was a woman—her stone skirts were drenched and held fast to her body, draping marble weighing her down. Her steed, a spectacular warhorse, his eyes wide with terror and determination.

Dumbcane's sunbeam threw itself to assist her, the light catching her outstretched fingers—and he sketched quickly. The beam scattered small pinpricks of sunlight down upon her dress, illuminating it, for one mere frustrating second, in a spray of stars.

This time he'd come as close as ever before in capturing the vision before him—but in the end, it had eluded him. He now stared blankly, as the fountain receded again into shadow, clutching his parchment before him, disgusted, and ready to crumple and discard it.

But something caught his eye in the gloom.

The vultures were rising with unpleasant yawns, and they raked their beaks against the marble of the fountain, sharpening them. The ugly scene was nothing like the moment of sunshine just before, and Dumbcane grew more dejected.

There, though, it was again.

A small bird. Drab gray-green along her back and pale busy wings, a curved downward-pointing bill. The drone of an insect.

What was a hummingbird doing here—of all places? Dumbcane wondered. What business could she have with the despicable vultures before her?

Chapter Fifty-seven

Irresistible Meals

Not far—not far at all—from the desperate fountain and turncoat hummingbird was a very notorious classroom, in a city filled with fearsome classrooms. Dumbcane knew nothing of this lecture hall—but Ivy did. Ivy, Rue, and all the students and graduates of the Tasters' Guild knew of the class held behind the brass emblem of the ox head. Rowan had failed the course three times before advancing to his Epistle.

Behind the ox head lay Snaith's class in Irresistible Meals.

The curriculum of the Tasters' Guild, a notoriously difficult and trying collection of requirements—all life-threatening—culminated in the lecture hall of the subrector Snaith. His imperviousness to pity and lack of empathy had caught the eye of the Director, Vidal Verjouce, when he needed a replacement for his treacherous assistant Sorrel Flux.

But even with his newly acquired administrational duties, Snaith still preferred to teach this one class in his roster. It was the one place outside of orphanages where he might perform dastardly experiments on unwitting children. All under the auspices of education.

And something terrible was indeed happening behind the heavy, metal-studded doors of the recessed entrance to Irresistible Meals. Something chilling and horrendous—borne from the depths of the bile that circulated through his soul, a place where normally patience and purity are found. But, in the case of Snaith, what virtue he might have possessed had long ago turned to sludge. Like the boils upon his face, Snaith's hatred had bubbled up from a place deep within him, a fearsome hatred for all but his master, Vidal Verjouce.

And since Verjouce was occupied with his terrible passion, Snaith had decided to take matters into his own hands.

Over his years of service at the Guild, Snaith had amassed a sort of list, and on it were the various people who had ever—even once—shown him some hint of unkindness, some measure of disagreeability, or perhaps he simply chose to dislike. And then, of course, there were the children—every one of them disappointing in some way or other.

So it was that the remaining students—a surprisingly numerous group, as the Guild had shut its doors quite quickly after the Deadly Nightshades were toppled—and a peppering of uncooperative subrectors had been herded into his lecture hall, where a vat was waiting. The room of Irresistible Meals.

Snaith, with his curved spine and uncooperative gait, took the lectern and looked around. Goblets lined the long table, glinting in the light of the chandelier.

"Welcome"—he interlaced his stubby fingers, resting them on his paunch—"to your *final* exam."

Chapter Fifty-eight

Nightmare

Dumbcane had begun to dream about the bewitching fountain and, in particular, about the horse and woman rider at its center. It seemed to him the cruelest of visions: a drowning woman and her steed, encircled by various onlookers (some quite fanciful and grotesque), helpless before the taunting crowd (and worse still: some of those gathered figures displayed a casual indifference, looking away from her plight—as if a drowning woman might be the commonest of things). The dream each time aligned Dumbcane with these jeering onlookers—and, in the way of dreams, he found himself horrifyingly incapable of action.

At night, Dumbcane thrashed and twitched in the airless room upon his straw pallet; in the day, he sleepwalked through his duties at the inkworks. At times, even, he fancied he heard a ghostly horse, galloping, urgent hoofbeats echoing off the twisting maze of Rocamadour's streets and walkways.

The woman, though he tried desperately to see her in these visions, was bathed in shadow. Remarkably—just as the sun shattered upon her dress at the fountain—her skirts were alive with starlight. Pinpricks of scorching light bounced about her as she traveled through the dark passages, jumping the small, greasy waterways with grace and ease. The stars were grouped in strange, unusual constellations from new and foreign skies. (Dumbcane, from his years of forging the Good King's magical documents, was familiar with them all.) His tiny room was littered with discarded attempts to capture the horse and rider on paper, for he was a man obsessed.

One particular haunting evening, when Hemsen felt feverish and the thoughts within his head echoed in an unpleasant and tinny way, he rose from his familiar dreams to search out his water jug. It was then that he heard it: the distinctive *clip-clop* of a large horse making its way clandestinely through the streets of Rocamadour—and then upon a nearby narrow passage that the scribe knew led up and let out eventually on top of the high wall of the city. The horse's hooves rendered a noise of stone striking stone, and Dumbcane soon assumed that the carved horse and rider from the fountain had finally come for him.

He raked his ink-stained fingers through his hair and pinched at his cheeks. He determined he was most certainly not sleeping.

Dazed, and not quite willing to trust his ears, Dumbcane wrapped his boiled-wool blanket about him hastily and went out, nightshirt flapping behind him as he ran.

Clothilde and Calyx rode as if there were no unaccounted years between them, rode as if both were fresh and new and the joy of simply being in each other's company was the greatest of all pleasures. Calyx would perform any maneuver Clothilde requested with enviable intuition—she need not dictate with her reins (and the whip she carried was reserved for other things). Such was his perfect anticipation of his rider, and his trust in her was complete. She had returned. It did not matter why.

They galloped throughout the darkened city on errands and scouting missions she devised, their knowledge of the twisting streets and walkways innate and unfailing. Calyx's new silver shoes grazed the mossy stones.

When he discovered that the ravishing figure of his dreams was indeed a living, breathing being, Dumbcane gave over any last resistance and devoted himself entirely to her command. He was free to do her bidding, the woman of the stars. Only then did his nightmares cease.

He enjoyed the sabotage he performed for her, for she seemed bent on disruption. She ordered various passages closed or obstructed; waterways were rerouted at her whim. She had an accomplished plan for everything, it seemed to

Dumbcane, who nodded mutely at each order she dispatched. The tarnished doors to the Chapter Room, with its macabre friezes lining the walls, had been flung open, the rooms aired, and a majestic drape mounted on the wall.

This weaving, she had told him haughtily, was from her personal collection, deep within a buried vault. It had held her warhorse Calyx's saddle for these many years.

Dumbcane unfurled it carefully, with heavy leather gloves. It was the image of a door with a porthole carved into it, through which the scribe saw stars upon a blue-black velvet sky. He had been given a set of warnings. Do not touch the ancient weave without your gloves. And be on the lookout for moths.

The woman was very precise on the placement of the wall hanging—and when Dumbcane was done, she stared at the thing, approaching it confidently. She blew away a speck of dust and nodded appraisingly. Then she spun on her heel, stars bounding about the dark hall and its woven contents like a string of lights on an evening carousel, and was gone.

Chapter Fifty-nine
Axle

he ravages of time had singled out for their pleasure the upper chambers of the central spire of Rocamadour. The very room that once held kings had now been redecorated in the theme of evil. Shadows draped the walls like malevolent curtains. Dense cobwebs sagged under the weight of grease and dust, forming small, ghostly hammocks. A carpet of decay and poison covered all else. Empty walls and pitted floors alike were splattered with dark, tarry ink, the stench of which was so cheerless, so desolate, that any visitor would instinctively beg for swift deliverance. Darkness prevailed, for light had been banished by a blind man.

In this inhospitable mess, the trestleman Axlerod D. Roux—arguably the wisest being in Caux—lay in a small gilt cage beside the room's lone window. His pleasant memories of

269

this room had long abandoned him. The slight rocking of the cage, suspended by a velvet cord, was all the trestleman had to remind him he was alive, and so great was his misery that he had begun wishing for nothing but stillness. A vast, eternal stillness.

Instead, there was constant noise.

The howling of the wind through the shattered window was like the breath of banshees. But, worse still, were the squeals and chatter of Vidal Verjouce's scourge bracken fiends, his grotesque ink monkeys. They clustered beside their dark master like nesting bats.

Axle watched as a squabble between two of them broke out beneath his cage. The ugly pair were tormenting a scorpion, plucking its legs off one at a time, and the disagreement appeared to be over whose meal the thing might make. The argument was forgotten when they turned their attention to Axle's cage, rattling the bars with little leathery fists for amusement. They shrieked mercilessly, baring yellow teeth.

An evil voice drifted over the stale air. "Soon," it said, "I shall have dominion over all things."

As Vidal Verjouce repeated his unfortunate promise, Axle was finding it hard to be impressed. To rule over this wasteland, he thought, could hardly be deemed a triumph. But the Director's words were not for him, Axle knew.

He turned his attention to the ink monkeys before him, the shattered light of the diamond-shaped window illuminating their dark velvety fur. Their nasty faces stared back eagerly,

270

small horn buds protruding haphazardly above their squinty eyes.

A bucket of ink lay at the Director's side, and in it he occasionally dipped the spiked tail of an ink monkey perched upon his wrist. The mixture was as thick as tar. Tail in hand, Vidal Verjouce continued his horrible composition—his masterpiece of ruin. The ink was now too caustic for paper, so Verjouce wrote upon the spire's walls, and where the scourge bracken touched the solid slabs, the stone was etched away.

Like a gravestone, Axle thought.

Suddenly he was compelled to speak. "What are you writing?" Axle asked.

"Your obituary," Verjouce responded. "You see—you're dead. You just don't know it yet."

The trestleman watched for a while longer while Verjouce muttered to himself in scratchy whispers. The walls were swirls of sentences, the letters incomprehensibly small at times, vastly oversized at others—all in the old tongue. Entire passages were underlined in places, while huge sections were crossed out with deep, ragged gouges. Yet the language was a familiar one to Axle, and he soon recognized a few key words and fragments.

"The Prophecy!" he croaked.

At the sound of the prisoner's voice again, the ink monkeys shrieked wildly, clambering upon each other in an attempt to reach his golden cage.

"Silence!" Verjouce commanded. "Can't you see that I am

concentrating? I do not toil over insignificant pulp, like you. No, I am rewriting the very fabric of life."

"You fool!" Axle rattled the bars of his cage. Half crazed, the monkeys gnashed their teeth and clawed at the air. "The Prophecy cannot be undone!"

"Now, Axlerod." Vidal Verjouce spun around, and Axle wished he hadn't. "We both know that this is not so." His face—the hollow pits where his eyes once were—was a mask of grim evil.

The trestleman regarded the dire scene before him. But he was not silent. Emboldened—and beyond caring—Axle continued, louder.

"Then you shall fail! For the Prophecy was long ago surrendered to the creatures of the air."

The monkeys hissed and shrieked at the trestleman.

"All things written can be unwritten. That is the power of this ink," Verjouce glowered.

Chapter Sixty

Tokens

he birds of Caux grow restless," Peps D. Roux observed from the window of Ivy's workshop in Templar.

"Soon," came Cecil's reply.

The pair were peering down at the courtyard, where a strange spectacle was unfolding. There Ivy and Rue had gathered, dispersing a thick carpet of untidy twigs and dried vines. They now stood in the middle, surveying their accomplishment. Shoo flew to Ivy's shoulder, and she whispered something to the old crow.

"This delay . . . ," Peps was saying. "For Axle's sake we must make haste! My men are ready at this very moment. Let us tell them they can go."

The loss of the beloved boar had galvanized the party in Templar, and it seemed that everyone was collected and accounted for, the various jobs dispensed and battle cries shouted—with the exception of Rowan. Rowan remained a source of great worry for the apotheopath, who hoped that the young man would turn back from his quest for vengeance and join them. Perhaps even with some news from the front.

"They won't wait much longer. Your brother will not be aided by an ill-prepared army," Cecil said quietly. "The scarecrows have marched," he reminded the trestleman. "It has begun."

Indeed, that very morning, Ivy had fortified Lumpen's army with bittersod, a weed known for its warlike traits. They departed wordlessly, after the horrifying discovery of the loss of the bettle boar. Leading them on were Lumpen's confident form and that of the much smaller Grig—and a caravan of half a dozen other trestlemen from the Knox. Their destination: the Lower Moors, and the imposing and impenetrable gates at Rocamadour.

"Yes, the strawmen issue forth—but to what army do we entrust our fate?" Peps muttered.

"To Ivy. And the Army of Flowers, Peps," Cecil replied kindly. "Have more faith in the ancient writings. Now, be quiet for a minute and watch. You're in for a treat." Cecil fell into a contemplative silence, studying his niece below.

A breathless silence had descended on the scene. The air was heavy and punishing, and it felt to the girls as if it might storm. Shoo opened his black beak and cawed loudly—three sharp, shrill cries—while Ivy and Rue scanned the skies nervously.

"Ivy was born with a particular talent with plants—they are simply more *alive* around her, and part of the Prophecy answers to this very point," Cecil whispered to Peps. "She can speak to trees—the very forest awakens at her command. Nature shall again return to its pure state. Only then will poison cease to be a way of life."

Peps frowned. It was a big burden on such small shoulders, he thought dismally, and he wondered if Cecil felt the same.

In the square, the two girls held hands. And then, in the vacuum before the clouds broke open and nature's fury was released, Ivy had a moment of doubt. She looked quickly to Rue, whose round face betrayed a similar nervousness, and her heart sank further. What if her plan failed? There was no time for additional regret, though, as for only the second time in her life, Ivy watched as the sky blackened to the color of pitch, and the winds picked up—and the birds of Caux descended upon her.

Ivy had called upon the crows, the jackdaws, the grackles, and the ravens—black-feathered, the color of night—for her secret errand.

Her golden hair whipped about, and the stark attire and soft moleskin apron, another gift from Gudgeon, pressed against her skin. The stones from the King were secured carefully in an upper pocket, sewn tightly closed. Ivy felt Shoo grip her shoulder. Above, the gale force of the birds threw open the leaded windows of the workshop, filling the room, and its occupants, with a whipping wind and their shrieks and cries.

And then the birds were gone, as quickly as they came, and the square was picked clean of the brush and twigs, each bird carrying aloft a small sprig of an invasive plant—a token of war from Poison Ivy.

In the aftermath, there were but two birds that remained. The albatrosses Klair and Lofft awaited the girls stoically. Ivy and Rue climbed on—the seabirds' bodies as light as the air beneath them.

Chapter Sixty-one

Departure

Cecil and Peps ran to the square.

"Well, Uncle." Ivy managed a smile. "Looks like this time we get a proper goodbye!"

"So it seems, young one. A first." The apotheopath's eyes shone. "But it won't be for long, this goodbye—we are all to meet, as arranged, in the Lower Moors, northwest of the Hawthorn Wood," her uncle assured her.

Cecil said something quickly to Lofft—it sounded to Ivy's surprised ears like a distant gull's cry carried over the sea and wind. Lofft nodded and bowed his regal head.

"You have the stones?" Cecil asked, a pained look passing over his old face.

Ivy nodded, feeling them in her apron pocket. Gudgeon had laced it shut against both the possibility of loss and their awful stench.

Earlier that morning, Cecil had finished deciphering Lumpen's scroll, and Ivy had one last conversation with her beloved uncle about the stones. It was a private—and awful— one.

Cecil had raised his head from Lumpen's parchment, his face wild and pale. "The stones . . ." His voice drifted off. "It is no wonder that traitor Flux understood them."

Ivy had waited, a cold dread growing in her stomach.

A blank, dull look overtook her uncle's face; he gazed unseeing out the window.

"Uncle?"

Ivy's voice brought him back—his attention, like a whip, sharp and pained.

"Ivy," Cecil began bitterly. "We were wrong. They are not of the earth, to be planted in the ground. Oh—a heavier burden I cannot fathom."

And then, haltingly, Cecil explained to Ivy just what was expected of her.

Now, in the courtyard, Ivy looked to Peps, who was a trestleman transformed. He had Gudgeon outfit him in a spectacle of warfare. There was the usual flamboyant cloak, true, but beneath that was an assembly of delicate chain mail—light and airy, but, as Gudgeon promised, impenetrable. A small, dangerous pick hung from a belt, and he brought only a skin of wine with him.

"Peps, you don't plan to eat?" Ivy teased her well-fed friend.

"I vowed not to eat until my brother can do the same," he explained seriously.

Ivy nodded. "Well, for the sake of all the fine restaurants in Templar—and for Axle—may that be soon, Peps."

To her uncle, she turned again. "The birds will drop the first offensive. It's the most invasive species I could find, but all the same, it will take some time to grow. And, Uncle, I will find Rowan. We have thousands of eyes—Shoo has sent out scouts. He will be at the Lower Moors."

"I dearly hope so."

There was something sad in the apotheopath's inflection that Ivy caught.

"Uncle? We *will* see you at the moors?"

"I have a small errand first. Should it keep me longer than I wish . . ."

Peps cleared his throat awkwardly and kicked a stray pebble with his boot. Cecil stared sharply at the trestleman, whose discomfort only grew.

"I will be there, Ivy," the apotheopath promised.

And then, before the tears could come, Ivy and Rue asked politely if the giant seabirds might now take them aloft—take them to the dreaded city of Rocamadour.

Chapter Sixty-two

As the Crow Flies

he Field Guide to the Poisons of Caux describes the
journey to Rocamadour in this manner:

> The ancient city of Rocamadour, composed of dark stone
> mined of a vein deep beneath the Craggy Burls, was serviced
> at one time by an unflinchingly straight road that cut a path
> between Rocamadour's wide, imposing gates and the capital
> city. While the road is no more, stretches of it remain—
> particularly in the encroaching forest of hawthorns, which
> guards the Tasters' Guild from the west and is deemed
> unfriendly to tourists and journeymen alike. Should you be

summoned to the dark, stone city, it is highly advisable to avoid this wood, as it is judged somewhat troublesome. The overgrowth of hawthorns, with their deep canopy of sharpened barbs and tearing thorns, is uncharted—and is a suspect in the disappearances of untold travelers.

For the ancient hawthorns are quite treacherous. They bind people within their ancient cloaks of bark and are said to contain imprisoned souls.

It was high above these very woods that Ivy and Rue would soon soar upon the giant albatrosses' backs.

"We go as the crow flies," Lofft was explaining to Ivy as they rose easily on an invisible updraft. "We are an hour's journey to the Lower Moors, where we will be sheltered by the hawthorns as we gather—although beware of their treachery. And from there, little more to the gates of Rocamadour."

Ivy clung to the silken ribbons of the harness with cramped hands. While flying upon Lofft's enormous back was a great honor, flying on this errand—to war—made the trip a dismal one. Punctuating her misery was the bleak winter landscape below them; the earth had heaved and shifted with the heavy frosts and seemed to be neither mud nor turf—but some new and ugly compromise between the two. The river

Marcel—the times they saw it—was a ribbon of greenish brown, a layer of sickly ice that captured felled trees and refuse in strange, shadowy clumps. This was no ordinary winter—Ivy barely recognized her land below. From this, she thought, no spring could ever be born.

They had been joined by a flock of great blue herons, and their wings worked in long, graceful strokes beside the seabirds. One bore the trestleman Peps upon his back—and at another time Ivy might find reason to smile at this were their errand not so dire. Peps was not ever a trestleman who appreciated heights (some did, living on bridges high above perilous gorges), but, in the face of Axle's captivity, he was a man reborn. Still, he refused all entreaties to conversation, holding his harness with white knuckles, and he kept his eyes upon the horizon stoically, never once looking down.

As the travelers got closer, the mountains fell back to their right and the land opened up into a stretch of rolling pasture—small, prickly hills and low, boggy glades. There they saw the startling sight of hundreds and hundreds of marching scarecrows, in orderly lines, making their way behind the figure of Lumpen Gorse—yarrow stick brandished high, a ribbon from Ivy's hair streaming from its pointed end.

And there was another sight, too, in the distance, one that Ivy could never forget.

Rocamadour.

Great plumes of filthy smoke hovered above the city

limits—the haze having taken on a weather system of its own, billowing greenish yellow clouds, the color of pea soup—here and there small orange flares from below. Ivy's blood ran cold. There, somewhere within the choking gases of scourge bracken, was the spire—and her beloved Axle. And his captor, bent on undivided devastation.

Her father.

Chapter Sixty-three

Escort

he great blue herons were to be their escort, and once aloft, they shifted their position wordlessly and advanced to the front, forming a streamlined V. The bird carrying Peps broke formation first and commanded the center point, most forward. The wind was strongest here and buffeted the tiny man's cloak violently, and Ivy could only imagine how Peps would feel about this rough indignity.

For some time, Ivy had tried to keep her disturbing visions at bay. In Templar, they seemed to have subsided, providing her some welcome respite, and she had kept them from Cecil lest he worry. But even there, if she moved her head too quickly or concentrated on a problem for any length of time, small purple sparks glimmered in the utmost corners of her perception. *A wounded healer,* she thought. *Never again right in the shadows.*

Now, as they approached the Tasters' Guild, the visions returned in force. Evil sparks bobbed and weaved, determined not to be consigned to the mere corners of her mind. The world before her rippled, like a dark, cruel flag—and on several occasions Ivy was struck with the terrible sense that reality was fraying, becoming undone. As if the fabric of life itself was being pulled apart.

She thought of her mother's treachery. Ivy was in the uncomfortable position of agreeing with Flux—her mother was a great disappointment. Clothilde seemed bent on her own success at any cost. Hadn't she nearly turned Ivy over to Vidal Verjouce in the abbey on Skytop? And in Underwood, she had casually poisoned Rowan to test Ivy's healing abilities.

Ivy felt the small, stitched pocket in her apron, where the King's stones resided. Shriveled now, they were beyond all recognition.

A sudden shift in direction brought Ivy back to the present.

"What is it?" Ivy leaned forward to speak with Lofft.

"Something approaches," Lofft explained, his words carried back to her on the wind.

Ivy scanned the horizon, but saw only the incessant purple flares of her own personal nightmare. The herons, and their sharp eyes accustomed to fishing, had keyed in on an intruder. Klair was flying with Rue off to the rear, on the right, catching an easier ride on Lofft's airstream, and she had no chance to communicate with Rue. Ivy waited for something to appear.

The herons were calling out to each other in their high, reedy voices—the otherworldly sound did nothing to calm Ivy's nerves. They were descending slightly, wings tucked, for whatever they sought was flying at a lower altitude. The air stung Ivy's lungs as she tried to breathe. Streaks of white were slashing by, and at first she took this for snow—but this was no snow. It was ash. She covered her face with the crook of her elbow, holding on tightly with her remaining hand, ducking down and sheltering her face from the stinging air. Below, the scarecrows had converged, milling about in great numbers— they had reached the Lower Moors.

The herons, in perfect synchronization, banked sharply to the left, pursuing their quarry, and the albatrosses followed. Ivy regained a firm hold on the reins, but all the same, the sharp turn nearly knocked her off. Recovering, she shouted to Lofft not to worry. But the words died upon her lips as she saw the enormous figure in the sky directly beneath them.

Ivy had but a moment to take the apparition in—its silhouette was a shadow above Lumpen's gathering forces. But through the silting ash and patchy cloud cover, she saw dark, greasy scales gleaming upon the frightening beast's wide wings, and it seemed to be hovering, peering down upon the gathering forces beneath it, working its way back and forth, searching, spying. This was no normal vulture, she realized.

What new, terrible creature had come forth from the bowels of Rocamadour?

They were descending quite quickly now, and Ivy lost the specter in the rush of nothingness and buffeting ash. But Rue hadn't. Klair had wisely held back, and Rue had a better angle on the beast.

"Ivy!" Rue called desperately, her voice strained upon the wind. "It's *Rowan*!"

Rowan—Ivy thought. The scales of Grig's wings flashed in her mind's eye.

Klair called a sharp, wordless cry.

"Lofft!" Ivy screamed. They were careering downward at great speed, and she was worried her dire warning would go unheard. "Tell the herons to stop their attack! That's my friend!"

Indeed, Rowan hovered above the gathering forces. He was bent on revenge and in search of Flux; his journey had brought him fruitlessly to Rocamadour and then here, to the Lower Moors and the gathering of Ivy's forces. Something in the Army of Flowers had caught his eye. He lost it, though, just as soon as he had found it, and, cursing under his breath, he began to methodically retrace his path. His wings seemed like natural appendages now, and he was able quite freely to hover, as a kestrel would.

There it was again; his heart raced. An unusually lithe

scarecrow, understuffed, a yellowish tinge to his features. This one seemed to break ranks often, and, even more strange, he wore impossibly shiny boots.

So engrossed was Rowan, he failed to see what gathered above. When he finally heard the shrill cries of war, it was too late. He threw his head upward and his eyes locked with Ivy's.

Ivy looked down upon her friend's face as he gazed skyward—his wings outstretched, a fierce look of satisfaction across his familiar features. And she realized they were going to collide.

Chapter Sixty-four

The Lower Moors

ut as the herons dived, with Lofft in their midst, another shrill cry from Klair reached the group. Instantly the birds fell back in an impossible array of dives and tumbles, each seemingly in defiance of gravity, and when they gathered again, they did so on the ground.

Peps, stepping off the great heron's back, looked pale and his knees threatened to fold beneath him, but Rowan was there with a sturdy arm.

"Peps." Rowan smiled. "You're a natural! We should get Grig to outfit you with a set of wings of your own!" He turned to the inventor, who had joined the welcoming party. "What do you say, Grig? Why not whip up this brave man a smaller set when you can?"

Rowan winked at the gathering, which included Lumpen

and Grig's assistants, while Peps, looking as if he very much disagreed, concentrated on trying to regain his breath.

Their remarkable arrival, while a surprise for those on the ground, was soon overshadowed by the business at hand. As Rowan folded his wings with care, Grig scrutinized them.

"Master Truax"—the inventor frowned—"these wings need immediate care. After every flight they need to be inspected carefully for rips or tears, and you've already ignored my warnings on two occasions. They need to be oiled and repaired. These conditions here, the ash and filth in the air, they gum up the works, and they are particularly hard on the small scales. I am afraid that flight is simply not recommended."

They stared at the dark walls across the moor, soot and ash raining down upon the stark heads of the gathered army.

"Well, it's time to do something about that ash and filth, then." Rowan turned to the group. To the inventor, he added privately, "Don't worry, Grig. The wings will bear me. There'll be time enough to examine them when we're celebrating our victory."

Ivy surveyed the dreary landscape. Nearby, Grig and his team of assistants had been overseeing the contents of his jingling caravan, which, from what Ivy could see, consisted of more of his complex and inexplicable inventions. Everywhere, deflated weather balloons lay on the frozen earth in lopsided shapes, the leather bladders waiting for air. Ivy knew that soon they would be inflated; the curious *tut-tut* noise of their paddles would fill the air, their baskets attended to by scurrying trestlemen. Packages, some large, some curiously small, were being organized upon the lifeless earth, crates pried open. Bundles and canvas-covered carts were being distributed to the scarecrows who gathered in orderly contingents. They formed a giant patchwork that stretched out as far as the eye could see, awaiting Lumpen's word.

In the gloom, the night birds stood guard—the owls, the nightjars, and the loons formed a watchful front. Shoo flapped noisily from Ivy's scarecrow, Jimson, alighting on her shoulder.

"Has my uncle arrived?" Ivy asked Lumpen hopefully. Cecil had said nothing about the nature of his errand to her, and Ivy worried at both his absence and the nature of his detour.

The well keeper, shaking her head, surveyed the thick walls of the dark city in the distance. The ramparts formed jagged openings like broken teeth, and in their dark recesses, untold Outriders awaited.

"They say these walls are impenetrable." Lumpen turned to Ivy and the crow.

Ivy turned, too, to the grim sight, and words failed her.

"Well, they should have asked Lumpen Gorse. Water's always got a way of seeping in."

"Ah, Lumpen!" Rowan sprinted over. "I would like very much to inspect the troops," he announced. "I do believe we have a stowaway."

Chapter Sixty-five

The Approach

Lumpen Gorse privately did not see the merits of searching a thousand scarecrows for one sneaky rat. She was one to believe that silt would eventually settle to the bottom of the pond. Instead, while Rowan and Rue attempted the inspection, Lumpen wandered over to the paler-than-usual trestleman Peps.

"You ready, then?" she asked, pulling on her pipe.

Peps sighed, nodding. He wrapped his fine velvet cloak about him and climbed up upon the wide cart beside the well keeper, picking his way carefully along the straw floor. Cecil had ensured that the cart was laden with rain barrels, of the sort water is transported in.

Lumpen turned to Ivy. "We go now, miss."

"But Cecil hasn't arrived!" Ivy panicked.

"In the end, it is water that conquers all."

"Peps?" Ivy looked desperately at her friend for counsel.

"Lumpen is right—there's nothing gained by waiting. Cecil will come when he can. Miss Gorse and I will go to the gates and announce our delivery. They know Lumpen. They have bartered for her water—and they will again. Only this time, I will be inside a barrel. And tonight, when all is quiet, I will let myself out. In the morning, you will find the gates of Rocamadour open and welcoming."

Peps did a small, flouncy bow, and Ivy couldn't help but smile.

Shortly thereafter, Ivy watched an impressive demonstration of Lumpen's strength, for she approached the forward end of the cart, designed to be pulled by a team of donkeys. Bending low, she hoisted the heavy yoke upon her shoulders and, setting her sights on the distant gates, lumbered off.

If there were two things Flux disliked in life, one was to be itchy. (The other was to be thirsty.) What more uncomfortable escape could Sangfroid have devised for him than this? The man must have made a study of his secret pet peeves and chosen to outfit him in a sack of straw thusly. He was happy he had taken his vengeance upon the old man—and he hoped his eternal rest beneath the waters of the old moat was wretched and cold.

Flux's yellowish skin, normally quite sensitive as it was,

was a carpet of red welts. Yellow skin, red welts—he looked as if he were a walking toadstool! And now, such a long walk! His feet were swimming in sweat in his leather shoes, but their high quality—he congratulated himself—had prevented any blistering. He despised these strawmen and cursed the very fact that his fortunes were currently tied to them. An army of weeds. Guttersnipe. Particularly that two-faced one directly before him—what nonsense was this? The thing had been given two faces, and the backward-facing one regarded him with an irksome expression. What was it? He tried to pinpoint it, but the blank look was elusive—which produced in Flux more annoyance.

The first chance he got, he relieved the thing of its gold pocket watch, and, whistling, he secured it to his own sacking.

When they finally stopped their tedious adventure, the former taster congratulated himself. In the distance, the gates of the Tasters' Guild stood like a beacon to his bitter, unlovely heart. Sorrel Flux had lived, had *served*, at the Guild for many long years, and he knew every crevice of the place. But service was no longer in his future. It was to be quite a homecoming.

The large, imposing gates caused him no dismay. At the opportune moment, with nightfall, he would simply slip away without a trace. He knew a way. He had seen it used before by that wicked, duplicitous woman—Clothilde. Yes, Flux knew her well. The woman had so captivated his Director, but Flux had seen through it all. Even then, when Clothilde called Ro-camadour her home, her loyalties were suspect but her errands and absences never questioned. Hers was a position rife with indulgence. She had borne Verjouce that wretched child, departing soon after with the tiny thing through an unguarded passage—returning empty-handed and arrogant. Together, mother and infant were the source of so much bother, so much inconvenience. Had Flux been able to drown the child, as he had offered to do out of the kindness of his heart, he would not be here today, itching and thirsty. Perhaps it was not too late.

At that passage's end, Flux knew, he might safely discard his straw stuffing—for it let out into the city's abandoned stables.

When his opportunity came, it did so accompanied by a little, angry-sounding hummingbird flitting by his side. These awful birds, he thought. The sky is filthy with them.

Chapter Sixty-six
The Gates

Lumpen Gorse, corncob pipe jutting from one corner of her wide face, sun-faded patchwork skirts a broad bell about her generous proportions, stood before the pitted gates of the Tasters' Guild. Her arms rested at her sides as she surveyed the ancient walls. The cart she had drawn—with many heavy water barrels and one trestleman—rested just behind her, and she pulled on her pipe contemplatively. She stared down the mighty walls.

"Well, Pips"—she blew a series of smoke rings—"it's showtime."

A patrol of Outriders, fierce shadowy robes and haunted faces beneath billowing hoods, regarded the well keeper silently from the wall.

"You there!" Lumpen's gravelly voice shouted. "Yoo-hoo! Down here! Yes—you. I'm talkin' to you."

A slight tilting of their shadowy heads was the only indicator Lumpen had been heard.

"Open up!" She gestured wide. "I got a delivery here for that Dumbkin."

Soon several more Outriders appeared beside the first patrol.

"Well? What're you waitin' for? How many Outriders does it take to open a door?"

There seemed to be little interest in fulfilling the well keeper's request, and several long minutes passed in stony silence. Lumpen glared up at the servants of the Guild—hand shading her face from the drifting ash.

"Have it your way," Lumpen shouted. She readied herself as if to go. "But that Dumbkin's gonna be one mad little feller. He might be small, but he packs a punch—" She gestured to her scarred forehead with a stout thumb.

Still nothing.

Lumpen spat into her hands and rubbed them together briskly. She frowned, thinking.

"Correct me if I'm wrong, but isn't this here water what keeps that Director of yours in ink?"

On this point, she appeared to have some success.

There was a small *pop,* followed by a well-oiled *click.*

Lumpen was genuinely confused.

A door appeared to be opening—but it hadn't been there before. Lumpen scratched her head. The door was a small one comparatively, cut right into the hulking gates. So that was it—it was simply expertly disguised! Not much got by the well keeper. But still, the door was confusing her, and she stared at it—at the small figure of a subrector standing within its frame. If only the slight sting in her haunch was less distracting.

Lumpen got her wish as a chilling numbness spread along her thigh and the world grew dim.

Chapter Sixty-seven
Revenge

Lumpen's cart sloshed as it was marched beside the gatekeeper. Her body had been flung ruthlessly upon the barrels and hung limply. The smaller doorway was designed to accommodate just these sorts of deliveries, but all the same, her head hit the doorframe with a loud *crack* as the wheels rolled through.

"Well, well," a high, sinister voice spoke. "What a . . . pity."

Snaith limped around the scene, long robes scraping the uneven cobbles. He stopped to inspect a puff of lace upon Lumpen's pantaloons.

"It appears an unfortunate acc*th*ident ha*th* befallen Dumbcane'*th* a*thoth*iate. Poor thing, she would have been well-advi*th*ed by our re*th*ident ink maker to tread lightly in the*the* time*th*."

A barrel was pried open, the contents analyzed. Snaith inspected the remaining contents of the cart, poking swollen fingers into cork holes and between wire hoops indiscriminately until he lost interest. Water held little appeal to one bent on blight and contamination. With a curt nod to the Outriders in attendance, Snaith turned to depart, red robes flaring briefly but settling askew again upon his limp shoulders.

"Roll thi*th* abomination to the Warming Room. U*th*e it for kindling. Oh—and throw thi*th* creature"—Snaith poked Lumpen's padded figure—"into the crypt*th*."

Gathering his scarlet robes about him, Snaith shuffled off to his lecture hall, where—a surge of excitement spread through him—he had students that needed to be taught a lesson.

The dejected cart sat in the dim light of the dismal city as the Outriders prepared to dispose of it. Between them, the tiny figure of Aster flitted around Lumpen's prostrate form.

Revenge is mine! she rejoiced.

But, in the way of revenge, it did little to quench the burning embers of hate in her heart. Instead, she sought ways to fan them further, ways to spread her small, insistent brand of misery.

High above the scene, on a quiet perch over Lumpen's doomed cart, Dumbcane was sketching feverishly on a section of the wall. He was always sketching these days, propelled by vivid dreams and strange voices. His interests in calligraphy, in ink, were supplanted by this newfound passion—he was a man possessed.

His subject of late: a particularly gruesome statue atop a stretch of a section of Rocamadour's thick wall. It was a hulking, winged gargoyle, ripped from the imaginings of a despot, and occupied a portion of the barricade often patrolled by the Outriders.

It had somehow eluded him, this grotesque but intriguing piece, until he began to be ravaged by its image in his dreams. Its pointed, twisted ears were pierced with bones; its teeth looked capable of tearing away at its own stony flesh. It stood three times the scribe's size, a specter over the dark city. Its wings appeared to be torn from the devil himself and slapped upon his broad back at irreverent angles.

It was a great work of art, thought Dumbcane.

He admired the creature's talons now, upon the very edge of the partition, and remembered his vision of the previous evening. Guided by the words of the lady of the fountain, dictated by his dreams, the scribe removed from his pocket a small penknife and began chipping away at the mortar that secured the demon to the wall.

Chapter Sixty-eight

Betrayed

n the Lower Moors, the scarecrows milled about restlessly, congregating in small, rustling groups. The distant tree line was heavy with Caux's birds. The townsfolk, rallied by Peps, looked pale and drawn. Ivy, studying her friends, saw faces tense with worry. Evening came, with no word—nor sign of Cecil. Skeins of gloamwort twine were strung around the encampment, spilling their faint glow in the absence of fire.

Springform tents had sprouted up—regal, billowing white structures that supplied a surprising amount of comfort—but Ivy preferred the counsel of the two albatrosses to four canvas walls. Someone—Gudgeon, Ivy thought—had sewn a banner that now rippled upon a pole atop the largest tent—a familiar three-pronged leaf. The sprig of poison ivy blazed across a white background of the flag.

"What now?" Ivy asked Lofft as she sat against his folded wing. Shoo hopped upon the earth at her feet.

"We wait." His voice sounded tired.

"For what?" she wondered.

"For morning," Klair answered.

Ivy pulled her knees to her chin and huddled between the enormous seabirds. She thought of the trestleman Peps—so much rested on his bravery. Would he and Lumpen succeed in opening the gates? Her eyes, heavy now, shut upon the barren scene, the green of her flag a beacon in the barren moor. A weightless blanket of down enveloped her; Klair had tucked Ivy beneath her wing, and, nestling her close, guarded her as she slept.

The morning did come, uneasily—not in glorious color or ripe with possibility. This one brought a layer of settled ash and dismay, and a dim light the color of gangrene.

It also brought with it a small warbler.

Even the worst of news, when delivered in sweet birdsong, can sound agreeable, and it was to this melody—the melody of betrayal—that Ivy awoke. She saw at once that the gates remained closed, and Lumpen had not returned.

Rowan, Rue, and Grig gathered to listen to the warbler. He had been sent ahead, a scout.

Teasel's report was long, for there was much he had discovered. On several occasions, as he sang, the poor bird looked on the verge of expiring, and Shoo was forced to prod him gently with his beak. Klair and Lofft filtered the warbler's exclamations and urgent *peeps* as a cold feeling of dread swept up Ivy's spine.

The warbler's news was this: they had been betrayed. A small hummingbird—one, in fact, known to Lumpen, and privileged with information from the caucus of the birds—had taken vengeance upon them. She had joined forces with the Guild. They knew of Ivy—and they were ready.

But Teasel saved the worst news for last.

Within the blighted city, something sinister was amiss. The remaining students had been herded into a lecture hall— one marked with a strange symbol.

"Ask Teasel to describe the symbol," Ivy commanded.

After an explosive burst of song, Lofft replied, "Teasel has never seen such an image in his small years, he says, having spent most of them in the regrettable parlor of Mrs. Mulk. But he describes a set of horns upon an animal of the pasture. And a swarm of insects issues forth—a swarm of bees."

"An ox head!" Rowan realized.

"Snaith!" Ivy and Rue gasped. "That's the door to Snaith's classroom. Irresistible Meals!"

The scene of Ivy's scourge bracken poisoning. Ivy knew personally that nothing good could come from that deadly course.

Chapter Sixty-nine

Courage

I t was as if a bolt of electricity had coursed through the camp. Teasel's news galvanized the Lower Moors, and collectively, everyone awaited orders.

"Where is my uncle?" Ivy demanded.

It seemed that no one knew. The answer perhaps lay with Peps—whose fate was equally uncertain.

The albatross Lofft was the first to advise Ivy. "Betrayal or not, we must move forward, my child. Lumpen and Peps will expect no less of us."

"Ivy"—Rue looked pale and pained—"I must go and help the remaining students. My grandfather. If there is a chance to save them, I cannot stand by!"

"But the Guild expects us!" argued Ivy. "Surely it is madness to continue with our plans?" She looked around the gathering, eyes straying to the shadowy tree line, to her waiting army.

Without the benefit of surprise, how would any of them survive?

"We are well prepared!" Rowan argued. "Well armed!" He turned to Grig. "Are you in position?"

"That I am!" the trestleman affirmed. "Just give the word, and I'll release the balloons. It should give you a head start. A distraction."

"The gates remain closed," Klair quietly pointed out.

"Then I will open them," Rowan announced. He held his folded wings out before him, shaking the dust from them, and strapped a pair of sharp-looking spurs from Grig to his ankles.

Ivy was silent, the faces of her friends and companions beseeching her. Her eyes were burning from the ash in the air, and she felt her courage wither. Flaming trails of deep purple surged in the sidelines of her vision, and looking down at her hands, she saw that they were shaking. The stones were heavy in her pocket.

She stepped away, Shoo upon her shoulder, hoping desperately for a sign.

Beside her a hazel thicket grew in the sparse moor; the dried leaves still clung to it in clumps. Together, they formed twisted, agonized faces . . . shouting silently ferocious things to the wind.

Her eyes fell upon Jimson, her scarecrow from the Hollow Bettle.

Courage, she thought. *Courage for Axle—his beloved trestle. Courage for Peps, for Lumpen. Above all, courage for Caux.*

306

Chapter Seventy
Balloons

Into the early-morning air, upon Ivy's command, went hundreds of Grig's fantastical weather balloons. Ivy and Rowan had encountered one such contraption before—in the heart of the dreaded Hawthorn Wood—only to see it torn to shreds against the spiked ceiling. Each inflated canvas sphere bulged within a crisscross of fishnet, which attached to a whimsical paddle, and it was from this spinning pinwheel that the balloons were propelled upward.

The sight of the sky thick with springforms did much to bolster Ivy's resolve—and quite soon, from above, a thick mist began drifting down. It was a deep mist—an elegant mist, Ivy would later congratulate Grig—and it tingled as it clung to their skin.

The mist was also to provide them with some element of surprise—the vultures and the spies on the ground would not

see them coming. As it drifted
down, the dispiriting silhouette
of Rocamadour receded, but in
the blankness, something new
and awful could be heard.

The clang of the alarm
had begun.

Ivy gave the orders. She
and Lofft would fly directly
to the shadowy spire in Rocamadour's center, while Rowan
would open the gates as the army
marched forward. He would act as
a decoy should they be spotted. Rue
and Klair would head to Snaith's lecture hall and Irresistible Meals.

The moors fell quickly away as they
rode up into the dawn mists, the Army of
Flowers below. As they flew, Ivy could not escape the feeling
that the very world was coming apart at the seams.

Damp Idyll No. VIII

A blur of calluses and crooked fingers worked the ancient loom as the Four Sisters performed their craft, the tapestry growing ever more, with the promise of being much larger than its predecessors. In fact, they were nearly done.

The tapestry cascaded upon the earthen floor from the olive wood loom, a pure, brilliant white. A blank canvas.

And as they wove, the world began to feel looser. The lines that kept reality separate from dreams were fraying.

Babette leaned in and grimaced, severing the final thread with her teeth.

"We have a visitor," Lola announced.

Or was it Lola?

Her voice was the same. But gone was her crumbling appearance, her rindlike skin. She stood tall and lithe, as if a weight had been lifted from her heavy heart, no longer the prisoner of an ancient enchantment.

The other two Mildew Sisters were equally transformed. Gigi had completely shed her cloak of greenery—it lay scattered about the great room—and Fifi's skin was as smooth and flawless as expensive porcelain. Only their hands were imperfect.

"We have been expecting you, apotheopath," Babette welcomed the newcomer.

Cecil Manx stood before the four ancient sisters and bowed his head. "Ladies," he greeted the beauties. "I received your invitation." In his hand he held a rolled scroll, wrapped in a white ribbon.

"It has been some time," Babette replied.

"Indeed."

Cecil leaned down to inspect their newest masterpiece but paused. He looked sharply at the sisters, a creased frown upon his brow and then a look of sadness, of longing. For a moment he sat in silence, the brilliant threads before him a wavering sheen of silk, an ocean of possibilities. And then, too quickly, he reached for it—but a sharp tut-tut from Babette arrested his hand.

"It is so, then?" he asked, a mere whisper.

This went unanswered.

Cecil wrenched himself away from the tapestry before him with some difficulty and cleared his throat. "I have come with thanks and with one, final request."

There was an air of some skepticism in the room.

"I bring gifts," he added, remembering the sack upon his shoulder. Opening the ties, he upended the bag before the Four Sisters. Precious tins of rare teas fell to the earthen floor. Gold scruples and silver minims scattered about a patch of dandelions. A silver tea set *of such loveliness that it rivaled its hosts' own beauty followed. At this, Lola peered in, admiring her reflection on the side of the teapot, and fixed a stray hair that had fallen across her majestic face. Her eyes narrowed at the apotheopath when she was done.*

"What is your request?" she demanded.

"The hawthorns," he said.

She straightened, lips puckered in thought.

"You are certain?" she asked. "Those are souls of poisoners and thieves. Men who followed, men who did not lead in life."

"Then they will make the perfect army," Cecil explained.

The four women conferred together quietly. Lola broke from the group and turned to the apotheopath.

"It was you who spoke the words that awakened the tapestries?" Her eyes narrowed.

Cecil nodded, holding her gaze.

"Then you broke the spell that imprisoned Babette. If we call forth the hawthorns, we are no longer beholden to you."

"Agreed."

Babette found a dandelion upon the floor—a remnant of the previous tapestries. Its life was spent, its yellow now a puff of stark white seed. This she brought to her lips. As she blew a small breath, the seeds scattered with surprising force. Soon the chamber was alive with the silvery white parachutes of the dandelion, more parachutes than Cecil ever thought possible, as if a thousand dandelions had taken to the air. They settled in his whiskers, in his hair.

Chapter Seventy-one

Visitor

Axle was awakened by a bright star—an unusual occurrence in the nighttime skies of Rocamadour, usually draped in a curtain of smoke and ash. He pried open a bloodshot eye, his pupil instantly dilating at the blinding light.

He marveled at it. A star! A sign from the heavens. Great enchantments are soon to be broken, the trestleman thought.

But the star was moving, he now realized. It bobbed and swayed. It was one of many, and it was *inside* the chambers. This was no star. It was a cloak, no—a dress, with stars shining out from its velvet depths. But it was a welcome break from the nightmarish reality of the caged trestleman's existence, and for that he gave thanks.

Soon the stars spoke. It was a greeting, something soft and lost to the trestleman. But not to Verjouce.

"You have come, my darling. I knew you would." Vidal Verjouce's voice was a hoarse whisper, but it woke the piles of sleeping ink monkeys that draped themselves about his desk. Their sulfurous eyes blinked open at Clothilde as they shook off sleep.

"I can't believe my eyes!" Clothilde declared. "Vidal, what has become of you?"

"I know—isn't it wonderful?"

"Wonderful? I see nothing to wonder at."

"Look closer. You'll see a genius."

"Is this your doing? The wall is covered in the scribbles of a madman."

"It is my manifest. I am writing our future. I am unwriting the past."

"I came to say goodbye—but you are already lost. I am too late—you have fallen to scourge bracken."

"It is *Kingmaker,* my dear—*Kingmaker.* And I control it, not the other way around. Do not for one second think otherwise." Verjouce stood suddenly, fiercely. Around him, the monkeys chittered and hissed, but Clothilde paid them no mind. Her voice pierced their racket easily.

"Or so your *Kingmaker* would have you believe," Clothilde scoffed. "I have known men who ruled, kings of all kings. And, Vidal, you are no king."

"On this small point we disagree." His voice was transformed, full of hatred.

"Who are your subjects—these pathetic creatures?"

313

Clothilde, in a surprisingly quick motion, grabbed a small monkey by its greasy scruff. The thing hissed and shrieked in a hopeless fury, and quite soon it was reduced to dangling uselessly from her long white fingers.

"So nice of you to come to say goodbye." A particularly unlovely smile spread across the Director's ravaged face. "But you are—at best—a relic, my dear. A relic from the past, and I shall think no further of you when you are gone. Your daughter's powers far exceed yours now." He grinned. "A lovely twist of fate. She shall rule alongside me in your stead. Dominion over Nature!" The Director paused, reveling in his new plan. "With her abilities and my, shall we say, resources—nothing can stop me."

Clothilde's eyes narrowed. "Not if I can help it."

"Ivy is coming. I know—I have my spies. . . ."

With a swift look of disgust, Clothilde swung the doomed monkey across the room, where it met with the wall in a loud thud. "Now you have one less."

Axle dared not move for a long time after Clothilde had stormed out. He was too buoyed by the news he had heard. *Ivy is coming,* Verjouce had said. Ivy was close. He must muster his strength to stay alive.

Chapter Seventy-two

The Mists

Grig's engineered mists provided deep cover for Ivy's journey. Flanked by Rue and Klair, and Rowan with his springform wings, Ivy and Lofft made the quick passage across the remainder of the moors surrounded by the first wing of the caucus. It was disconcerting flying blind—the veil of cloud was thick and obscuring—but the birds flew true, guided by a sixth sense. Nor did Ivy wish the mists away. She dreaded the moment when they would clear—for only then would she be treated to the fearsome image of their enemy.

When the mist did finally melt away, it mingled with the inkworks' smoke and ash. Morning had yet to come. The group hovered above the dark city. The air smelled of decay.

Something small and fast whizzed by Ivy's ear, and suddenly Lofft was taking evasive action—jackknifing, careering chaotically through thin air—and Ivy held on desperately. A chorus of shrieks rose from the gulls, who were armed with great stones that they dropped on the city beneath them, pelting the wall and inner courtyard with a hard rain. Angry, guttural shouts rose up as the alarm continued to clang.

A further volley of small, burr-like projectiles ripped through the air, and with horror Ivy saw a cluster of several birds fall—as if the magic that propelled the creatures away from earth abandoned them in an instant. The air was filled with feathers.

Great searchlights were lit, illuminating the stark underbellies of the bobbing weather balloons, a ceiling above the city. The powerful flares cast about the skies, everywhere. Birds darted and soared through the pillars of light—there one minute, vanishing the next into the gloom.

Rue and Klair banked steeply to the right, carving through the rancid smoke at a sharp angle above Dumbcane's fountain, heading for Snaith's lecture hall. For a brief instant, Ivy spotted Rowan. His beautiful wings were cupped beneath him; he appeared to be floating as he searched her out. Their eyes met—he smiled—and Ivy was struck with a sudden surge of hope and fondness for her friend.

Then, on all sides, harsh, chilling cries rose from below—vast drifting shadows were grasping for purchase in the air. Here were the Rocamadour vultures, and a great dread swept over Ivy's body. So many of them, she saw. She was sickened by their numbers. Dark, swirling sparks floated before her eyes, and she resisted the urge to wave them away.

They flapped wildly. The terrible birds were slow to gain altitude, though—their great wings, made for soaring on thermals or catching the winds from the cliffs, did not serve them well for the swift needs of aerial warfare. They were at a disadvantage. But they made up for it by the true horror of what they carried upon their backs.

For the vultures of Rocamadour, great beasts that feast on death, each carried with them a passenger. Seated behind each of their gruesome heads and gripping roughly at their feathers was an oily, cruel ink monkey. Yellow eyes glinting and teeth bared, they urged the vultures on with their spiked tails.

Ivy watched in horror as several of them fixed on Rowan and, rising on an invisible wind current, surrounded him.

Chapter Seventy-three

Calamity

uddenly the wind picked up, and the sky was full of the soaring monsters. Rising like a dark spike in their center—the sheer black spire and its shattered window.

"Hold on, Ivy," Lofft cried as he fell into a tumble, descending dramatically.

Black shadows flashed past, tinged with the smell of rot, the screeches of the ink monkeys upon their backs piercing her ears. The ink monkeys hacked mercilessly at the air with their spiked tails, their shrieks louder even than the alarm. Smaller birds, the juncos and sharp-billed nuthatches, pursued the vultures in packs, plucking at the larger birds' tail feathers to destabilize them. One vulture, off balance and top-heavy, groaned. Wobbling, it began a slow roll, careening to earth, its furious monkey with it. It was a small victory, for Ivy saw as soon as one was toppled, another rose to take its place.

Shoo led the crows and ravens, and as their collection of sharp talons and dense numbers held off the nearer vultures, Ivy and Lofft were able to soar through a small area of unguarded air. Lofft righted himself; they had descended through much of the sky battle, and below Ivy the maze of Rocamadour's tiny streets was in perfect miniature. They raced to the spire, its diamond-shaped opening a terrifying beacon.

Ivy craned her neck upward, desperate to see Rowan, the searchlights mercilessly revealing their losses as they swept about the sky. The early-morning air was murky over the city, except for the wild beams of gray-green light, which were punctured with the silhouettes of creatures in flight— long-billed thrashers, trogons, and a scattering of sparrows. It seemed to Ivy as if the heavens were tearing apart. Great and small birds battled, the injured falling to the earth like dark stars.

Lofft again corrected his course, bearing down on the lone window—and this slight shift brought Ivy a welcome sighting: Rowan, high above his former school, effortlessly floating. He was surrounded by three large vultures, his mechanical wings outmaneuvering them with ease. Ivy watched her friend; a strange mixture of pride and homesickness nearly overwhelmed her. Rowan tucked his knees in and tumbled, opening wide his arms and hacking at a vulture with his spurs.

The doomed creature squawked once and listed to the side; like a sinking boat, it began a slow dive.

Turning about, Rowan slashed again at a nearby ink monkey, and his feet landed solidly on its greasy fur. It shot off into the night, shrieking, its mount meeting a similar fate.

The former taster now faced the last of the three vultures. It was rattled and uncertain, its monkey jeering it on. Rowan was close enough to smell the stench of the thing. He stared into its tar-pit eyes.

But something was wrong—desperately wrong.

Where one of Rowan's wings should have been was a broken coil of wire and canvas fluttering at an awful angle. The springform hung limply from his elbow for a moment, and then the former taster began spiraling down—his one good wing desperately cupping at the empty air. Down, down, smashing brutally through vultures and caucus birds alike— farther down, his broken wing delivering him to the Tasters' Guild below.

Chapter Seventy-four

The Return of Six

As Aster flitted about, darting from fountain to fountain, exploring untold dark alleys and silent, scowling Outriders, she allowed herself a moment of congratulation. Above her, in the air, the birds of the caucus were clashing wildly with the vultures of Rocamadour, getting all that they deserved. Their bodies were piling up upon the cobbles, and there was no one but themselves to blame. She had given them a chance at the caucus, and they had turned on her.

They got what they deserved!

The bird-snacking well keeper was dead.

Aster flew about her new home. Within these walls there was a dark order, of the kind only oppression can bring. It was lovely, thought Aster. Outside the walls, her very own pandemonium was loosed.

But the long list of creatures she had wronged was not to be contained by these walls.

One such creature, adept at climbing (for his fierce claws could grasp any surface) and silent stalking (for he was gifted with thick pads upon his twelve toes), lurked patiently within the deep shadows of a ravaged fountain. He yawned, and half his face disappeared into a set of intimidating fangs. Composing himself, the enormous, matted cat Six looked about.

He sniffed the air. Six had feasted once upon man, and now he craved more. It had drawn him back to Rocamadour, this particular taste. There was a heavy scent of the scribe from the Knox—Six knew him well from his forays into the man's shop and his inkwells. But the cat was not interested in this man.

No, there was only one man in particular—a meal interrupted.

He crouched and waited for the subrector.

Six smelled him nearby—he was close.

His lair lay behind stone and wood. His prey's scent mingled with the distinct scent of fear—not the man's, but others'. Many others'. *Fear, and what else?* the cat pondered.

Fear and *ink*.

In the meantime, spying a distracted hummingbird beside the forgotten fountain, Six would make do with a snack.

 In a quick, bright instant, Aster's short, wicked life ended in the jaws of the cat Six. Her bones—as light as air— crunched pleasurably in his powerful jaws.

Part VI

The Stones

And in his folly—let him be sure to see.

—Prophecy, Tern fragment

Chapter Seventy-five

The Spire

Child," came Lofft's voice.

Ivy was having problems seeing properly, the closer she flew to the gaping hole in her father's spire high above the city of Rocamadour. The small purple-black spots in her vision were now streaks of pent-up lightning, ravaging her vision with their flashes and voids. Her heart beat with a tinny echo in her ears, and she felt both drawn and repelled by the awful entrance. She was plagued by the last image of Rowan, falling helplessly to the earth.

"We must soon part," the albatross announced.

Ivy nodded. She was staring desperately at the swiftly approaching diamond window—no light to guide her within.

Would Axle be there? she wondered. Or would she have to fulfill the Good King's command on her own? The small stones felt their heaviest now, dragging her weight to one side, and she prayed Gudgeon's stitching would hold.

"I will pull up as best I can," Lofft advised. "You must be ready, for there is no perch for me."

"All right, Lofft." Ivy's mouth felt as dry as dust. "And thank you."

They made a first, unsatisfactory pass, and Ivy's nervousness grew. The window tapered off at a cruel angle at the diamond's lower lip, and there was very little room for error.

The second pass was no better, and Lofft's calming tones did little to bolster her courage.

But on the third approach, she steadied her nerves, and, timing it just right, Ivy pushed off the seabird, leaping with all of her might into the ashen air. Something, though, had caused her to miscalculate—and she realized only too late that the heavy stones in her pocket had upset her delicate balance. Her body hit the smooth black wall with a smack—the crook of her arm just managing to grasp the open window.

There she dangled.

Until two things happened.

First, a sharp, warning cry from Lofft filled all the air, reverberating through the city's twisting paths and recessed doors, and then a small knot of frantic black feathers was suddenly beside her.

And second, her hand—already tired from supporting her weight—felt something truly awful. Little leathery fingers prying at her own, pinching, stabbing with sharp nails, poking at her.

Ivy's strength began to fail.

Chapter Seventy-six
True Nature

vy's nails scraped against the ledge, grasping at any groove, any chink, but her nails were too weak and began to give way. The small hands of the ink monkeys assisted in her predicament—prying up her fingers and wrenching them in their sockets—anything to dislodge the girl. Her feet scrabbled for a foothold—but there was nothing. The spire was as smooth as glass.

And then, there he was at her ear, gently urging her, the knot of black feathers. Her beloved crow, Shoo. He had answered Lofft's cry and had come to her rescue.

Shoo was there to bolster her courage.

But it was scourge bracken that invited her inside.

All at once, she felt a surge of strength, an inscrutable potency in her limbs, and her hand found the edge of the window where there was a slight lip before the void. Flashes of deep purple lightning glazed her eyes, and she felt herself suddenly fearless. Her body performed with great ease when asked to pull itself up, through the window, and when she arrived, she took great pleasure in kicking several of the oily monkeys that awaited her. Their limp bodies broke upon the etched stone.

Her eyes adjusted to the terrible chamber instantly, but everything was tinged with inky purple. She sought out Axle's cage—and found it directly above her. But a deeply unhandsome, thick-spittled voice arose from the darkest corner of the room, and in its wake the ink monkeys fell upon each other for shelter.

"Where have you been, my child? I've been *so* worried."

She looked for movement in Axle's cage—there was none—and she debated rushing to open it, but stopped short at the hungry glare of the monkeys.

"I had a little problem getting by the welcoming committee, Father," Ivy explained.

"Hmm. I'll be sure and punish them. Severely."

Vidal Verjouce stood from behind the stone desk. A clatter of scorpions fell from his cloak, skittering around confusedly on the tabletop. He was a ravaged specter of poison and deceit.

"You're looking well, Father," Ivy said. "You must tell me your secret."

She peeked again at Axle. She could barely see the trestleman, his body was so depleted and her eyesight was so infected with dizzying flashes and pops. The cage appeared to be filled with giant, menacing shadows—ghostlike—which hovered over him in a vaporous halo. The scourge bracken within her was awakening, demanding and insistent.

Axle. She willed a thought at the trestleman. *Courage!*

She reached for her pocket, sharply pulling on a knotted thread Gudgeon had left dangling. The protective stitching fell away. She inched a step forward toward the blind Director.

"My secret?" Verjouce now turned his horrid face to her, his blank sockets and ink-splattered skin an apparition of the grave. He produced a demoralizing smile. "Why tell you, when I can *show* you?"

A crown of shadowy violets encircled Ivy's head, appearing from nowhere. As she felt their delicate petals in surprise, fireflies convened around her suddenly. They hovered about her crown, bobbing, weaving, echoing the shape with flickering pulses of purple light—as they had when she was first poisoned by Snaith, her dark power made visible.

The monkeys had recovered from their fright and were surging upon her, pinching her black-and-blue. They prodded her with their pointed horn buds and pulled at her hems. One tiny arm snaked its way up her apron—grasping at the heavy secret pocket. A horrible fascination grew within her as she gazed upon them. Each monkey was separate and distinct from the rest, a haphazard collection of defects. Horns emerged from unreliable places. No spiked tail was alike; their eyes shifted about their greasy faces.

"Plants are returning to their true natures, assuming their mantles of power—with scourge bracken in its rightful place at the top. Apotheopaths are mere children playing with dried, suspect plants—lifeless, unpotent ones," Verjouce said.

As Vidal Verjouce spoke, a procession of dark monkeys formed a jagged row, parading toward her in a display of pomp. Scorpions surged at her across the dull stone. Ivy felt her crown grow, the fireflies pulsing to the spectacle unfolding before her. A chilling mingling of ink monkeys and fireflies began.

"Your gift—your enviable gift of dominion over the plant world. Kingmaker has chosen you; it senses your power. It wants you, Ivy. Together, there is nothing we cannot attain."

As Vidal Verjouce droned his dreams of domination, the ink monkeys and fireflies continued their peculiar display.

"It was destined," Verjouce continued. "You cannot refuse me."

Before her, the monkeys were sprouting ridiculously small insect wings that glowed with a purple vengeance. Their distended bellies took on a lamplike display, illuminating the room in flashes and beats. Creeping vines from a pair of funerary urns strained in her direction, taut as rope, reaching, grabbing at her.

But while Ivy was captivated with this grotesque display, a

small contingent of monkeys had gathered in a dark corner. Something was trapped there.

"Ivy—" Axle's hoarse whisper carried across the room.

The monkeys had captured the crow, chittering and squealing at their new toy.

Chapter Seventy-seven
Seeing Is Believing

he chamber in the sky held many secrets within its walls, and Axlerod D. Roux was privy to most of them. It was here that the fires that destroyed the vast and magical Library of the Good King were devised. And it was here that the Director chose to abandon his sense of sight—to put out his own eyes—and devote himself more fully to that of taste.

Had Axle examined the stones now in Ivy's possession, he most certainly would have identified them correctly, not as a fruit pit or stone, as Ivy had concluded, but as what they actually were: the remnants of Verjouce's self-mutilation. Axle would have known the depths of the burden the Good King had passed on to Ivy. Axle would have recognized the stones— not as stones—but as the Director's sightless eyes. But Axle was unavailable for comment.

The King's stones—once Verjouce's eyes—were in Ivy's hands now, small and withered, gruesome and heavy. They were also a distraction, a nameless one, for the man who had forsaken them.

As Ivy removed them from their secret pocket, the Director froze—his head cocked, as if listening to the sound of distant drums.

"*Ivy . . .*," Axle warned again with the last ounce of his strength. This time the appalling commingling of the monkeys and Ivy's fireflies ended abruptly, the dreadful spell broken. In its wake, Ivy was left with a deep void, a stab of anger as scourge bracken still called to her, muted, muffled—as if from beneath the grave.

Blinking, Ivy looked around—and with horror, she saw Shoo.

He was being roughly held down by one ink monkey while another attempted to pluck the feathers from his tail. The crow's eyes were wide, and his beak was open and panting, calling out to her silently. More monkeys piled upon him, jeering and taunting, reaching their leathery hands in for a turn.

Shoo desperately needed her—but this was her one chance. Her father was lost in a moment of confusion, as he sensed some *presence*—something long ago forgotten.

Ivy bounded across the room in a wave of purple trails and pounced upon the stone table to face her father. Her hands ached from the heavy stones; she could no longer feel her heart pounding in her chest. The haunted, ink-stained face of Vidal Verjouce loomed before her, the face of her ruined father.

With horror, she saw oily scorpions were nesting in the Director's hair. They arched their deadly stingers at her, a crackling electric charge flowing between them. But her fireflies tightened into a savage crown upon her head, and jagged purple tendrils of power coursed from them, scattering the scorpions—their legs clicking awfully against the table as they fled.

"You overestimate me, Father," she whispered into the Director's ear as she shoved his heavy eyes into the scarred sockets. "I never learned how to share."

There was a moment of utter silence.

A ravaging howl filled the room then, reverberating upon the dank walls and floors and shaking the trestleman's golden cage. The stunned monkeys cowered and whimpered their own symphony.

Vidal Verjouce pawed desperately at his eyes. Scourge bracken was abandoning him—sensing his defeat—as it had Dumbcane, and those who came before him. For that was the nature of the weed. It was fickle, and desirous, and in Ivy—in the Child of the Prophecy—it now had found boundless power.

Ivy stood before the broken Director, her face blazing with dark knowledge, her hands on her hips. All around them the

337

walls, Verjouce's mad scribbles, glowed like embers. The cryptic words suddenly were all made clear, and danced before her eyes.

"Ungrateful child!" The towering Director gripped his face, stumbling. "After all I've done for you!"

He whirled about, his long cloak caught the edge of his boot—and suddenly he lay humbled and confused upon the floor, more helpless now than he was when blind. The light— a stranger to him for so long—burning his eyes.

Chapter Seventy-eight
The Cure

In the corner, the ink monkeys now turned to Ivy, Shoo forgotten. She narrowed her eyes, ready for the onslaught, but instead a look of rapture spread across their gruesome faces. Then, like rats, they surged across the uneven stones and began flocking to her, scrambling to be first. They poured over the Director, who was quietly sobbing, trampling his heaving figure indifferently.

The ink monkeys rushed Ivy—grasping at each other with their leathery hands, biting, gouging eyes with their awful horn buds—as they made their way to their new mistress. They leapt at her, an eerie adoration washing over their faces.

But in an instant, they were gone.

Where they had been but a moment before, nothing but silty outlines of their unlikely figures remained, their hollow insides small, drifting dust motes, hovering for a moment and then falling finally to the soiled floor.

As Ivy stood in the room atop the spire, she felt a surge of furious power, of infinite possibility, course through her small form. She heard the great cries of the caucus in the skies as they warred in her name. For Kingmaker rules alone—it does not share power, and Ivy's dominion over plants was the ultimate attraction. She was surprised to find that she was crying, and, wiping away her streaming tears, she was stunned to see they were as dark as ink.

The Good King's stones were in their proper place, his burden lifted. Verjouce lay at her feet, shattered by his loss of power and stunned by the return of his sight. Ivy had cured her father's blindness. It was Axle's turn, and as she rushed for his cage, the room began to sway.

The floor buckled.

And as the world began to peel away, fraying like a mildewed tapestry, she braced herself for the return to the abysmal Mind Garden.

The last thing she saw, as the room descended into darkness, was a strange, jaunty scarecrow loose in the room. One with particularly shiny shoes.

Chapter Seventy-nine

Flux

Flux was no stranger to his former master's blindness. He had, in fact, had a hand in it. He had nursed Verjouce when the injury was fresh, and had he not endeavored to dispose of his master's discarded goods, he was quite sure no one else would have. As he set out for the long walk to the Infirmary, a thought occurred to him. He suddenly, gleefully recognized that a blind master was the best sort of master. His laziness and penchant for insubordination would surely go unnoticed now.

And as he was finding the trip to be a tiresome one, Flux placed the Director's eyes in a trash pile, bound for the incinerator.

But as he turned on his heel, Flux saw a strange thing. A dark bird—a pitch-black crow, he thought idly—plucked them from the pile of Guild refuse and flew away.

Even better—thought he. Now the evidence of his indiscretion was thoroughly eliminated.

Here he was, Sorrel Flux mused, back in the spire now, after what felt like so long. He had been watching the proceedings in his former master's chamber closely before revealing himself. Flux watched unemotionally as the brat bested her father—the clash of their deep purple insects a mere curiosity to the traitorous assistant. He bided his time as his master was stricken with the return of his sight. And then he pounced.

As the ink monkeys dispersed to the wind, evaporating in a twinkling vision of dust motes, he dashed at Ivy, coughing through their remnants.

He was quick.

His polished boots trampled through the fine silt that coated the room now. His straw hat and wispy silhouette perplexed Ivy, and only too late did she see her attacker was Sorrel Flux. Inconceivably, her former taster was dressed as a scarecrow. A familiar pocket watch draped luxuriously from a frayed buttonhole, and a jaunty hat sat slightly askew on his irregular head.

Before Ivy knew it, a burlap-clad arm had encircled her neck. Flux's other arm snaked its way up to her face, and his hand pinched at her cheeks roughly, then her nose as he attempted to pry open her mouth. In his fist, a small vial.

"This won't hurt a bit." He held her head roughly. "Although, come to think of it, all the people who have tried it are dead."

Without warning, Shoo was upon them—talons flashing, sleek feathers batting Flux's face furiously, a hoarse cry in his ears. But Flux would not be distracted. He felt his face slashed open, and a spill of scarlet blood met the hay of his collar, clotting there. Still, he held the child.

But oddly, the brat's body felt spongy—no, *airy*—his grip on the child unsatisfactory. He pulled her closer, trying more urgently to unlock her clenched teeth. She was a mere wisp of a thing—skin and bones.

Then, impossibly, she was nothing.

Flux was left staring at the defeated figure of his former employer, who, squinting, stared back.

Chapter Eighty

A Tour of the Grounds

A howling, screaming, bitter wind scooped up Ivy and Shoo and deposited them before the now-familiar forsaken gates of the Mind Garden. The fireflies seemed to be nowhere, but her crown of flowers glowed in a vivid darkest purple, encircling her golden hair.

Ivy rattled the rusting doors, and they opened.

Gnats and blackflies descended upon them, but with a wave of her hand, they vanished. Marching into the dark turf, the terrain of her father's imagination, she looked about.

"I'm your master now," she announced. Her father's Mind Garden was crumbling as scourge bracken abandoned him.

It was becoming hers.

Just ahead, the mounds of tarry earth rose, the place she had seen the gardener tending to the ink monkeys. She ran at the small hills and kicked at them, spreading a black viscous goo upon the field.

Hands on her hips, she circled the Garden.

"You are finished!" she called to the wind.

The insect buzzing ceased. The only thing to be heard was the lapping of the waves at the lakeshore.

Shoo rode upon her shoulder as Ivy continued her tour of the grounds.

Along the pea-stone path, her father's gruesome topiary reared—its carved hedges a collection of fearsome grimaces and lurking beasts. Ivy walked. She was not afraid.

The small leaves of the topiary's statues were blighted, she saw, dark patches infecting the tiny veins. Small wormholes formed lacy patterns on the larger leaves, tracing a secret long-forgotten language. The dull sky filtered through the hedgerows now—the walls and carved bestiary were made less of leaf and more of deadwood and air, like a moth-eaten tapestry.

In fact, the entire Garden seemed as if it were crumbling. A vast graveyard rose where the ruined topiary left off. Ancient, jutting stones with terrible symbols. The dead of Caux.

Ivy approached the abandoned folly. In a previous visit, it had housed charcoal-colored peacocks, birds almost a shadow themselves. But, like most within the Garden, they had been forgotten, left to a dreary end by her father's disinterest.

The folly loomed at her, its silhouette much changed.

Walls bulged at unlikely angles, and the thatch upon the roof was unkempt and mangy. Yet there was something familiar about the place—deeply familiar. New, honest-looking apple trees sprouted in a small, homey copse. Balls of mistletoe dangled from several of the taller branches.

She gasped as she approached.

There, clacking in the hot wind, was a sign, written in a young girl's handwriting. The ink upon the sign was still wet—it ran in dark, moody streaks beneath the letters.

The Hollow Bettle

Ivy stared at her childhood home. Or rather, an apparition of it. She sighed deeply, her heart opening to a heavy homesickness. This Hollow Bettle was tinged with scourge bracken—the entire vision, she desperately knew, was false. Yet her heart leapt at the thought of seeing Cecil again, at home behind the tavern bar. Inside the dilapidated door, Ivy saw nothing at first—small, birdlike bones on the floor and dust.

A strange, anemic light drew a crack in the shape of a door on one wall. Her secret workshop. The walls—once listing the outdated menu—were covered with her father's mad scribbles and etchings. Shoo cawed a low, throaty warning, but Ivy was drawn forward.

The workshop was cloaked in shadow, somehow bigger than it should have been, and shelves that once held notes and apotheopathic medicines now displayed unearthly bottled specimens floating in amber fluid. On a far wall, plants were speared on straight pins, straining at her, waving about helplessly. Botanical specimens and graveyard rubbings littered the floor.

Her alcohol stove was lit, and in the copper vat something bubbled, giving off a thick, bitter cloud—but the concoction was ruined, she saw, nothing but a burnt and tarry sludge. Ink.

As Ivy stood in the facsimile of her favorite room, a great longing filled her.

In the corner was something new.

A set of oars rested against the wall, an elegant extravagance in the murky Mind Garden. They appeared silvery, made of hard olive wood.

Chapter Eighty-one
The Lake

Although her father's Mind Garden was crumbling, the vast and still lake remained. Ivy decided to take the oars.

The old folly—or the new Hollow Bettle—creaked as she left it; the hinges of the tavern door needed oil even in the confines of her mind.

At the shore, she stopped.

The water was the same steel gray of the sky and stretched on to the very edge of sight, where it became vague with mist. The shore was strewn with black, slick pebbles, and here and there Ivy noticed a few misshapen shells. A dirty foam licked the banks.

But there was something new. A marooned boat awaited her now—bleached from age and as light as driftwood. At its bow a carved figurehead, at one time painted in glorious colors, was now peeling and despondent. It was the face of a beautiful woman; her blank eyes stared out across the water.

Ivy righted the boat. She threw the oars in and called to her crow, who alighted easily on the head of the carved figure. But as she made to lift a leg over the boat's side, Ivy found she could not. It was as if the very soles of her feet had sprouted roots and held her fast to the shore. To move them was agony.

Having had the pleasure of her company, the Mind Garden would not relinquish her so easily.

Over her shoulder she saw the eerie Hollow Bettle, a palish, sickly light flickering in the windows, mysterious shadows moving about inside.

Her heart ached to return to her home—but this was not it.

She clamped her eyes shut. *It is the scourge bracken,* she realized.

And with that thought, a surge of recognition snaked its way up inside her—she was tainted. She would never again feel right in the shadows. In that case, she would stick to the light.

Her crown of fiercely glowing violets was still solidly upon her head. She had bested her father. Like it or not, she had inherited the Kingmaker mantle. The Mind Garden was *hers* now.

And if it was hers, she would do a little redecorating.

She began simply, with the bettles. Her father's macabre Garden had their dead husks as ground cover. Now, with but a simple wish, Ivy gave them life. The air burst with their glorious colors and delicate, crystal wings. And, like in Queen Nightshade's own garden, everywhere the bettles fluttered, a darkness was conquered.

An unknown power coursed through her body—a not unpleasant one—and with a shock, she knew at once that this was how her father felt as he cast his poisoned web from high atop the spire of Rocamadour. A passage from Axle's *Field Guide* echoed through her mind.

With true knowledge of plants comes extreme power. Power, even, to be king.

And with that, Ivy Manx willed the lights to dim behind the smoke-stained glass and slammed the door upon its rusty hinges. She saw to her false workshop, making its grotesque contents molder and then turn to dust. Jars and beakers shattered, and brown syrupy fluid congealed on the floor. She stoppered up the belching chimney and folded the half-timbered walls into themselves like a house of cards. With a final snap of her fingers, the tavern's inky sign clattered to the ground, the script glowing a scorching red and then fading to nothing.

And then, with her crow, Ivy Manx set out upon the still waters of her mind, barely a ripple in her wake.

Chapter Eighty-two

The Island

vy rowed.

She dipped the slick oars into the smooth surface of the water and moved forward.

Shoo flew at times, his dark reflection mirrored in the steely water, until he tired and returned to rest upon the blank-eyed maiden.

Eventually, wisps of silvery white down appeared in the air beside her, settling on the surface of the lake, an iridescent blanket. Many wisps of silvery white down. The oars swirled them into small eddies with each plunge. They became thicker, settling in her golden hair, her crown of violets, upon Shoo's sleek black back.

Ivy soon realized they were dandelion tufts, airborne, hovering.

Still, she rowed through the lake of her new Mind Garden.

Spent dandelion silk coated the oars.

It seemed that the world was made of only the girl and the crow and the dandelions upon the water. But then a voice filled the air, accompanied by a splintering noise from the front of the boat. Shoo took to the air.

"All of this is yours now, Ivy Manx, Shepherd of Weeds," the voice creaked.

Ivy looked around—there was little of her domain to see, other than sky, water, and silken tufts. Not wanting to insult whoever it was that addressed her, she wisely kept quiet. The voice was that of a woman, melodious, with a distinct wooden tone—the maiden figurehead, Ivy realized, and she listened eagerly.

"I am carved from barrel wood," the maiden began, by way of introduction. "Of oak." There was a slightly haughty tone to this, as if this fact granted her some position of import within the hierarchy of figureheads.

After a lengthy pause, in which Ivy wondered if something was expected of her, the lady resumed her speech.

"Oak begets acorns. Ivy, do you remember what it is an acorn symbolizes?"

"Why—eternal life." Ivy thought of Flower Language. "Or imminent death."

"It is all in how it's presented," the maiden continued.

"Exactly," Ivy agreed. "It depends how you look at it."

"Nothing is set in stone."

Tell that to my father. Ivy thought of her father's crazed etchings on the walls.

"Tell me," Ivy blurted suddenly. "Is it true that all things written can be unwritten?"

The figurehead had resumed her wooden silence, and Ivy wondered if she had insulted her, until, quite some time later when Ivy had nearly forgotten her, the maiden proceeded to sing. It was a beautiful melody, a song of the lonesome lake, but also, it seemed to Ivy, of something else. . . . But try as she might, Ivy could not grasp it. The mournful melody continued for some time, and then, suddenly, it was over. And with it, Ivy knew two things.

The Prophecy would not be fulfilled.

But that all depended on how she looked at it.

Ahead, there was a small island drenched in fog. Only, Ivy soon realized, this was no ordinary fog. It was in fact not fog at all. It was a mass of dandelion tufts, a cluster of spores hovering over the island, rising like the moon from the edge of the sea. As she alighted, stepping onto the shore, they tickled her skin—her cheeks, her neck, her hands. Her whole body tingled in the presence of a great enchantment.

Turning to the figurehead, for she stood beside it now, Ivy saw no evidence of the nameless song, the wise words. The carved maiden's eyes were rubbed blank with the salt and wind of the sea. Seized by an urge, Ivy kissed her polished cheek.

She walked away from the boat, and the dandelion parachutes parted for her, these tufts, swirling into rich whorls as she passed through. The oars dropped from her hands and vanished into a downy cloud of whiteness. From behind her, the carved figurehead creaked. Ivy turned to see the woman's wooden cheeks puff out with a deep breath—two bright pillows—blowing a sea wind ashore. The tufts responded and began to clear.

Ivy waited, Shoo upon her shoulder.

As the wind picked up, Ivy noticed there were shells beneath her feet. The breeze was a delicate one, but the dandelions were caught up in its caress, gathering in small pools upon the beach. Very soon none remained, whisked away with the breath of a giant. In the distance, birdsong.

Ivy looked around the small island in the lake of her Mind Garden. She saw that where she had thrown her oars down, olive trees had sprouted. A small path led between them, and at its end was a familiar structure.

A King's Cottage.

Chapter Eighty-three
The Battle

In Rocamadour, the battle was raging in the air high above the dark city. Shadowy vultures with grotesque ink monkeys on their broad backs were falling upon the birds of the caucus; the air was choked with smoke and ash—as dark as night.

But for Rowan, time stood still.

Here I am, falling again, he thought. There had been a time—it felt like years ago—when he had plummeted down a long passage in the sewers of the dark city. But that was nothing compared to this. That time, a river ended his fall. Today, he would be delivering himself to his enemies upon the battle-field.

Grig's springform wing had failed; it trailed behind him as he began to tumble downward. A mass of bent wire and canvas dangled from his left arm, but still the thought did not occur to him to jettison it. All around, the clouds were filled with shrieks and battle cries of a desperate war, and beneath him, as he tumbled head over feet, Rocamadour was laid out like a terrible maze of cobbles and gutters.

The air roared in his ears.

The first wave of the caucus, the tenacious gulls and formidable birds of prey, was outnumbered by the clumsy vultures, and Rowan fell through air laden with their screams. At one point, he saw the scarecrows at the entrance to the dark city, huddled in formation beside the closed gates. They drew dark bows, brandished pointed sticks. Many were mounting hairy vine ladders from Grig, which clung to the dark stone with spidery barbs, or assembling springform catapults. Somewhere within their ranks would be Grig, and the other trestlemen, and the loyal townsmen of Templar.

Then, with mounting horror, Rowan saw what awaited them.

Upon the walls above the strawmen, old-growth logs—simply massive in girth and drenched in flammable paraffin—were being rolled into place alongside pots of tarry sludge, positioned between the jagged ramparts. Weapons of fire. The Outriders readied their flints, waiting for orders, and orange sparks sailed through the wind.

As he fell, time slowed. The noise from the battle quieted, and Rowan's eyes were drawn to a silvery speck, seemingly bobbing before his eyes. At first, he mistook it for a stray downy feather, but a searchlight from the towering wall cast a stark beam upon it. It glowed like spun silver. His eyes were glued to it, rapt.

It was a small tuft. A dandelion parachute.

Ivy, he thought, gazing upon it. *I wonder if she made it to the spire.*

The dandelion seed shone, weaving through smoke and ash, a tiny beacon of hope. But it was soon lost as the rush of the air had returned, taking with it the unearthly silence, and soon he had lost sight of the silvery tuft.

I must reach the doors! Rowan remembered desperately. They were all depending upon him. Ivy was to fly to the spire and Rue to Irresistible Meals. The job fell to him to open the vast gates when Lumpen and Peps had not returned.

The roar again ravaged his ears—ill wind, the smell of rot, of the acrid inkworks. The clang of the terrifying alarm reverberated about the dark stones of the city, and Outriders—more Outriders than Rowan ever thought possible—surged through the twisted streets, bound for the high walls.

With his one good wing desperately cupping the air beneath him, he began a dizzying downward spiral. Everywhere now were swirling, peaceful wisps of dandelion silk, and as he passed through them, they touched his cheek, snagging upon his worthless wing.

Down, down he fell. Faster, he approached the thick, iron-studded gates to the Guild. Dropping by them helplessly, he reached out an arm, but grasped at nothing but air.

The earth approached too quickly.

Spinning, dizzy, the former taster shut his eyes to his doom—which is why he did not see what ended his fall.

A cradle of night velvet, lit up by small, shining stars.

Chapter Eighty-four
Horse and Rider

O utside the gates, the battle was going extremely poorly.

Grig and his trestlemen companions were shouting orders and readying various contraptions from the meager shelter of his canvas-topped cart, repairing ones that could be saved, lost in a sea of clashing strawmen. Downed weather balloons littered the area, their empty canvas bladders sagging dejectedly, pierced with burr-like arrows. Atop his tinkerer's cart, a tattered flag blew—the three-pronged Poison Ivy.

"The gates remain closed!" Grig lamented, shouting in the ear of his companion, his apprentice Crimble.

"What?" Crimble cupped his hand to his ear, but thought better of it and returned his attention to the taut wire of a loaded springform catapult beneath him. At his feet were burlap sacks of slingshots ready to be paired with giant spiked chestnuts.

Grig motioned at the black, solid barricade and then gave up. It was patently obvious that the gates remained closed, and further discussions on this topic were fruitless. What had become of Peps and Lumpen? he wondered, shivering. He waved away a small dandelion spore that floated before him. Several were snagged in his wiry hair.

All around them, chaos.

A guttural roar echoed through the dark city from behind the closed gates—whatever awaited them there was not going to be pleasant.

Before the gateway, fallen scarecrows littered the battlefield, vultures perched upon them—pulling their straw innards out with hideous abandon. Strange, slick monkeys surged from the vultures' backs, gleefully picking at the spoils, rooting about for wounded birds. They covered the battlefield like swarms of greasy rats.

The enormous stones that made up the foundation of the heavy walls were piled high with the burning embers of spent logs, where they had been thrown like fiery comets from the high outposts. Thatch drifted through the air. The garments and primitive weapons of perished strawmen glowed in the bonfires. Against the smooth walls, the rope ladders were nothing now but an outline of ash and cobweb.

Cecil had not mentioned to Grig any possibility for

retreat, but the trestleman, his heart a dismal pit within his small chest, could take no more.

"Fall back!" he shouted, his small voice carrying no farther than the nearest shadow.

Dandelion parachutes swirled about the air, covering the atrocities before them in a layer of white lace.

"Fall back!" he called again, with all his might.

His tiny voice was answered, not by the mute scarecrows, nor the shrieking of the caucus still waging war above, but by a low rumble of the earth.

"What evil befalls us now?" he called desperately to Crimble.

But Crimble did not see him, did not hear him. He was staring up ahead. For the walls were cleaving as great chains pulled the heaving doors aside. A grouping of startled Outriders fell from their peak, cloaks streaming out behind them, smashing to the ground. And when the gates were opened, the dark city of Rocamadour awaited, its twisted streets and soaring spire lurking within the thick shadows.

Before it all, a figure, framed in the giant doorway.

A horse and rider.

Chapter Eighty-five
Clothilde

Rowan watched mutely as Clothilde replaced the shining hairpin in her silvery hair, the one she had used to open the gates of Rocamadour and, once before that, with Ivy, an icy lock atop the Craggy Burls. After she had deposited him unceremoniously on the dark cobbles, the former taster attempted to regain his bearings. The very sight of Ivy's mother upon such a noble beast as Calyx, resplendent in their war finery, left him dumbfounded. And while he recovered, a few more brightly shining constellations burnt from Clothilde's dress, which fanned out beneath her.

"You!" Rowan was incapable of finishing his thought. He was both grateful and repelled. Ivy's mother at one time had poisoned him capriciously, to test Ivy's powers. But here she was, having saved him from certain death—the gates to the impenetrable city of Rocamadour stood open behind her.

Rowan fell into a deep, shaky bow.

"Rise, Rowan Truax," she commanded.

And then, as if to illustrate her duplicity, she summoned a slight figure hiding in the shadows, who Rowan recognized with great confusion as Hemsen Dumbcane, the forger from the Knox.

Rowan recoiled, his sharp spurs scraping the ground as he tensed.

"Rowan Truax?" Hemsen Dumbcane repeated. The forger inspected Rowan carefully, a slight leer upon his face.

In the battleground, through the gates, loud cheers could be heard, along with a few off-key trumpets. As word of the breach spread, Rowan remembered his duty. The doors were open—but the battle had just begun.

Dumbcane moved to one side of the gatehouse and fumbled with a set of keys. Finally, a pair of tall doors opened. These were made for the gatekeeper and delivered quick access to the topside of the walls. The spiraling passage led up at a steep angle, and a great chandelier hung beside the entrance, but it was a sad fixture—long forgotten, abandoned to dust and disuse.

Without a word, Clothilde rode off, the silver from Calyx's shoes sending small shooting sparks into the darkness. As she passed beneath the darkened ring of lights, the chandelier blazed to life again, its crystal prisms and flickering lamplight a salve to the pressing shadows.

A clear voice floated back to the taster. "Now is your chance to redeem yourself, Rowan Truax," Clothilde called. "Command your army to storm the gates."

Chapter Eighty-six

The Gargoyle

The warhorse Calyx galloped up the remainder of the sloping passage, emerging finally in the open air at a far section of the outpost. The wall that circled Rocamadour was high—but it did eventually end, and its topside formed an open and well-paved run, and it was upon this parapet the Outriders patrolled. This run was punctuated here and there with turrets, as well as large stone gargoyles perched upon a jagged rail.

Calyx was finding that the air was caustic; straggling weather balloons bobbed heavily, armed with Grig's noxious combinations of blisterbush and bitter mustard, and the stallion snorted, nostrils flared. Birds—great ones, small ones— dived and swerved about these lazy, floating springforms, clashing with the careering vultures and the ink monkeys.

A small bird alighted on Calyx's bejeweled mane. It had a beautiful song—even through the clatter and discord all around them. A warbler, he guessed.

The bird sang, and his mistress answered in low tones. Raising her head high, Clothilde steered Calyx toward the dark side of the city, away from the battle that was pouring into the open corridor below them with the gates now breached. His silver-shod shoes clattered against the cut stone.

They were not alone.

The wall was a chaotic place for the horse and rider—Outriders, in their black billowing robes and flailing beards, and other dark figures of the Guild scurried from rampart to rampart, monitoring the battle playing out beneath them. Occasional fires scorched the air as these men struck their flints, releasing liquid flames down on those unfortunates below.

Calyx knew of these guards called Outriders—men in dark robes with guttural language. Still, he had never seen so many of them—theirs was normally the place that few chose to tread (and horses simply couldn't): the mazelike crypts beneath the city.

The warhorse towered above even the largest of these cloaked men, and with his mistress guiding him, he felt no fear. They were soon spotted. The horse and rider charged, and when the guards troubled their progress, Clothilde threw them aside with her long spear—dashing them to the ground below.

They galloped the length of the great wall heedless of the

battle playing out about them. The distinction between horse and rider—where one stopped and the other began—was blurred, not only by their blazing attire, but by their wordless communication. An imperceptible touch of his mistress's knees halted Calyx. They had reached their destination.

They stood before Dumbcane's blighted gargoyle, overlooking the city below.

The dark soldiers of the Tasters' Guild were surging along the walkway behind them, closer now than Calyx would have liked—still, Clothilde held him steady. More approached now from the other direction, and the warhorse reared—a splendid sight—pawing the air, sending several of the first line of Outriders to their deaths below.

Clothilde plunged her spear into the air, lashing at the dark statue, and then with the back end of the weapon, knocked down several men. With each fallen enemy, a new star pierced her gown.

The warbler flitted from rampart to rampart, tense and watching.

Again Clothilde struck, and the dreadful gargoyle groaned. Calyx faltered and nearly spooked, his mistress's hand soothing him. A rending noise followed, and the statue was suddenly gone—vanished—and where it once sat a gaping opening in the facade appeared, followed by a shattering far below. A half smile graced her face. Now, with this small weakness, let the dam break, she thought. She turned, spear raised high, and jeered at the men—they were scores deep. She dug her heels into her stallion's side, and he answered in an about-face, his braided tail lashing out as he turned and reared.

Dumbcane had done his job well. Down the Guilds' servants went—as they rushed for the horse and rider. With a sweep of her silver spear and flash of her whip, a dozen Outriders fell through the jagged break in the wall that once housed the gargoyle. But these first guards were the lucky ones. Those that foolishly lagged behind were treated to the pointed end of her weapon, which pinned them through their scarred throats only to heave them, too, through the break in the wall.

Forty men in all fell like this, and when forty stars appeared on her skirts, Clothilde allowed herself a moment of congratulation. Here was something she was quite good at: war. So much easier than mothering. The birds screeched and called around her—the Keepers of the Prophecy. But Clothilde was nothing if not wise, and she knew, too, fragments of the ancient augury.

A warning trill from the small warbler pierced the air.

Only too late did Clothilde realize that more had come— more Outriders surging at them from behind.

Calyx's battle instincts fired: *We are trapped.* As the swarms of Outriders ran at them—*An endless enemy,* Calyx realized— Clothilde turned her mount and steered him unflinchingly at the break in the wall. She nodded at the small, earnest warbler.

The warbler sang, its song shrill, and sad.

Clothilde laid her white cheek on her horse's damp neck, a lather of sweat. She allowed herself that moment, eyes closed, and then she straightened, casting aside her spear. The new horde was upon them.

Faithfully, the horse Calyx allowed himself to be urged forward, picking up speed—a trot, then a canter. Her knees guided him; they had never steered him wrong. The Outriders had bottlenecked, and, tumbling through the impasse, a mountain of the dark creatures were upon them. Calyx galloped, full speed. Looking behind her, Clothilde shook free her silver hair from its pin as Calyx leapt into the thin air—his saddle and war finery shining with the light of a thousand stars. Clothilde's hair streamed like fallen moonlight all around her.

All this, she knew, was prophesied.

Ivy must succeed at all costs. Clothilde hoped to take as many of the Guilds' servants with her as she could. And indeed, the enhanced patrol followed them over the edge, rushing through the void after her, a cascade of dark billowing cloaks and confusion, catapulting to the earth below.

A small warbler, Teasel, hovered in the air beside Clothilde and Calyx. He had no song to sing.

And still—even as they fell to their deaths—Calyx believed by the simple touch of his mistress's hand that yes, a horse can fly.

Chapter Eighty-seven

Snaith's Hall

ou may wonder why I've a*th*ed you here." The subrector Snaith's voice was singsongy before his large lecture
hall. "Indeed, thank you all for coming!"

He stared out at the pale faces of the remaining students,
the various disappointing subrectors he had corralled into his
hall. He saw the pinched features of the failed Librarian,
Malapert, beside the doddering old professor Breaux. One
smallish girl in the front was crying quietly, and in this Snaith
took great pleasure.

"I reali*th*e that thi*th* i*th* quite la*th* minute, but I'm afraid
there'*th* been an error—a *th*mall over*th*ight. You *th*ee, I cannot
po*th*ibly allow any of you to advan*th*e in thi*th* cour*th*e, to con-
*th*ider your*th*elf ta*th*ter*th* of any merit—product*th* of the e*th*-
teemed Guild—without fir*th*t ta*th*ting thi*th*—"

With a flourish of his scarlet-clad arm, he indicated a hulking blackened vat behind him, the contents of which had previously dripped from its bulbous rim and now sat hardened in unappetizing rivulets. The stench from the ink filled the hall. Carved into an archway above the terrible scene was the familiar phrase of the Tasters' Credo: *Taste and Inform,* and it was with this slogan in mind that Snaith now commenced.

"Pen*th*il*th*, plea*th*e." Snaith's tone took on that of a lecture.

Few of the once-earnest students complied, and for the most part, the audience sat motionless, staring at the horrifying vat.

"What we have here today i*th* an ink compo*th*ed of the rare and imminently to*th*ic herb, *th*courge bracken. That'*th* th-*c-o-u-r-g-e,* a*th* in ruinou*th* plague. Do not con*th*ern your-*th*elf if it i*th* unfamiliar—that i*th* why we are here today! It wa*th*, until quite re*th*ently, con*th*idered extinct. But we are in luck! And for that, we have our dear Director to thank. For today we will *th*ample thi*th* potent weed, and if you have paid attention to my lecture*th*, you *th*ould find your*th*elve*th* eminently prepared for thi*th* examination."

Snaith approached a white-clothed table set with myriad goblets. His split tongue slipped from his mouth, wetting his lips. He donned a thick set of leather gloves and balanced a long ladle in his hands, his hunched back bulging. If he were to experience a moment of regret, it would be now, he reasoned, but, as the caustic ink dripped from ladle to goblet, he felt nothing but exhilaration.

372

Pivoting his ruined neck back to his class, he gestured at the row of waiting goblets. "Bottom*th* up! Oh, and pay no attention if it burn*th* on the way down."

As Snaith busied himself with dispensing the poison, the lecture hall descended into a silence of the doomed. It was into this that his former apprentice Rue slipped silently from the shadows.

"Professor Snaith," Rue called. Her hair was windblown from her journey upon Klair, and her body still frail from Mrs. Mulk's, but her eyes were alight with fire.

He spun around, off balance.

"Ah," he snarled. "Look who'*th* coming to dinner! If it i*th*n't Rue Breaux." Snaith's smile was sinister. "I like you, Rue. I'll kill you la*th*t."

Six was nothing if not a patient cat, but his hunger was getting the better of him. The small hummingbird had done nothing to quell his appetite—especially now that he was so close to his prey.

Man flesh, the cat wanted. Having tasted man flesh, nothing else would satisfy him. And his patience was about to be rewarded. The girl who traveled with Ivy had left the door open a mere crack as she slipped through.

And a mere crack was all he needed.

The scent of the subrector Snaith wafted out the recessed door, mingling with the overriding mildew of the city—and drew Six nearer to the entrance. His padded feet made not a sound as he prowled along the cobbles, pausing at the threshold beneath the symbol of the ox head. He nudged the door, relishing the aroma from within. And then, pushing through the small opening, the tattered cat found himself inside the inner sanctum—so near to Snaith he could almost taste him.

Chapter Eighty-eight

Stormbird

f Rowan's encounter with Clothilde left him shaken, he soon recovered at the incredible sight with which she left him: the impenetrable gates of the Guild stood open and, framed starkly in the vast, jagged archway, the Army of Flowers just behind. Dawn was breaking in the distance, and in the small crack of pale sun, a wonderful thing was happening in the skies.

From the moors, the remaining caucus had regrouped and was bearing down on the battlefield—their dark shapes clustered together as if a squall. But this was no mere flock. They flew together tightly, a huge mass, while a panic spread through the vultures. The fiendish birds were turning away, to the dismay of the ink monkeys, their lumbering bodies barely able to keep aloft.

As the caucus drew nearer, Rowan saw why.

They had pulled together into a single form—a giant monster of a bird, its wings spanning the horizon. It was a whirlwind of chaos and feathers; the vast thing had great talons, which dangled far below into sharp curves, scratching the earth. Where the sharp curves left off, a few stragglers flew—mere specks in the sky.

The swirling, massive apparition drew up on the dark city, and the air was suddenly filled with the sound of wingbeats and the shrieking of the ink monkeys. As the sun rose unhurriedly behind the great flock, its yellowed rays slashed through its midst like flames.

A stormbird, Rowan thought.

He wrenched his eyes away from the dazzling scene with renewed determination. Grig was rolling through the hulking iron-studded doors of the city of Rocamadour before him. His cart jingled and clinked with industry, the canvas cover sewn everywhere with pockets meant for supplies, coils of rope of varying thicknesses and lengths neatly aligned on the vehicle's front posts. His cluster of trestlemen, Crimble included, flanked his entry, defending against the few guards that greeted them with their broadaxes. The scarecrow army surged on by them, the few of Peps's townsfolk rallying in their midst, brandishing ragtag weapons.

"Where are their forces? Their brutal weapons?" Grig shouted to Rowan, his eyes sparkling.

They were coming, Rowan knew. But Grig was still too far to call out his orders. He attempted a quick calculation. How many Outriders awaited them? Theirs were the secret nether regions of the city, deep and unknown. There was no telling how many men Verjouce had sent, tongueless, to those depths.

The corridor following the gate was a bottleneck of sorts, and the Army of Flowers was corralled within its walls. Twisted, cobbled streets led off it—a desperate place to take the fight. Looking up the high wall, Rowan saw it was unpatrolled. Not a single Outrider. *Clothilde*, he realized. She had somehow opened the doors for them and eliminated the upper guard. She had bought them some valuable time. All that greeted them was the resonant *clang* of the alarm, echoing off the slick stones and alleyways of Rocamadour.

The ink monkeys had recovered from their initial fright and were urging the hulking vultures upward, whipping them with their bone-tipped tails. They screamed at one another in displeasure and gnashed their teeth as they rose high in the air, the vultures teetering unsteadily with the sudden ascent.

There was a moment of silence, as before a cloud bursts open with thunder, and Rowan held his breath.

As he watched, the giant stormbird shattered into a million pieces as it fell upon the vultures midair. The noise was deafening. Tiny martins, hulking eagles, giddy magpies—all battled as one; the air rang with their shrill war cries. But the foul ink monkeys were merciless, and Rowan's heart sank as wounded birds began to rain about him.

But suddenly, confusion was everywhere. In an inexplicable moment, the hissing and screeching of the vicious monkeys ceased. Where the monkeys were but an instant ago—they quite simply were not. Their greasy hides and gruesome horn buds had vanished, their unsettling remains sifting about in small whorls of dried ink. A silken powder drifted down on the battlefield. For, unbeknownst to Rowan, in the spire, scourge bracken had found a new mistress—and as the fickle weed abandoned Vidal Verjouce, the ink monkeys, too, were forsaken.

Rowan stood upon the base of a lamppost, shouting orders.

There was no time for further thought—at any moment more of the Guild's forces would answer the alarm and fall upon them.

Grig and his handful of trestlemen companions were to head to the spire in search of Axle. The remaining army would hold its position, keeping the gates open and fending off any further strikes.

Jumping down from the post, Rowan readied the cleavewood club he had taken from a fallen scarecrow. He turned to Grig and continued privately. "You won't find Axle unguarded."

The inventor smiled, patting a burlap sack of charcoals

and tidy packets of gallthorn. "Then we'll smoke him out. And you, Master Truax?" Grig appraised his friend. "Where in this forsaken city are you off to?"

"The inkworks," Rowan replied. "They must be destroyed."

Grig nodded, desperately coiling a length of uncooperative rope from the side of his wagon.

"Take backup," the trestleman advised.

Rowan shook his head. "There's no one to spare."

"Then take this—" Grig removed a plain, brown paper box from his jingling cart.

Rowan frowned.

"Pulverized staunchroot," Grig explained. "From Ivy's workshop."

"Grig—" Rowan broke into a wide smile. "You're a genius!"

Giving the inventor an admiring pat on the back, Rowan ran off. He was a graduate of the Guild. And just like the Director, he could find his way to the Warming Room blind.

Chapter Eighty-nine

Dumbcane

The inkworks were vastly expanded since Rowan last set eyes on them with Ivy on their way to Pimcaux.

Coils of copper tubing, performing mad twists and studded with zigzagging rivets, crowded the upper reaches of the tall space, and beneath them a mayhem of industrial machinery was unleashed. He skidded to a halt.

The former taster oriented himself with the enormous set of bellows that breathed air upon a great fire pit, which in turn warmed immense vats of Lumpen's water. The dreaded scourge bracken was brewed in these and in a series of smaller vessels that followed. Any steam that was produced was captured, and when it condensed, it was ushered into a drip hose and returned to the mix to be refined, capturing the volatile oils. A series of pumps pushed the clotted brew through to a rasp and strainer and finally to a wooden screw press. Through a maze of receding glass pipes set upon glowing flames, the ink gradually darkened, becoming ever more concentrated, until it reached a minuscule funnel, which emptied its bitter contents into a tiny beaker. Here Dumbcane had a worktable erected. The ink was tested for potency and then sealed in a glass ampoule for the Director's pleasure.

As Rowan inspected the dizzying array, he gripped the brown box from Grig. He had planned to disable the inkworks the old-fashioned way—with the aid of his borrowed club—but this was much, much better. Stepping up to the largest of the open vats, Rowan suppressed a wave of nausea. The putrid smell was overpowering, and the former taster's eyes began watering in the heat and stench. A few stray tufts of dandelion silk caught upon his cloak. He wrenched Ivy's box open as the roiling brew spewed out its deadly scent.

Too late, he saw a movement just behind him.

"Rowan Truax." A hoarse whisper was at his ear.

A splattered arm snaked its way around the former taster's neck. Rowan was coughing now, his lungs rebelling against the foul air. Whoever it was that held him seemed unaffected by the stench, quite at home in the inhospitable room.

"I couldn't believe my fortune when my lady called your vile, worthless name!" the raspy voice continued. "I thought: What luck! What destiny shines upon my wretched soul! *Tru-ax, Tru-ax...*" The voice sang a small lullaby of hatred.

"I swore in that dank cell my vengeance on you—how I planned your suffering. Those Taxus brutes, their lien upon you, brought me utter misery! It is all your fault, Rowan Truax! I am here, in this befouled city, because of you."

Shooting specks of light erupted before Rowan's eyes as Dumbcane's arm tightened around his neck. He summoned up a last, urgent surge of strength and elbowed the forger, aiming for the ribs, but found nothing behind him but empty space.

In his last few moments of consciousness, Rowan frantically dropped the open box of powdered staunchweed into the simmering vat before him, and, falling back, he met the ground in a disturbing heap.

Chapter Ninety

The Hayman

"What vapid thing, this light—this dreary scrim! It dulls my senses as it burns my retinas!" Vidal Verjouce wailed. "Agony! Oh, agony—Snaith!" he howled. "Snaith! Get me a blindfold!"

The Director stood unsteadily, hands desperately clawing his face.

"Snaith is currently . . . unavailable," Sorrel Flux replied in his thin, nasally voice. Flux, in a burlap shirt and overalls and with straw jutting from his collar and cuffs, was seated in the Director's chair, his feet upon the stone table.

He was thoroughly enjoying himself.

At the sound of his former assistant's voice, Verjouce spun around. "Who—who's there?"

Verjouce removed his hands from his eyes and squinted. His vision had indeed returned, but his brain was uncooperative, and the world was a swirl of lights and darks, spun shadows of dreary, pale color and hints of shapes. After a minute, he managed to determine that a scarecrow was seated before him (at his desk!) and immediately dismissed the hallucination.

A new question bubbled up within him.

"What is this place?" Verjouce knew himself to be in the room atop the spire, but what he now faced was unrecognizable. Etchings, like gravestones—endless epitaphs—lined every inch of the walls. He was in a tomb of his own making. Gone were the elegant, rich tapestries that once lined the chamber, alongside vast bookshelves of immense, leatherbound books. Where gold letters once glinted were ruined walls, pitted and stained. The floors, too, were soiled with hardened puddles of dark lacquer. His hands, the nails broken and blackened, and his robes and collar—everything had been abandoned to this oily blackness. The frigid wind blew about him from his shattered window, his ravaged hair whipping about his face. Sight, he thought, was overrated.

How had this happened?

He saw nothing but decay.

Decay, and that persistent scarecrow.

Vidal Verjouce closed his eyes and steadied himself. *My Mind Garden. My source of strength*, he thought. It was the one place to which he might return and find solace. He tried to imagine it, to conjure it up in the dark recess of his imagination—but there was nothing.

His Mind Garden lay crumbled, in ruins.

With the return of his sight, his mind abandoned him, overwhelmed and misfiring. Nothing remained but confusion. He fell to his knees, howling.

"Those watery things rolling down your cheeks are called *tears*—remember them?" Flux piped up. "It's a regrettable thing that eyes do. That, and allow you to see."

"Yesss—" Verjouce whispered. He was grasping to make sense of the shreds of visions, the wisps of light and dark returning to him. "A girl!" Verjouce told the scarecrow. His voice trailed off. "I saw a girl, here—in my chambers. Princess Violet!"

"Hardly," Flux scoffed.

"My eyes deceive me, then. Surely it is so—for it appears I'm talking to a scarecrow."

"The King's daughter is dead." The scarecrow yawned. "What you saw was your own daughter. Ivy, she is called. A tedious creature at best—but, yes, admittedly, she does bear a striking resemblance to Princess Violet."

Verjouce stared at the creature before him, this strawman. His face was pinched and his nose long and crooked—his skin the color of marigolds. Verjouce's newly acquired eyes narrowed as a deep memory stirred. His mind had returned him to the time before his blinding, the events that followed it— the truly awful events that followed it. Everything was now curiously relegated to a dark fog.

"Princess Violet," the Guild's Director continued. "What's become of her?"

"Poison hemlock," Flux gloated. "One of your favorites, wasn't it, Vidal?"

The Princess's death had the distinction of being the very first poisoning—a new and horrible crime, and her sad end began a new chapter in Caux's misery.

Vidal Verjouce blinked—a new sensation. The terrible Director of the infamous Tasters' Guild was responsible for many, many poisonings—but not this one.

"There, there," Flux soothed. "I can hardly take all the credit. I *did* have a wonderful teacher."

"Bite your tongue, you traitorous minion! I will be sure to give you all that you are due. Now fetch me my cane!"

Flux stood, hayseed floating in the air about him. "Looking for this?"

He flaunted the Director's infamous barbed cane triumphantly. In an instant Flux was before his former employer, brandishing the weapon.

"We're going on a little field trip, master and servant. You will take me to the place where this Kingmaker grows. And hurry. Your current state of weakness is revolting—it must be so very disappointing for you. I hope redemption isn't catching."

And with that, the former servant ushered the Director from his ill-gotten chambers, the poisoned tip of his own cane at his back.

The King and the Crow

Ivy stood before the King's Cottage.

She had found her way to a King's outpost before—once in the Southern Wood with Rowan, at the beginning of her adventures, and then again at the glorious Lake District before flying to the waiting hovel of the Mildew Sisters. But she had never traveled so far as this.

She had vanquished her father, toppled his Mind Garden, and sailed across a still sea to find herself at this familiar hut—an enchanted cottage, a place frozen in time, waiting to welcome King Verdigris.

But unlike the others, this cottage was occupied.

The flower boxes before the tidy windows sprouted small yellow flowers, cinquefoils, the flower of the King. Candles glittered with sparkling life upon a table within. Smoke drifted amiably from a plump chimney, and the door was unlocked. Shoo alighted happily upon a windowsill, peering in, shifting his weight from side to side in an effort to defy his own reflection.

Ivy stood on the threshold, suddenly unsure. She thought of the small boat—it wasn't too late to turn around. She could just see the still lake in the distance from where they came. A great nervousness swelled inside her, and as she made to call for Shoo, she saw that he was gone.

"My dear Ivy," an exquisite voice spoke.

Inside, a figure stood at a simple stove with his back to her.

"King Verdigris?" Ivy asked, hesitant.

The man turned from his preparations to face her. It was indeed the King, Ivy saw—but the King transformed. Gone were the cruel hawthorns, the imprisoning throne from their first encounter. His blue eyes were sharp and unhindered by age, and his cloak of green was replaced with a rich fur of the purest white, which draped regally across his shoulders, sweeping down to the floor. His long hair and beard were still tied in erratically placed ribbons, as they had been in Pimcaux, but his body seemed insubstantial somehow—as if made more of light than of flesh. And more amazingly, Ivy noticed, the old man cast no shadow, for he was made of something as rarefied as the stars.

Ivy looked anxiously around for Shoo, but he was nowhere to be found.

"Great-granddaughter. Noble One," the King addressed her. "Welcome."

Ivy frowned, looking about the room. Where had Shoo gotten to?

"You must be hungry from your travels."

Ivy was indeed aware of a growing hunger—and whatever was on the small stove smelled captivating. Soon they were at the table, a single bowl before her. Ivy examined it—a clear broth, small yellow cinquefoils floating at the surface. It smelled sublime. But Ivy's bowl went ignored—the lump in her throat was ruining her appetite.

After poking at the floating flowers, Ivy raised her head to the King, who sat at the far end of the table. She inspected Good King Verdigris closely. He had chosen no bowl for himself. Ivy cleared her throat, summoning her courage. A few stray dandelion wisps floated by lazily.

"Er, excuse me, Great-grandfather. Have you seen my crow, Shoo?"

"Shoo? He has gone on ahead."

"Ahead?" Ivy looked around, her eyes falling on the stone-studded fireplace. She remembered what her mother had once told her, at a similar cottage at the Lake District. All the King's Cottages led to just one place.

"Underwood?" Ivy asked excitedly.

"Yes." The King nodded.

A great surge of relief now swept over the girl—leaving her both thrilled and drained. Underwood. The improbable retreat beneath Southern Wood—so very close to the tavern she grew up in. She was returning home.

"And if we hurry, we'll be just in time for tea," King Verdigris announced.

Chapter Ninety-two
The Four Sisters

hey turned from the homey table, the King and Ivy, and walked to the ample fireplace. Rounding the far side, where in each cottage Ivy knew a hidden door was located, the King paused. At his touch, it sprang open.

Together, they entered a length of stone stairs. The King shone slightly in the darkness, a twilight halo about his figure. Ivy felt for her crown of interlaced violets, which encircled her head still. At the end of the stairs, the great King placed his long fingers upon the wall of entwined twigs that grew before him. These parted, dripping sap, as a door sprang forth in their midst. Ahead, the familiar cavernous great room of Under-wood.

Ivy felt the solid earth beneath her feet, and indeed knew that they were home. And while all of Caux stretched out above them, ahead Ivy was greeted with a spectacular sight.

391

The twining roots of Underwood pulsed with life, small green shoots sprouting from larger, more substantial stalks, unfurling new tender leaves. Underwood marked the beginning of her adventures, and the place where she had met her mother. The first time Ivy had seen the immense room, it was brown and dormant—or worse, dying. But new life flowed now into the roots from the trees above, and everywhere it felt like spring.

The room was illuminated by some unknown source, as if the light was filtered through woven leaves of a shady canopy, and this conspired to make everything appear to be a more brilliant version of itself. The greens were newer, brighter. The wildflowers ridiculously attractive. But nothing compared to the beauty of the four ladies Ivy saw standing before her.

They were timeless, these figures from a childhood dream, and their attire bewildered the eye. Yet each bore a strangely familiar presence, as if Ivy had met them before—and indeed Ivy felt she might place them at any moment.

It was with the last of them, a woman in a gown as white and weightless as spun sugar, where Shoo was to be found. He sat, perched upon her shoulder, as he had in the tapestry that imprisoned them both. Ivy opened her mouth to call for her crow, but stopped.

"The lady from the tapestry!" she gasped. Babette was the great mystery of the Verdigris tapestries; Shoo had been imprisoned upon her shoulder when Cecil spoke the potent words that made the tapestries come alive and then recede. And here she was—in the flesh. But where were the familiar tapestries? Searching the room, she saw not one. Instead, among the flourishing plant life, she saw her uncle.

"Uncle Cecil! How did you—"

But her uncle, indeed the entire gathering before her, fell into a deep bow, and Ivy stopped, confused. She felt the color rise in her cheeks.

"King Verdigris," Ivy mumbled, lowering herself into a formal curtsy.

The ancient king beside her lifted her chin, touched her crown, and in turn a few new violets bloomed.

"My child," he said, his voice deep and kind. "They bow for you, too."

The Four Sisters had moved away from their informal line, revealing an empty olive wood loom and a small table with a silver tea service set upon it. The ornate teapot exhaled a thin line of steam from its spout.

"Ah, I see we have not missed tea?" the King asked, a sparkle in his eyes. "You're in for a real treat, Ivy." He turned to her.

"Your Highness." Babette smiled, arranging the small dainty cups upon their saucers.

Tea was poured and served, but strangely, not to Ivy.

And even stranger, it was not drunk. For the Four Sisters

each inspected their cups carefully, sloshing the contents about severely and then dashing the tea leaves to the ground between them. They leaned in eagerly to divine.

Ivy blinked.

Could it be?

Could these ladies before her be the ruined, moldy sisters from the Eath?

Ah, life's rich tapestry.

Chapter Ninety-three

In Which Fifi
Redeems Herself

"My dear sisters," Lola began. "The tea leaves do not lie."

"Indeed." Gigi nodded thoughtfully. "It is merely a matter of precise interpretation."

"After you." Lola gestured magnanimously.

Gigi's eyes sparkled.

As the sisters prepared themselves, Ivy felt suddenly crowded. It was as if the room were host to spectators—not just herself, Cecil, and the King. Slowly, she became aware of a ghostly audience, vague people cloaked in dusk. Her skin tingled.

Cecil had found Ivy and held her by the hand, his solid arm alive with warmth. Together, her uncle's great form and her small one pooled on the floor as their shadows mixed.

"They have come to glimpse you before they go." Cecil indicated the crowd.

"Go?"

But the reading was commencing, and Ivy was shushed. A pile of spent tea leaves sat on the floor.

Gigi daintily cleared her throat. "How very strange." She coughed slightly into a gloved hand.

"Yes, extremely *particular*." Lola nodded. "I can't seem to make heads or tails of it."

Gigi moved her hands in vague circles over the tea-leaf dregs, concentrating.

Ivy looked down beside her and saw a white boar, and she reached to stroke her old friend's ear. It felt of wool, as if woven of filament, and her hand came away with a frayed thread.

"Poppy," she sighed, as the boar nuzzled her.

Still more shadowless people drifted in, some with their faces hidden, but others were known to Ivy. There was a low murmur as these new arrivals greeted each other. Hollow Bettle regulars, many whose lives were cut short under the Deadly Nightshades, mingled together. A few in the gathering were clothed in attire from an earlier time in Caux's history, and still others were like drifting smoke—faces formed of air and shifting in the wind, insubstantial, mercurial.

Ivy was pleased to notice a figure beside the King and Shoo.

Princess Violet, Ivy realized. King Verdigris's beloved daughter. The King smiled at Ivy then, and a great, indescribable feeling of relief washed over her. Everything was going to be all right.

Gigi cast a sharp look at her sister Lola.

"Just a minute, and it will come to me," Gigi muttered. "It's so . . . so . . . irritatingly *obscure.*"

Together, the pair peered in closer.

Ivy noticed that somehow a large warhorse had joined the proceedings. The animal stomped, silver bells upon his saddle tinkling. He greeted Ivy with a nod, and Ivy returned it, smiling. And when Clothilde stepped forward from the animal's broad side, her dress was as pristine and as white as the day Ivy had first met her back in the Southern Wood. Ivy was happy to see how well she looked. Her mother was finally at peace.

Meanwhile, the sisters were enduring an awkward silence. Their reading was not going as planned, and it was Fifi's turn.

Fifi, once stricken with a bulbous fungus upon her face and skin, was now clad in a gown like the rising sun. She was the most petite of the foursome and the youngest. She was also an uneasy fortune-teller, and the sisters held little hope for Fifi's interpretation.

But Fifi was staring at the tea leaves before her, transfixed.

She held her hands out above the sodden pile of spent tea as if warming them upon a fire. She swayed slightly, her wondrous gown floating like a bell. Suddenly, from somewhere deep within her corseted waist, an unlikely baritone emerged.

And, turning to Ivy, Fifi spoke.

"Poison and deceit are vanquished," Fifi's voice boomed throughout Underwood. "The King has returned to Caux, with his shepherd. A new day dawns. And while his chapter comes to a close, a new one begins. Long live the Shepherd of Weeds!"

The ghostly gallery murmured their approval.

Ivy frowned, looking sharply at her uncle, then the King himself. *A new chapter begins?*

"Life is a pleasant mix of contradictions. Ivy will have to make her way herself. It is not for even us to say if hers is a tale of success—or failure. Sisters, the tea leaves are imperfect— they have limitations. Plants have much to say, much to teach, if you are willing to listen—but that is a talent beyond most. Ivy speaks the true Language of Flowers. The future of Caux now rests with her—the last of Verdigris's noble and magical line."

There was a profound silence.

"One thing *is* for certain," Fifi continued. "Her magic will someday exceed even the King's, and our looms stand ready to weave her tale."

The feeling of people pressing in, interest renewed.

"But it will not be easy," Fifi continued. "Her enemies await, biding their time, for they are not all vanquished. Scourge bracken has found a new mistress."

A few aghast cries from the ghostly gallery.

"When it senses a weakness, it will emerge—for it is the destructive weed's nature. The next battlefield is not on the green grass of Caux, but *within* the Child. Hers is the decision as to whether the world outside our door is lush and green, or black and barren."

There was dead silence. Babette, Lola, and Gigi wore a look of utter astonishment.

Fifi raised her eyes from the tea leaves unsteadily, blinking once. "And one last thing. She will remember the moment that's just to come with great heartache."

Fifi shuddered and closed her eyes. When, an instant later, they again fluttered open, she frowned prettily and shrugged. In a flurry of adulation, the sisters rushed to congratulate her on her accomplished reading.

Together, they walked off, Ivy forgotten.

Ivy was left beside her uncle, and Underwood felt suddenly vast and dreary to her; the sunny feelings she just possessed were dashed and trampled. All eyes had turned from her to what hung on a far wall—the sisters' newest masterpiece.

A tapestry of clouds.

Chapter Ninety-four

Eternal Life ~ Imminent Death

A person is capable of a great many emotions, and it is generally agreed that those Ivy was currently experiencing were some of the worst. A heady feeling of shame and failure settled in on the girl, and she battled to hold back tears.

All of this, she thought bitterly. And for what? I am forever tainted with scourge bracken. I have failed the King.

"You have not failed, Ivy Manx." The King spoke to her from somewhere nearby. "In fact, it is just the opposite."

"I am too late!" Ivy mumbled, heartsick.

"For me—yes." The King smiled. "But you will see that there are many others that need you still—if not me."

"You cannot cure the dead," Ivy stated miserably, looking across the cavernous hall to Poppy—she had been too late for her, too. Indeed, the entire gathering was proof of the finality of poison.

"No, you cannot. Not in this life, anyway."

"So what's the use?" Tears were rolling down her cheeks now. On her shoulder, Shoo paced, agitated.

"Think of the acorn, Ivy. It is all how you look at it. If life and death are really one and the same—perhaps you need to change how you feel about death."

"But—you were meant to return to Caux—" Ivy cried out.

The Good King placed a hand beneath her chin.

"My dear Ivy," he said softly. "I already have." King Verdigris gestured around the vast room of the underground retreat, a world built with his hands from the twining roots of the great trees of Southern Wood.

"Your Highness," Babette called to King Verdigris. "Your new kingdom awaits."

The King turned, and Ivy walked hesitantly beside him and Cecil, her feet scraping the soft floor, Shoo a comforting presence at her shoulder. Midway, they came to Clothilde, and her mother bowed low. King Verdigris placed both hands upon her mother's face, closing his eyes. After a moment, Clothilde rose, and the two embraced, great tears rolling down her mother's pale cheeks.

Ivy's mother turned to her. Her white dress, her hair—she positively glowed. She leaned down, gazing intently into Ivy's eyes.

"As a mother, I have had, perhaps, some failings," Clothilde said with some difficulty. "But I hope that in the end, you will see that everything I did, I did for you."

Ivy and King Verdigris stood now before the stark white tapestry.

"What is this?" Ivy asked. Clouds of dandelion seed and thick mist rolled forth, like the sea.

"It is what comes After," the King answered.

"After?" Ivy squinted into the clouds. "Why can't I see anything?"

"It is not your time."

Suddenly she understood.

"All things in life—and what comes after—are made from these looms?" She turned to her uncle, who nodded imperceptibly. The Mildew Sisters—the Four Sisters of the Haberdashery—wove the very fabric of life.

The visitors were gone now, the ghostly entourage of Caux's dead—Poppy, Calyx, her mother, the tavern regulars—for they had drifted into the billowing mists.

King Verdigris stood before the tapestry, his features smooth as marble. He turned to Ivy. He let the fur cape drop from his shoulders, and as it met the ground, it became a white rabbit—twitching its long pink ears idly and then loping away.

"Ivy," the Good King said. "Your journey ends here. You must remain in Caux. All this—Underwood—is yours now. Use it, as I did, as a retreat. A place to renew."

"No!" she cried. "I want to go with you!"

Shoo flew from her shoulder to the King's outstretched

hand, and Ivy felt her heart break—the warmth where he sat beside her neck fading.

"Your place is here, child." His voice was soft and sad. "Where I'm going is not a kingdom for the living."

"No!" she cried again, bitterly. "Shoo—do not leave me!"

Great tufts of dandelion had picked up again, their whiteness matched only by the brilliant tapestry. They swirled playfully, their numbers growing thick. The room was a blur suddenly, their soft touch cushioning Ivy, gathering, trapped in her tears. She sank to her knees in despair, her uncle's hand upon her shoulder her only comfort.

Chapter Ninety-five

Will-o'-Wisp

he *Field Guild to the Poisons of Caux,* Axle's preemi-
nent reference book, is uncharacteristically dismissive on the
topic of the will-o'-wisp, the ghostly vision that is blamed in
many a traveler's death. The writer prefers to take the cynic's
role, stating on page 1274:

> While charming, the folktales surrounding the will-o'-wisp serve
> as a more practical warning for any nighttime traveler. It is
> said the glowing apparition lures travelers to their untimely
> deaths, but this author chooses to take these tales as a
> collective lesson on the dangers of night voyages. Journeymen
> have occasionally reported seeing inexplicable and eerie lights,

usually off at some distance, and floating or bobbing suggestively. The beholder is then seized by the irresistible urge to approach the mysterious illumination. In doing so, the fool is lured to his death.

Many such sightings can be dismissed as phosphorescent weeds such as gloamwort or shepherd's balm—or even swamp gas—yet others' tales cannot be as easily ignored. Might the will-o'-wisp be a specter from those lands that lie beyond ours? Although the finality of life cannot be underestimated, there is one purported exception. The ancients say that twilight, as the day dwindles and night's dark veil unfurls, is a time of some great magic. Here it is said that the dead walk along with the living.

"Hurry, you miserable wretch," Flux growled at his former employer. "This way! Faster!" Flux had spirited away the Director, urging him quickly down the spire's long stairs. Yet it seemed that at every step, the old man stumbled. "You were better off blind," Flux muttered.

The unlikely pair swept past the dismal fountains and crooked alleys, keeping to the shadows. Everywhere, Outriders darted past on their murderous errands, black cloaks streaming out behind them. From deep beneath the city they surged, dark ants from a wrecked hill. They searched their fallen comrades and fell upon any unfortunate in their way.

Broken-winged birds fluttered uselessly upon the ground. Heaps of old clothes and straw stuffing were all that remained of the scarecrow army. The Outriders had upended Grig's eclectic cart, and its contents were spread about the cobbles— broken flasks and untidy coils of hemp rope were flung haphazardly about the square.

It was easy to overlook the drifting tufts of dandelion seed, silvery spores upon the dank air. They were everywhere now, drifting silently throughout the city. They caught in the gutters and slipways, bridged the dark grates that led to the sewers. The black stone of the slick walls held them fast, slowly turning to gray, then white.

Outside the breeched walls, in the thick forest of hawthorns that girdled the city, the silvery parachutes snagged upon the cruel barbs and stuck fast, their numbers growing. The enormous trees groaned, as if carrying a great weight.

This was the scene that was reflected in Vidal Verjouce's new glistening eyes, and so strange a sight was it that he stared back uncomprehendingly. A great battle had been waged, and was winding down. Who was the victor? He shut his eyes finally, to return to his cherished darkness, as the poisoned barb of his own cane pierced the boiled wool of his cloak. With his eyes closed, he found himself more surefooted, and it was in this way that he passed through the Warming Room blind to the dim fires and smoldering embers—the chaos that Rowan had wrought.

Onward Flux urged Verjouce, for the ink, while a great temptation, was not the ultimate prize. They wandered beneath the very foundation of the city, passing massive cut stones placed by ancient hands, and down the lonely, dispirited hall to the door of the dead.

"Kingmaker," whispered Flux. They drifted beneath the depths of the city in search of it. And like so many before him, his was a vision of crowned glory at any cost.

The catacombs were once a source of strength for the blind Director, a fear-inspiring place of pride and dominance. A place to house his dark servants, to imprison his enemies. Without his eyes, Verjouce would have confidently found his way to the small crypt—the hallowed ground in which scourge bracken grew—in a matter of minutes.

Now, he was racked with uncertainty and confusion. Everything was unfamiliar—his sense of sight a burden in the gloom. His hands felt desperately at the walls, searching for any familiar landmark; his ragged fingernails scraped at the chipped mortar.

"Where is it, you doddering old fool?" Flux demanded. His scrappy burlap shirt was itching, and he dreamed of ermine robes and golden scepters. "What a pathetic spectacle you are!"

Verjouce had finally settled upon a direction and had taken a few hesitant steps along it when he stopped short—and no amount of prodding from the cane in Flux's hand would make him continue.

"What now?" Flux sighed, exasperated.

"Do—do you see that?" Verjouce's voice was hoarse, barely audible.

"What?" Flux waved his torch about recklessly. "See what? Where?"

"There." Vidal's long, ink-stained finger pointed off into the heavy darkness ahead. "Do you not see? A will-o'-wisp!"

After a moment's deliberation, Flux shook his head. Vidal had begun babbling in tired, hoarse whispers.

"There's nothing there, you fool. See?" Flux snorted, turning to his former master. "Get up from your knees immediately! I've got Kingmaker to find."

But Verjouce did not hear him. He was cowering now, beyond reach, withered and defeated.

Ahead, a bobbing, glowing light both enthralled and dismayed.

There, in the dark catacombs, beside orderly stacks of the bones of the dead, stood King Verdigris, glowing, wavering, the passage ahead vaguely discernable through his translucent body.

Chapter Ninety-six

The King Is Among Us!

ndeed, everywhere in Caux, people suddenly reported seeing the Good King.

Here he was, sidled up to a bar, sipping from a golden goblet.

There, a green sapling in his hand, fishing from the Knox.

A disgraced Librarian, contemplating a ruined book, raised his head to the vision of his beloved King, a sigh escaping his burnt lips and settling on his sooty robes.

A dying solider was comforted by the King beside a city of dark stone, a bouquet of meadowsweet and cinquefoils in his hand.

At once, everywhere, and for the briefest of moments, the glowing, refined apparition of the King was to be found.

"The King!" they cried. "The King! The King is among us!"

There, before the glazed eyes of Hemsen Dumbcane, a faint, glowing outline. He watched numbly as it grew stronger, finally taking shape.

He sat stricken with grief beside the lifeless body of his mistress and her horse. His hands, his face—his entire body—trembled, but he took no notice. The last of Clothilde's stars had extinguished from her skirts, fizzling in the water of the fountain where they had perished. Her body, and that of her mount, were now indistinguishable from the agonized statues. Soon all that would remain of the doomed pair would be an indistinct clump of driftwood and lichen that—from just the right angle—could be mistaken for a horse and rider.

Tears ran down the forger's gaunt face; a bitter sob escaped his lips. Looking up from the spectacle, he cursed his hands that they might have led to this. He shivered uncontrollably.

King Verdigris removed his flowing cloak, and, walking to the scribe, he placed it on his trembling shoulders.

Axlerod D. Roux lay cramped and desolate in the gilt cage, high above the city, more dead than alive. Dandelion tufts covered his small, frail body, erasing the soil of the cage's floor in a white blanket.

The trestleman had not moved in many days. Yet now his eyes fluttered open.

The room was dark; he appeared to be alone. No ink monkeys, no vile Director.

No—wait.

A man was at the ruined window, studying the chambers. His outline was vague, and Axle had no problem seeing the stars right through him. The regal visitor called something to the air, and a magnificent seabird answered, and the wingbeats of some enormous creature filled the heavens. The King now turned to Axle, and the trestleman nodded.

His desperate mind, he reasoned, had given him a gracious gift. The vision of his beloved King would carry him through this dark night. He shut his eyes and slept peacefully for the first time in weeks.

In the morning, with the first streak of dawn, Axle would awaken to the welcome sight of Peps, the most unlikely warrior, at his side. Peps had freed himself from the barrel and, true to his promise, returned for his brother.

Through the shattered window, circling the clear skies, a pair of simply enormous albatrosses waited to take them home.

Chapter Ninety-seven

A Place for the Dead

"Get up! Get up, I said." Sorrel Flux's voice was growing raspy from pleading. But no amount of prodding could get the Guild's Director to shake his debilitating fit. "There is nothing there, I tell you! I see nothing at all."

So, torch in hand, Flux set off on his own. The crypt could not be far and, in it, his small, stony heart's desire: Kingmaker.

His first few strides were long and jaunty, but quite soon thereafter they shortened some, until he found himself inching forward on mere hubris. The catacombs, after all, were a place for the dead—not the living—and Sorrel Flux was feeling a strange chill on the back of his straw-studded neck. The dead kept to their own, didn't they?

Again he took to waving his torch about him, but the shadows it created were troubling, and he soon stopped.

What if the Director had been right—that something lurked before him in this passage?

His swagger gone, he paused uneasily.

He seemed to be in some small chamber, skulls and bones stacked neatly in rows on an upper shelf, larger vaults resting upon the earthen floor. There was one way out, ahead. Peering carefully in that direction, Flux jumped.

Something was glowing red in the gloomy passage, a small prick of firelight. It bobbed ever so, floating at eye level. Squinting, he dismissed it, finally, as a trick of his imagination—only to see the small ember flare from crimson to a burnt orange, and back again. Stepping back—and cursing Verjouce—he dropped his torch. The heavy dark pressed in—for there is no dark like that of a crypt. A bead of cold sweat trickled down his pounding temple as he struggled to maintain his composure.

His torch—he saw it now, glowing dimly against a near wall. Floundering about on the cold floor before him, eyes never leaving the strange floating ember, he regained the lantern—along with a surge of relief and renewed confidence.

There is nothing to fear, Flux scolded himself.

But his torch disputed this, its light falling upon a figure—an ample figure—standing before him. He screamed, after which he endured a moment of confusion—the figure was one easily mistaken for a scarecrow, like he. But as recognition dawned, he again shrieked, dropping the torch for a final time.

"You!" he cried.

The light flared from the corner, where it had come to rest.

Standing before him was Lumpen Gorse, arms crossed over her broad chest, corncob pipe aglow. She had survived Dumbcane's inky thumbprint and Snaith's poisoned burr—for Lumpen was made of some sturdy stock, and there was life in those old bones yet.

Chapter Ninety-eight

Cat and Mouthe

naith scurried like a crab, his ruined body refusing to face forward, instead skittering along with an awkward sidestep. He threw a backward glance over his left shoulder, but his hood fell forward and his vision was blocked by the scarlet velvet. The cat—that awful, monstrous, mangy beast—had been pursuing him for nearly an hour, and he was beginning to seriously tire. He had been forced humiliatingly from his lecture hall as the thing pounced at him; Snaith had pushed his former assistant Rue at the attacking animal—offering up the girl in hopes she would quell the thing's hunger. But it was as if the cat had not even seen her—his amber eyes never left Snaith's own. He had felt his robes captured, snagged—but with a terrible rending noise, he had managed to rip free.

Snaith had scurried in wild abandon, darting, hiding, only to emerge to the evil moon face of that beast at every turn. The thing was *toying* with him.

Again his progress was thwarted by his attire. He shook his hood roughly from his head. What he saw made him shriek—the scream fell on his own ears harshly, high-pitched, that of a young girl.

Incredibly, Six waited *before* him. He was certain he had left the cat many twisting streets behind—yet here the thing was, swatting the turf with its tail. Blinking uncivilly. He raised a paw to preen, spreading wide his padded toes and stretching out his glinting claws one at a time, torturously.

Back-stepping, the Watchman was off again, stumbling, tripping on his long cloak, desperation writ upon his scarred face.

Six watched placidly for a moment, and then meandered off after him.

Soon Snaith had retreated as far as his slippered feet would carry him, and he stood breathless against a slick pillar. He had fled through an open door, into the Chapter Room. His chest heaved and he bent forward, catching his breath. His delicate feet were blistered, hobbled.

When he had regained his composure and set off limping down the carpeted entryway, he found himself drawn to a particular wall hanging. He knew the contents of the Chapter

Room thoroughly, for he often hosted dignitaries or devised secret punishments within its solid walls. Yet this was something new. A wall hanging.

A childhood dream returned to him then.

As a young boy, it had been a recurring dream, a pleasant one, where in a hallway, he would find himself at a door that he was certain had not been there before. He would enter the door, and, behind it, he would be treated to a delightful number of unexplored rooms and unexpected surprises. (Perhaps here was the seed for the pleasure he found in the catacombs.)

To the subrector Snaith's delight, the wall hanging now before him bore the very image of a door. So realistic—the knob was even newly polished.

A guttural meow issued from the entrance of the Chapter Room. The cat was meandering toward him slowly, pausing every now and then to sniff the air. Snaith was cornered.

He made a quick decision.

As in his childhood dream, he opened the door upon Clothilde's tapestry and stepped inside.

His ugly heart surged at what he saw—indeed, there were rooms, many, many rooms of all sizes, one leading to the next, and all thrilling to the subrector's sense of endless possibilities. An utter quiet descended.

As he stepped farther into the ancient tapestry, and further into the enchantment, Snaith's footsteps became increasingly matted, like he was walking upon a fine weave. His velvet cloak—the color of which was a rich span of scarlets—now faded to a single swatch of red dye. His throat felt scratchy. He coughed once—an intricate knot of thread fell from his mouth. The raised and bulbous scars upon his face flattened—indeed, his entire body seemed uncomfortably thin and stretched, and, as he regarded his hands, he found them to be perforated with seams.

Soon all thought drifted away, all memories of his childhood, his recurrent dreams, the Tasters' Guild, his evil ambitions. He was conscious only of a lightness inside, a dryness, and then this final awareness was gone—extinguished forever.

Chapter Ninety-nine

Hawthorns

t was the edge of night—daylight's last tendrils were rising up from the west—and Ivy Manx and her uncle Cecil stood huddled together before the impenetrable Hawthorn Wood. Together, they had traveled from Underwood to the dreaded forest with a single goal. Ivy was needed here, Cecil had explained, before their return to the battlefield. In exchange for releasing Babette from the tapestry, the sisters had granted him this one concession.

The gloomy forest was expecting them.

"Are you sure this will work?" Ivy asked, a shiver of doubt creeping across the back of her neck.

"These ancient trees contain the souls of poisoners, murderers, and villains—and the occasional lost traveler. They will answer to you," Cecil explained. "Without them, Ivy, all is lost."

Hawthorns bind and imprison people, Ivy knew. But this was also their advantage. Before her was an imprisoned army, and Ivy would free them. Everywhere the silvery tufts of spent dandelions swirled, and the perilous trees were made ashen.

Something moved beneath Ivy's cloak. Reaching into one of the many pockets, she removed the white rabbit, bringing him close to her neck and feeling his warmth.

Ivy nodded to her uncle. She was ready. She had spoken to the silver and gold oak trees in Pimcaux, and she would speak to the hawthorns. She would call forth the forest to her aid.

"I am Ivy Manx," she said, her small voice carrying farther than she thought it could, reverberating throughout the shadowy barbs, the sinister thorns. "And I release you."

First, nothing.

Ivy shivered in the cold.

Then, a great rending noise—the cracking of hundreds of limbs, the unpleasant splintering of green wood—shook the earth. The rabbit disappeared, shivering, beneath Ivy's wrap, but Ivy stood her ground.

A wind blew in from the west, and it gathered strength, carrying the dandelion seeds everywhere. It coursed through the ancient wood, picking up speed, until, in a massive gust, it rose high, high above Ivy's and Cecil's heads.

The air was suddenly clear.

Where the forest stood were the twisted figures of dreary souls, ghostly pale faces clad in moss and tangled in ivy, a mass snarled together in bitter entrapment. They wore on their eyes tarnished coins of gold and silver—minims and scruples—and their mouths hung open in silent screams.

The brutal wind was whipping Ivy's and Cecil's cloaks against their bodies, but the pair held still. Cecil nodded at his niece, and she spoke two words to the waiting army.

"The Guild."

The wall of souls reared above the two—agonized faces pressing outward at its limits, a surging crest that threatened to engulf them. For a brief moment, the ghostly army loomed silently above them. Then, with a deafening roar, they dashed down to the earth behind Ivy and her uncle, tumbling over each other in confusion and bedlam, bound for Rocamadour.

They were not long.

They came in a deluge, as if a tidal wave, and reached the city gates at twilight—when the dead are said to walk among the living. And there the lost souls of the Hawthorn Wood scoured the city of its mold and mildew, its remaining Outriders and Watchmen, and then, just as quickly, they were gone, leaving behind the broken statues and fountains of the famed city and a single shining star. A silver hairpin.

Elegy

The air brimmed with sunlight and dew

His enemy lay vanquished

Behind him, an Army of Flowers.

—The Ballad of King Verdigris

Axle's Trestle

fter a long period of gentle rain, the sun was finally shining, its yellow beams thrown down to the earth from between mountainous white clouds. It shone on rolling hills and deep wooded thickets of Caux alike, warming the land into an early spring.

Small green buds had opened on the maples and oaks, and there in a humble walled orchard, Cecil's apple trees had finally burst into bloom—white and rosy pink flowers welcomed the bees. The air was alive with their persistent, happy buzzing, for spring was finally here and there was much to do. On a low branch a mockingbird sang.

Today the river Marcel was muddy, silt from the runoff being swept downstream, scrubbing clean the river floor. It rolled patiently alongside the limestone shore, cutting a watery line between Ivy's childhood home and the Southern Wood before meandering beneath the old iron grid of one of Caux's most cherished trestles.

There was activity beneath this trestle, with several stately houseboats and polished travel crafts docked in the water. Above, royal footmen and servants were patiently scraping the rust from the iron of the old bridge and, onshore, applying new paint to the old tavern. A white flag rippled upon Cecil's old flagpole—where once the Belladonna flew, now the three-pronged leaf of poison ivy hung, a vivid, lively green.

And within the trestle—Axle's trestle—preparations were being made for a spectacular celebration.

Or rather, preparations were being burnt.

In the trestleman's sunny kitchen, a place that held the memories of many a good meal, Ivy was neglecting a bubbling pot on the small polished woodstove, while smoke billowed from one of the tiny oven doors. Stacks of dishes awaited washing, and a sack of flour had rebelled, coating most of the floor in a conspicuous dusting. Ivy blew a stray lock of hair away from her eyes as she arranged a vase of purple and white violets. Her face was streaked with both flour and stove black, which she now successfully transferred to the bouquet. Discovering the oven, she cried in dismay and grabbed a flowered towel— but the tray that emerged held only random, blackened lumps.

Waving away the smoke, she flung open the small window

and looked guiltily over her shoulder. Out the window went the entire ruined contents of the tray, which fizzled when they landed in the river. With all the best intentions, Ivy had planned the menu for the day, but from the start it seemed that everything had gone wrong.

The door did open then, and Ivy assumed what she hoped was a casual pose. Rowan entered, and she relaxed somewhat, but scowled when he burst out laughing.

"Just look at these!" she said, displaying an earlier attempt at corn fritters. They were runny in the middle and charred on the outside, and Rowan was pretty sure this was not her desired goal. "I don't know how Axle does it! Everything he makes is so . . . perfect."

"Hmm." Rowan smiled. "How refreshing!"

"Refreshing?" Ivy eyed him suspiciously.

"Yes. Apparently, you can't do *everything*." He patted her on the shoulder when he saw her glum expression. "Ivy, it's the gesture that counts. Maybe it's time to let Axle back in his kitchen?"

"I wanted to surprise him!"

"I think it's too late for that. The poor man is pacing back and forth in the hall, wondering when you're going to burn his house down!"

"Oh, I give up."

"It's okay. Potion-making and cooking are quite different talents, you know."

"Maybe, but I haven't been able to do either since—"

Rowan looked down as a white rabbit loped by.

"—since Shoo left."

She bent down and tenderly lifted the rabbit, dusting off his heavy coating of flour and cradling him around her neck.

"Come." Rowan held out his hand. "Your friends are waiting for you in the parlor."

It was a fine gathering indeed, albeit slightly cramped. Beneath the trestle's low ceilings an array of bright faces awaited Ivy. It had been a few weeks since she'd seen most of them, and, after a brief pause, the room erupted in welcome.

Grig was there, sipping on mulberry wine, with many of his familiar assistants. Cecil sat beside the small men, stuffed uncomfortably into a tiny chair, and a plate of burnt cookies sat conspicuously in their midst. In one corner, the trestle's renowned owner fretted beside his brother, Peps, but as Ivy entered, Axle brightened, and he raced to join her. After nervously inquiring about the state of his kitchen, he vanished to inspect it himself.

"How did everyone like the cookies?" Ivy asked, regarding the room. "Grig—you've hardly touched yours!"

Looking sheepish, Grig leaned forward and, taking one, attempted to bite it. The resulting crack did not bode well for his teeth.

The trestleman looked around helplessly. "They're quite . . . toothsome!"

"Yes—delicious!" Peps added quickly.

"I simply must have the recipe," Rue enthused. She whispered something to her grandfather, Professor Breaux, and the old man cleared his throat. "A respectable attempt," he pronounced thoughtfully.

"I'll second that," Malapert, the Guild's disgraced Librarian, agreed.

The room was silent.

"You're all awful liars!" Ivy burst out laughing. "But don't worry; I suspect Axle is in charge now."

And indeed, as they mingled, excitedly speaking among themselves, somehow a plate piled high with hot biscuits and peach jam replaced Ivy's blackened attempt, alongside a pitcher of sweet spiced cider.

"I don't know how he does it," Ivy said, turning to her uncle with her mouth full.

"We all have our particular talents." He smiled, eyes twinkling. "And apparently cooking is not one of yours."

A Toast

toast!" Cecil stood, stooped beneath the low ceiling. He held his glass high.

"Well, let's hear it." Peps smiled, raising his own.

They were gathered around the bounty of Axle's table, the trestleman finally looking relaxed as he served platter after platter of scrumptious food. The meal was nearly over, and their bellies full.

There was the sound of chairs scraping against the polished floor as one by one each guest stood.

"To Ivy," Cecil said, turning to face her. "Whom I've been proud to call my niece. Without you, we would not be here to enjoy this—or any—bounty."

Ivy felt the color rise in her cheeks. She stood now, looking around the table at the welcome sight of so many of her beloved friends. "Thank you, Uncle," she said. "But I suspect we each have many things to be thankful for. And I'd like to offer a toast of my own." Ivy adjusted the particular silver pin that held her hair in place, and as she did, the light caught it, dancing wildly across the crowded walls. She raised her birch beer. "To those whose faces I do not see here today."

The room sat silent, thoughts of the fallen still heavy in everyone's hearts.

Axle was next, standing chest high to the table. "I have one of my own," he spoke softly. "To my brother, Peps. For without him, you'd all be eating Ivy's cooking!"

The room cheered. Peps had rescued Axle from his prison in the spire with the help of the albatrosses Klair and Lofft and, with Ivy's help, nursed him back to health in his beloved trestle.

"I shall write a ballad for you," Axle informed his brother brightly. "For never has there been a more deserving trestle-man about whom to sing. Right after I finish my current project, that is."

"What project, Axle?" Rowan asked.

"Ah, such an undertaking has never before been done. A new *Field Guide*—to Pimcaux! But first, I need to finish a truly important work," Axle replied. "I'm calling it *Potent Prophecy: The Complete Chronicles of Queen Ivy.*"

Ivy smiled at Rowan, who now stood.

"I have one, too," the former taster began.

Ivy watched her friend with interest. She remembered their last time together in this trestle, as their adventure was just beginning. Then he wore his tasters' robes with great pride, and Axle had somewhat impatiently told him he had a lot of unlearning to do. Today she was proud to see how much he'd changed. He stood as tall and confidently as he could beneath the low ceilings, and he raised his glass to her. Ivy noticed with a shock that it was she who blushed, not he.

"To my great friend and companion, Ivy Manx." Rowan bowed. "Whose place is in my heart—not the kitchen." He winked, and then grew serious. "To our Queen."

Ivy frowned—glancing quickly at her uncle. She preferred the name the birds had given her long ago, the Shepherd of Weeds, to that of Queen. In the days following the fall of the Tasters' Guild, her uncle had tried to prepare her for this, her new incarnation. The two had returned to Templar, huddling together in her workshop as Cecil had readied her for the monumental changes that her new role would bring. Yet the title *Queen* was a foreign one to her, one that held distant undertones of poison and tyranny, and sent her scurrying to her small alcohol stove to tinker, or to the comfort of Axle's *Field Guide*—her own battered copy had been retrieved from Rocamadour.

"And there's still the little issue of your studies." Cecil had smiled. "For they've been woefully neglected."

The Tasters' Guild had been vanquished by the Hawthorn army in a matter of moments, their howling, screaming faces sending the surviving Outriders retreating for their lair in the catacombs. The doors to the dead were sealed from within, and the unlucky subrectors and Guild loyalists that remained on higher ground were captured. And with that, the imprisoned souls of the Hawthorn Wood were gone.

The invasive weeds dropped by the caucus grew wildly up and over the city's sheer walls—with Ivy's urging—twisting up the dark spire, and finally covering the entire Guild in a thick blanket of greenery. The Tasters' Guild was but a shadow, a shroud of thick shoots of ivy and bramble, destined forever to exist in a woven twilight. The needle-sharp point of the spire, the vast halls of learning, the Chapter Room—all were transformed by the overgrowth, their contours dulled like a rusted ax blade, trumped by nature. Rocamadour had become unrecognizable.

Grig had rescued Rowan from the inkworks, which were destroyed by the staunchroot.

"Hardened like glue," Grig pronounced happily. "There will never again be ink made in that forsaken hole."

But no amount of urging would convince the forger, Hemsen Dumbcane, to abandon his vigil beside his beloved fountain. In the end, he was left there to fend for himself in permanent dusk, his grieving shadow blending with that of the desperate horse and rider in the fountain's center.

There was a knock on Axle's door, and Cecil stood.

The door swung open and the full figure of Lumpen's patchwork skirts and corncob pipe filled its frame. Her ruddy cheeks bristled with health, and her very presence made Axle's trestle seem smaller than ever before.

"Lumpen!" Ivy smiled, standing joyfully at the sight of her traveling companion. The well keeper performed a clumsy curtsy.

"Come, let me see you," Ivy beckoned.

Axle emerged again from the kitchen and set down a pair of bowls upon the floor—one holding the delicate arch of a small fish, the other a froth of fresh cream—as the hem of Lumpen's skirts bristled and lifted.

"Six!" Ivy squealed as the cat made his way indifferently into the crowded parlor. He eyed Ivy coolly.

"Six, all is forgiven?" Ivy asked, leaning down to pet him.

Blinking once, he paused. The cat contemplated Ivy, and answered finally with a raspy purr before settling himself upon his lunch.

"Uh, Ivy." Rue stood, shyly. "We have a little souvenir for you."

Together, Rue, her grandfather Professor Breaux, and the Librarian Malapert presented Ivy with a bulky roll of cloth, tied with a ribbon.

"What is this?" Ivy asked as Rue helped her unroll it upon the cleared table.

434

The gathering pressed in, curious.

There, the flattened but unmistakable image of a familiar face in a scarlet robe.

"Snaith!" Ivy gasped.

The professor of the dreaded Irresistible Meals wore a perplexed look; his hood lay bunched upon his shoulders, his gloved finger gesturing in the air—a pose he often struck when lecturing. But whatever the subrector wished to say was lost—frozen forever in the ancient weave.

Six padded over, sniffing the tapestry, as Ivy inspected it closer.

It was a work of much distinction. Snaith's bulbous face, his potbelly, and his scrunched spine bulged unsettlingly from the textured surface, even as the weave contained him.

"A little too lifelike for me." Ivy shivered, rolling the tapestry carefully. She knew what mischief such tapestries might bring. "We'll let Six keep an eye on this one." It was propped in a corner, where the cat began sharpening his claws upon it.

Axle laughed merrily. "Another toast!" he called. Mulberry wine was poured, in ancient tribute. "To life's rich tapestry." The trestleman raised his glass, and the room followed.

Still, one question remained. It was a big one.

Ivy looked around the room. "What of my father? Flux?"

Lumpen glanced at Cecil and lit her pipe. Then she began her story.

The well keeper had made it inside the gates, she explained, but was shot with a pointed barb in her thigh. According to Peps, who was listening from within the barrel, Snaith ordered her thrown in the catacombs, where he left her to die.

"I guess he underestimated me." Lumpen exhaled a few smoke rings, and continued.

She awoke to a strange sight. A wisp of an old man hovered over her, and he visited with her, sitting beside her for some time. They chatted unhurriedly. He told her of the sea, its great tides, describing it in detail—a place where water stretches out as far as the eye can see!—and then he was gone.

Soon after, Lumpen heard voices, and she crept forward. There she spied the Guild's Director in the company of a yellowish scarecrow. The scarecrow was in a foul temper, stomping its feet and shouting. She had no problem sneaking up and capturing it—and only then did it become clear to her that it was the fugitive taster Flux.

With Flux under one arm, she threw the Guild's Director, weeping, into a cell—the very one that once imprisoned the forger Dumbcane. Verjouce gave her little trouble. She jangled the keys loudly, and hung them on a rusty nail nearby for the Outriders to find.

"His power gone, the Outriders are no longer beholden to him—in fact, just the opposite. I suspect, in the utter dark, he found himself swept away by rough hands. They have a score to settle. These are the very men Verjouce had silenced by stealing their tongues," Axle explained.

436

But the scarecrow captive was a different story, the well keeper continued. He was loud and impertinent, and Lumpen found holding on to his scrawny collar to be more difficult than she imagined. She thought for a while about what to do with him. Ignoring his bleating, she grabbed Flux by his straw scruff. She would bring him with her.

"I figured you'd want a word with him, miss," Lumpen explained.

Only, she had no idea how to get out, and the weasely one could not be relied on for directions.

As they began the journey through the mazelike catacombs, Flux protested heartily. He talked absurdities, dreams of crowns and thrones. He offered bribes, then threats. They walked for hours—and when Flux refused to walk any farther, Lumpen carried him. Soon enough, Flux abandoned his complaints, his indignity complete.

"He was a wisp of a thing—even lighter than you or Rue." Lumpen looked mournful.

Lumpen and Flux continued on in silence until the well keeper finally reached the stone steps marking the way out of the land of the dead.

Here the well keeper paused her tale, looking down dejectedly.

"Where's Flux, then?" Ivy asked.

"Miss, when we got above that wretched ground and into the light, I looked into my arms. There I carried not that scoundrel but a scarecrow—mind you, a scarecrow made to

437

look exactly like him, yellow hide and all—but a scarecrow, all the same. Blank, button eyes. Hat sewn right upon his head, straw inside and out. You can be sure I tore him open to be certain, but I found only a rock where his heart should be."

The well keeper removed a small stone from her bosom, black and jagged, and placed it on the table, where it languished in the withering looks from the guests.

"Flux escaped?" Ivy asked sharply.

"It's hard to say for sure," Axle admitted, pocketing the dark stone thoughtfully.

A distant cry of a seabird filled the silence, and Ivy straightened.

"Well, then." She smiled brightly at her friends, reserving a particular look for Rowan. "A little fresh air, perhaps?"

Outside, Ivy cast an expectant look at the skies, but they held only a few scarce clouds. From a nearby maple, a flock of red-winged blackbirds lifted from the branches, darting in consort through the spring air, only to settle again in the tree. Ivy and Rowan navigated the rails and wide gaps of the train trestle, as they had at the beginning of their adventure, Rowan more tentatively than his friend.

"Do you have it?" She turned to him when they reached land.

Rowan nodded, digging deep into a pocket. He produced a small, silvery object, holding it out to her in his open palm.

"Where should we plant it?" he asked.

Ivy looked around. There was the Hollow Bettle, her childhood home, bright and lively—brighter and livelier than she had ever seen it, with the aid of her royal staff. A new well garnished the exterior, courtesy of Lumpen and her yarrow stick. It was marked by a tidy outcrop of stones, and a sturdy rocking chair sat to one side.

Ivy's rabbit peeked out from her robes, sniffing the air timidly.

"Here," she indicated, after the pair walked along the riverbank. "Wasn't this where we first met?"

Rowan smiled. How could he forget?

They dug a quick hole in the earth, and Ivy dropped the silvery acorn from Pimcaux into it. As they waited together, Ivy reached for her friend's hand.

As Ivy smiled at him knowingly, he saw something new in her face—she seemed older, different—but it was a fleeting thought, replaced by the excitement of new arrivals. Rowan's eyes grew wide as a familiar noise filled the air, for great wings were settling upon the arched roof of the trestle. The albatrosses Klair and Lofft called out their sharp greetings in voices of faraway seas. In their midst, a small warbler, Teasel, flitted about.

Soon Axle, Cecil, and the rest of the welcoming party

gathered expectantly, their attention drawn downriver. Peps gestured with his small arm, excitedly. Work ceased on the tavern and the grounds as everyone waited with great anticipation.

Down the river, a distant boat approached. It was still far enough away that its elegant lines appeared wavy—watery, even. Billowing flags, the color of seafoam, crested the mast. White gulls escorted the ship, soaring beside it like kites. Soft, dreamlike chimes filled the air.

Ivy smiled. The alewives were coming home.

Here was the last gift from King Verdigris: the crumbling of the doorways had begun. A mingling of Caux and Pimcaux. At Ivy's feet, the acorn had begun to sprout, silvery flashes reflecting off its young leaves, lighting up the hems of her impeccable gown. It would grow someday to be a marvelous oak—rarefied and pure—with potent healing properties. And beneath its vast canopy, two old friends might be seen sitting in its shade, marveling as the sunlight casts thousands of prisms down upon them off its polished leaves.

APPENDIX
Final Exam (Partial)
from Irresistible Meals

Please complete as many of the following questions as you can before you die.

1. The contents of my goblet are
   a. Bitter
   b. Burning
   c. Caustic
   d. All of the above

2. As my life flashes before my eyes, I am surprised by
   a. The grade I will receive in Irresistible Meals—I thought I deserved more.
   b. How short and meaningless it all was.
   c. The quality of care in the Infirmary.
   d. The fact that Kingmaker betrayed me in the end.

3. As you writhe in agony, how would you rate your professor's performance in this class?

a. Genius
b. Evil genius
c. All-knowing
d. I wouldn't dare—for who am I to judge things I know nothing about?

4. My opinion on cats is that they are
a. Awful, needy things.
b. The devil's spawn, filthy with fleas and dander.
c. Rats with hairy tails. No—that would disparage the entire race of rats.
d. Excellent creatures upon which to test my questionable potions.

5. Are you still alive? You obviously have not drunk enough ink. See me.

Acknowledgments

The three books of Caux were, in many ways, a lifetime in the making, and there are many people to whom I am indebted.

My chorus—the very important cheerleaders along the way: Karmen Ross, Steph Whitehouse, Mark Shaw, Jana Potashnik, Lisa Jack, Marissa Rothkopf-Bates. Jim Anstey and Jessica Golke for the late-night huddles, Marcy Pianin, Monika Wuhrer. Ray Bradley (and Seven and Not Seven) and Iris Kimberg—for meals even a trestleman would envy. Moshe Siegel for inexhaustible help with the hardest part. Alysa Wishingrad, Robin Jacobowitz—my early and thoughtful readers—Virginie Lefeuvre.

I am forever grateful for my husband, Neal, and my children, Harper and Henry. How hard it is to have a writer in the family! I am so thankful for their patience with my early-morning absences and scattered retreats. Caux would not exist without my father, David—distinguished scholar of Cauvian affairs. My brother, Joshua, and the lovely Katy Bray. Kate Hamilton for, among other things, bringing Poison Ivy to life in costume.

And most importantly, I am beholden to Craig Tenney for answering a note not addressed to him and then following it up with such perseverance, and to Joan Slattery for her thoughtfulness, expertise, and encouragement. And finally, to Allison Wortche for all of the above—and for being the first at the door when she heard Ivy's small fist pounding.

Susannah Appelbaum

(With apologies to both W. C. Fields and the very real, and very glorious, city of Rocamadour.)

About the Author

Susannah Appelbaum comes from a family of doctors and philosophers, which instilled in her both an early fascination and a great deal of caution with bottles marked "Poison." She worked in magazine publishing for many years and now lives with her family in New York's Hudson Valley and in Cape Breton, Nova Scotia, where her garden prefers to grow weeds.

The Shepherd of Weeds is the final book in the Poisons of Caux trilogy, following *The Hollow Bettle* and *The Tasters Guild.* To learn more about the author and her work, please visit susannahappelbaum.com.